MW01074080

THE
EMPEROR'S AERONAUT

SHELLEY ADINA
R.E. SCOTT

© 2022 Shelley Adina Bates and Regina Lundgren

License Note

This eBook is licensed for your personal enjoyment only. It may not be re-sold or given away to other people unless it is part of a lending program. If you're reading this book and did not purchase it, or it was not purchased for lending, please delete it from your device and purchase your own copy. Thank you for respecting the authors' work and livelihood.

This is a work of fiction. Names, characters, places, and incidents are a product of the author's imagination. Locales and public names are sometimes used for atmospheric purposes. Any resemblance to actual people, living or dead, or to businesses, companies, events, institutions, or locales is completely coincidental.

Cover design by Tugboat Design. Images used under license.

The Emperor's Aeronaut / Shelley Adina and R.E. Scott—1st ed.

ISBN 978-1-950854-40-0

❀ Created with Vellum

PRAISE

"Adina and Scott launch their Regent's Devices series with a witty and whimsical flight of fancy in a subgenre they call *Prinnypunk* (Regency-era steampunk); it plays out as a delightfully fun mash-up of Jane Austen and Jules Verne, right down to the hint of sweet romance and the array of ingenious inventions."

— BOOKLIST ON *THE EMPEROR'S AERONAUT*

Five Stars! "Regina Scott's books make me happy! I can always count on her to provide a story that is witty, adventurous, and sweetly romantic."

— AMONG THE READS

"The Magnificent Devices series continues to wow me book after book."

— AMY'S BOOK DEN

For those who wanted more.
This is Prinnypunk. You heard it here first.

FIND MORE DARING ADVENTURE TO LOVE

Sign up for Shelley Adina's mailing list at https://www.subscribepage.com/shelley-adina and begin the adventure with "The Abduction of Lord Will."

Sign up for Regina Scott's mailing list at https://subscribe.reginascott.com/ and learn what happened in France while Celeste was in England.

Don't miss out!

IN THIS SERIES

The Emperor's Aeronaut
The Prince's Pilot
The Lady's Triumph

THE EMPEROR'S AERONAUT

CHAPTER 1

TRURO, CORNWALL

May 1819

"*F*or the love of Saint Piran, Loveday, this is not your mother's kitchen!" Thomas Trevithick's red hair practically stood on end with rage. "Either give that hammer to someone who knows how to use it, or go home and learn how to cook."

Loveday Penhale braced herself against the overwhelming urge to apply the hammer to Thomas's nose. Only the fact that it had already been broken once, thus rendering her efforts redundant, saved him. That, and the fact he had inherited the steam manufactory from his uncle, the great Richard Trevithick, whom she had worshipped and now mourned as lost forever. She would not willingly damage any relative of her mentor.

Instead, she simply applied the muffled hammer with increased force to the sheet of copper she was shaping for the new boiler design. The sheet gleamed in the light of the manufactory's isinglass windows, kept sparkling clean by their concerted efforts so that they might see what they were doing, even on the gloomiest winter's day.

With the back of one heavily gloved hand, she smoothed away a lock of wavy blond hair that had fallen out of its knot and somehow escaped the kerchief she had tied over it. She was hot, and the leather apron was heavy. Emory Thorndyke had cut it down to fit her when her old one fell to pieces, but on this May day, with the sun slanting in the windows, she felt every inch of its protection.

An hour later, the sheet of copper had submitted to her persuasions and become part of the boiler for the high-pressure rolling engine, which would be complete, if all went well, by the time of the Tinkering Prince's royal visit. Provided, of course, that happy event ever became more than a rumor.

Her arms ached, her back had a kink in it, and she looked a complete fright, she was quite certain. But no one here cared about anything except the pleasing curve of the boiler and the neat row of rivets that marched down the seam between today's piece and the one she had installed yesterday.

In the distance, the bells of St Mary's parish church in the center of Truro began to toll the hour. One. Two. Three o'clock.

"Oh, dear." Loveday scrabbled at the knot in the ties of her apron, finally gave up, and heaved it off over her head.

She did not look at Emory, who made a point of staying hours later than she on Wednesdays. He was a man, independent and free to manage the hours of his day as he pleased. She was not even supposed to be here, and it was only because as a girl of fifteen she had assisted the great Trevithick himself that his nephew permitted her to continue the association. But on Wednesdays, when her father was in Truro, meeting with his friends on market day, Loveday must perforce be home in time for tea, washed, combed, and with the flush caused by the hot metals and oils subsided to a ladylike pink, before he himself rode in.

Piffle, she thought, gritting her teeth as she slid the stable door aside. The stableboy, standing next to Rhea, already in the cane whiskey's harness, grinned. "Three of the clock, miss."

"Thank you, Toby, I heard. Give this to your grandmother, will you?" She dropped a shilling into his grubby palm. "My sister reports that the elderberry syrup has soothed her cough. She is very grateful."

Gwendolyn had not specifically said so, nor would she have thought to send the coin, but Toby's shining face was its own reward.

"Thank you, miss."

Old Mrs Protheroe was an herbwoman of some renown in Truro. Some called her a white witch. Likely the same prattle-boxes who called Loveday a hoyden and a disgrace and oh, wasn't it a shame that George Penhale, the heir, had been killed in France and that reckless tinkering girl could do nothing but add to the burdens their poor parents had to endure in their mourning?

Loveday slapped the reins over Rhea's glossy brown back, and startled, the horse lurched into motion across the stable-yard of the steam works. They lived only six miles from Truro, but on market day, the road was clogged with farmers' wagons returning empty, with women walking home carrying laden baskets, and with the occasional smart group of soldiers of the local militia, who fancied themselves cavalry, trotting in toward their billets.

It took every bit of skill Loveday possessed to keep Rhea from dancing and shying, especially when the soldiers passed four abreast and did not have the courtesy to give way to a lady driving a cane whiskey. "Move your blasted beast, you stupid potted wilkie!" she shouted as poor Rhea slowed to a walk while her left-hand wheel did a proper job of cleaning the mud off the soldier's leather boot.

"Harridan," the soldier muttered.

"Pillock!" she flung over her shoulder. Her hearing was quite acute, which was useful when one had two younger sisters.

Honestly, was the militia so desperate for recruits that it had to settle for men such as these? Why had they not joined the army proper, and gone to fight Boney like George—Jory to the family—had? England would never win this war if Napoleon was not stopped on the sands of his own shores. The militia was supposed to be composed of fierce old men who would give rudimentary training to boys too young yet to enlist, not able-bodied boors like the ones who had just passed. If the news sheets had their facts in order, the war was at an uneasy stalemate. A breeze blowing one way or the other could set it off.

If only the King had not bought Upper Canada! For once Napoleon came to power, he had taken that sum and gleefully invested it in engineering science, inventing engines that staggered even Loveday, who was no laggard in her studies of such matters herself. What twisted mind could have taken the engine invented by Papin and created the steam behemoths that rolled over the battlefield, crushing all before them? And what about Fulton's *sous-marin*? Because of that wretched invention, England's shipping industry was not only crippled, she had lost the battle of Trafalgar because of the nuisances below the waves. It was only by the grace of God that the sneaky French had not yet figured out how to give the *sous-marin* a size sufficient to carry troops.

Rhea crested the hill, and in the distance Loveday could see Hale Head, the cliff promontory giving their family its name, crouching in the sea like a watchful lion looking out into the Channel.

Halfway home.

At least they had steam cannons, Loveday consoled herself. Their use had netted General Wellington a dukedom and set the French back on their heels when the pressure-powered balls had breached the behemoths' skins. But they had not suffered such a setback long. Their repeating rifles that turned on a crank had harried Wellington's troops repeatedly at short range, after which the French troops would run back into their hideouts in the dry hills. Where the cannons could not find them.

Rhea's hooves made a hollow sound on the arched bridge over the Gwynn Bourne, the river that formed the western boundary of their neighbor's estate, Gwynn Place. Such an elevated name for a rambling brick and stone farmhouse set in acres of hay and tenant farms. She preferred the Cornish: *plas-an-gwynn*. The place of the winds. Overlooking the estuary on its rolling hills, it was a pretty enough property. The Trevelyans had suffered, too, at the hands of the French, though not nearly as badly as the Penhales. At least Arthur, the son and heir, was alive, unlike dear Jory. He'd had one leg smashed by a piece of an exploding behemoth and could not yet walk.

Loveday sighed as Rhea climbed out of the bourne's little valley and thence to the Penhale acres. As the Trevelyan twins might say, there was a distinct lack of heirs in the neighborhood. It did not affect Loveday personally, for she had other plans for her life. But at eighteen and sixteen, her sisters Rosalind and Gwen felt it keenly.

Just one more thing to hate Napoleon for.

Loveday turned Rhea's head and they plunged into the cool green depths of the long lane that led home.

"WHAT IS the news from town, Papa?" Rosalind took the plate on which their father had just laid a slice of roast pork and helped herself to apples cooked in syrup, buttered beans, and the first lettuces of the season.

The carving for his family completed, George Penhale senior flipped his coattails out of the way and sat down to his own dinner. "There is talk that the Prince Regent will make his progress here as soon as July," he said.

"At Christmas, it was to be March," Loveday complained, eating as fast as she dared. "Now it is July? Perhaps he will not come at all. He is not the sort of man to enjoy being paraded about the countryside. He is still in mourning, even if the *ton* is not."

"And what would you know of him or the *ton*?" mocked

Gwen. "None of us have even seen him, never mind become so well acquainted with the royal character."

"I have a mind, and I apply it," Loveday informed her loftily. "Besides, the newspapers have so much to say that we might all be as well acquainted with him as anyone at court."

From all accounts, Prinny, as he was affectionately known, was a man of medium height and slender build, his myopic blue Hanover eyes hidden by thick spectacles. After the death of his only daughter, the lovely Princess Charlotte, he had gone into seclusion, having no use for the social whirl of the *ton* or for making himself a leader of fashion. Rather, he preferred his laboratory that filled an entire wing at St James's, or living the life of a country gentleman at his castle in Scotland, well out of sight of critical eyes. Caroline, the Princess of Wales, her character the opposite of his in every way, preferred to hold her own court under the domes of her Pavilion in Brighton, an edifice that looked to be every whit as silly and fanciful as she was herself.

"Poor Prinny," Mama said sadly. "His father gone blind and mad as a hatter out in Windsor, his daughter and baby grandson both dead, his wife a social butterfly living a separate life…" With a shake of her head, she addressed herself to her roast, and did not finish her sentence out of consideration for her daughters' delicate sensibilities.

Loveday had heard the rumors of the princess and her Italian count. But such was not a suitable topic of conversation at Papa's table.

"He would probably have been much happier in a cottage than a palace," Rosalind offered. As the middle daughter, she did not speak up much, but when she did, it was usually to the point, and with more insight than one would expect of someone only eighteen and not much inclined to company.

"Perhaps," their father said. "But a man of his talents ought to be turning his hand to solving the French problem, not gallivanting about the country, much as you girls want to see him. Such a great inventor he is supposed to be, and yet he has not found a way to end this war with an English victory."

"Now, dearest—" their mother began.

"Dash it all, Mrs Penhale, it is the truth." Papa sawed at his slice of roast with energy. "At the very least, he ought to form a Ministry of Engines or Devices or War or some such, and let the First Admiral have a go at it."

"You have signed the petition, haven't you," Loveday said on a sudden burst of realization. "To have the Prime Minister insist on the formation of just such a ministry."

Papa gazed at her. "And how did you come to that conclusion?"

Loveday flushed. Once again her inability to hold her tongue had tripped her up. "Because it is common knowledge in Truro that Lord St Aubyn has signed it." Head of the leading family of the district, where his lordship led, the other gentry tended to follow.

"Mr Trevelyan has signed it, too," Gwen put in. "I heard it from Cecily and Jenifer when I called this afternoon."

Their father glared, clearly displeased—not that his news was no longer so fresh, but that his daughters were engaging in politics. Or as good as.

Loveday could only feel grateful that she was not the only black sheep in poor Papa's fold. Well, Gwen and Rosalind were merely a pale grey, not black. But still. He would be so angry to know that she was still assisting at the Trevithick

Steam Works. Every day, she was in danger of his ringing such a peal over her head that she would likely go deaf. But until that day…

After dinner, she excused herself to go upstairs and put off her pale lawn dinner dress with its whitework embroidery all around the hem. She liked pretty things as well as the next girl; she was a competent needlewoman and had embroidered the overskirt herself. But she was practical, too, and knew it would never survive a moment in her workshop in the barn. She put on an ugly chambray dress that was too short to wear to the steam works, but which served her well at home. Then she slipped down the servants' stairs to the door to the kitchen garden, hurried down the burgeoning rows of peas and carrots, and through the gate in the wall to the older of their two barns. Here, in a room that had been the tack room before they'd built the carriage house and stables, was her workshop.

Her current project was a piece of furniture. Emory would laugh at her making something so prosaic, something that did not require steam power and therefore should be beneath her notice. Emory was a man of singular interests. She couldn't wait for the day when some young lady knocked him off his intellectual pedestal and explained to him that he was a man like every other and ought to have a more well-rounded life. Or at the very least, a life.

This piece of furniture, a kind of sideboard, had been brought home on a tea clipper by some seafaring relative during the previous century. Her mother disliked it—said its ivory and black wood was too stark and unbeautiful to have in her pretty rooms. Loveday had a sneaking suspicion that it was the seafaring relative she hadn't liked, not the sideboard. In any case, Loveday was experimenting with its repair.

"Now, me dear," she said to it, "let us make another attempt, shall we?"

The original sideboard had once been designed to move on its own, but the cogs and pulleys were rusted and broken and it was difficult to see what their original movements had been. Loveday had just read a monograph from London in which automatons—which were essentially as devoid of life as a sideboard, were they not?—had been made to move and even provided simple services to the scientist, such as carrying a tea tray. If the same rudimentary principles had been applied years ago by some foresighted genius in a far country, could she not both learn from them and bring them up to date with her own modern knowledge?

Its weights, gears, and connectors had clearly once been meant to get the boxes to assemble themselves into various configurations. If she could make it over, the sideboard would be useful again. It was all in the physics and the mathematics... and in a few modern parts.

Granted, she was mostly self-taught in those subjects. The education that Papa had seen fit to give his children had mostly been for Jory's benefit, but she and Rosalind had been rather good at stealing his books and putting them back before they were missed. Loveday had read every book the subscription library had possessed on the two sciences and spent her pin money not on bonnets and ribbons—well, perhaps only a little of it—but in the bookshops in Truro and St Mawes. And then, of course, there had been her training in engineering under Richard Trevithick, which was every bit as good as a man would have received at Oxford. Probably better, since she had not had to waste time on Latin and history.

Her Latin was appalling, her history not much better. But she knew nearly as much about mechanics as Emory, who had actually been to Oxford.

What Papa did not know about her education would not hurt him. He knew she had been underfoot at the steam works, but he thought she had grown out of her fascination with engines. Little did he know that with every year, every obstacle, it only grew.

With a tiny turnscrew, she made a last adjustment to the connector between two of the boxes. "Let's see how you do now that I have changed the size of these wheels."

After laying down a saddle blanket to protect their glossy wood, she positioned the two connected boxes on the shallow stone steps of the workshop. Then, with one finger, she gave the topmost box a nudge.

The two boxes fell over and sprawled on the blanket, still connected.

Loveday let out a long breath. "Bother."

She seated herself on the step and, chin in hand, gazed at them as the light faded in the sky and the lamplight from the workshop behind her glowed on the wood. Where had she gone wrong?

In her mind, she pictured what should have happened. A change in weight distribution. A fall. The wheels taking up the slack to slow the fall. The forward motion that would have set the second pair of wheels spinning. The second box following the first.

Slack. Spinning.

Tension.

There wasn't enough tension on the gears!

"Loveday!" She heard Gwen's voice, faintly, from the flower garden at the front of the house. "Mother is looking for you."

"Coming!" she called back, tamping down the rush of excitement. Tension. She couldn't wait for the next bit of free time she could steal in which to make the adjustments. "Come along, then," she told the boxes as she picked them up. "We'll try again tomorrow."

CHAPTER 2

PARIS, FRANCE

May 1819

$\mathcal{N}$o good scientific advancement went unpunished. Celeste Blanchard didn't realize she'd grimaced at the memory of her father's favorite saying until she noticed the modiste's assistant gazing at her in alarm from where she knelt at the hem of Celeste's gown.

"How well you trim it," Celeste said, forcing a bright smile. She twisted to look over her shoulder at the drape of blue silk. Like the sky on a summer's morning, her mother had said, as if consoling her that a blue gown was as close as she'd get to the sky.

Non, Maman. I will reach the stars. You'll see. I have already accepted punishment for my advances.

"*Plus haute?*" Marie asked around her mouth full of pins. "Do you want it higher?"

Celeste took a step back from the trio of standing mirrors that encircled the dais where Madame Finett's illustrious clients stood for fittings. The high-waisted gown with its puffed short sleeves was now weighted by row upon row of frothy white satin ruching along the hem. And the low neckline was edged with Spanish lace, so hard to get now that Spain had declared its independence once more.

Still, the color accentuated the dark, curly hair she had inherited from her mother and the deep-set walnut-colored eyes her father had bequeathed her. The Emperor liked to call her his *petite elfe*, as if she had no greater purpose than to adorn his court. He'd change his mind when she proved herself.

She swished the heavy skirts from side to side. "*Parfait!* This will do nicely for the next court ball." She turned to face Marie and lowered her voice. "And the yellow silk?"

"Bundled and sent to *l'École*, Mademoiselle Blanchard, just as you asked." The young woman stood and met Celeste's gaze, then dropped her voice as well. "I do not know how long we can continue refurbishing your older gowns before your mother and my mistress notice."

Celeste reached out to give her hand a squeeze. "This is the last. I promise. With the yellow, we have enough for our purposes."

She sighed. "Oh, to soar into the heavens! You are so brave. Just like your mother. But why must you hide it from her? Surely she would be proud to have you follow in her glorious tradition."

"Perhaps not as much as you might think," Celeste allowed, releasing the girl's hand to turn about. "Now, *vite!* Get me out of this. There is work to be done, and when it is done, then *La Blanchard* will be proud."

At least the mere mention of Madame Marie Madeleine-Sophie Blanchard, Napoleon's Chief Air Minister, still brought instant obedience. The assistant was only a few months older than Celeste's nineteen years, but she knew the legend. There wasn't a man, woman, or child in Paris who had not witnessed one of Madame Blanchard's ascents. She starred in any entertainment the Emperor planned, was front and center at every event. Sophie Blanchard, famed cofounder of *l'École des Aéronautes*.

Her mother.

As soon as she had been pinned back into her muslin day dress and slipped the serpentine velvet short jacket over the top, she gave Marie a hug and hurried out the rear entrance of the shop. There, she adjusted her wide-brimmed, tall-crowned hat and tied it securely under her chin with a pink satin ribbon. Few of the fine ladies and gentlemen of Napoleon's court would have peered down such a backway, where sunlight failed to reach what remained of the cobblestones through the tall stone buildings. If they had looked that way, they might have wondered at the fashionably dressed young lady straddling a curious contraption that resembled nothing so much as a child's drawing of a horse. The crossbar back was low enough that it only raised her wide white skirts a few inches above her ankles. The taller head of her iron steed reached the middle of her chest, with enough of an ear on either side for her hands to steer it. The high, proud flat of the tail provided a rest for her back.

"Gravity is all that is required to set it in motion," her father had explained when he'd spread out his plans over blankets that covered his legs, which would never walk again.

"Oh, perhaps the judicious application of the feet from time to time, but that could be said of any fine mount, *non?*" His dark eyes had twinkled, as if he'd appreciated his own wit. Very likely her eyes had twinkled in return.

They had been a pair, Celeste and her father. She'd followed him and her mother all over Europe. When he'd been injured eleven years ago, she'd been only eight, too young to understand what a fall from a thousand feet might do to a man, much less how her clever, bubbly Papa could have fallen to begin with. A seizure of the heart, the physician had said afterward, as if anyone but an angel might have stolen her father's heart at such a height. As she'd grown older and assumed the nursing duties that so ill suited her mother, she'd learned something new about her *cher* Papa.

He liked to tinker.

Oh, the drawings he'd shared with her, the journals he'd left behind. What wonders that agile mind had envisioned. And not one of them had worked, until now.

She kicked off against the crooked stones of the alleyway, and the velocipede began its bumpy glide. It slowed at the first turn—she'd have to adjust the gears again—then picked up speed as she reached the pavement of the Rue de Rivoli. Less friction always increased the pace. The air rushing past her face set her eyes to watering, and she reached up a hand to tug down the goggles hidden by the sweep of her bonnet's brim. The carriage ahead leaped into view.

She leaned right, and the velocipede veered around the lumbering beast. She caught the startled gaze of the coachman as she shot past.

It was the in-between time—too late in the day to pay calls

or shop, too early for dinners and balls. Few vehicles clogged the streets as she turned down Rue du Renard, then swept onto Rue des Aeronautes, where the largest, grandest stone building was her parents' school. She swung the velocipede into the wide, flagstone-paved front courtyard, which had seen its share of ascensions, and brought her iron steed to a stop at the base of the stairs leading up to the double oak doors. The frame slid easily into the brackets Marcel had installed for it. His velocipede was already waiting.

Celeste patted the cool metal as she stepped over the frame. "At least I don't have to carry an apple to please you into giving me a ride."

She traipsed up the stairs and into the entry. Her heels clacked against the marble-tiled floor as she followed the corridor toward the back of the building. Once, the school would have been abuzz. In the great hall, first-year students would be studying her father's history curriculum on ballooning and the current state of the art, including the location and harvesting of the precious lifting gas. On the next floor up, second-year students would be designing and constructing their own balloons—models at first. In the center courtyard, third-year students would be working on a few life-sized prototypes they would test and launch in their fourth year as they graduated to join Napoleon's elite forces. And everyone would gather in the outer court to watch her mother as she prepared for her next ascent.

Now the corridors were silent, and a pair of doves had made their nest in a stone urn in the center courtyard. Who wanted to join a school when one founder had died in the art and the other was known to be in disgrace with the Emperor?

It seemed the angelic *La Blanchard* was mortal after all, for she had not found a way to give the great Napoleon what he most wanted.

Voices rang from the rear workshop as Celeste shoved open the door. Here was where all materials were stored, waiting their turn to be fashioned into balloons. The bins of silk were empty now, depleted of all but what she'd been able to smuggle from her fittings. But her mother's performances meant they must keep kegs of lifting gas filled so she could gratify the Emperor's whim. Still, there was plenty of rope hanging from hooks like the bananas in the Emperor's conservatory, and several baskets from previous performances leaning up against the high walls, the wicker fashioned into whimsical shapes like seashells and birds of prey.

"You have returned," Amélie cried, waving a hand as Celeste ventured deeper into the cavernous workroom. She and her sister, Josephine Aventure, the last of the third and fourth-year students, had the yellow silk draped over the oak worktable, a bright flash against the green and blue of the other panels.

"We are becoming quite colorful," Josie announced, already threading her needle with the triple-ply cotton thread that had proven strong enough to bind the panels together. "This should finish the envelope."

Amélie bent her head closer to her sister, until their golden ringlets bumped. In their blue muslin gowns, white fichus around their necks, they might have been sitting in a withdrawing room, waiting to receive callers.

"Such tiny stitches!" Amélie marveled. "You always were better at embroidery."

Josie laughed. "And who would think such skills could serve the Empire?"

"The Emperor needs all our skills. France cannot be contained." Marcel's voice echoed as he swung down from his perch on one of the empty steel racks to land in the square woven wood basket they'd decided to use. With his dusky skin and dark curls clustered around a strong-jawed face, he could have been a pirate on the Moorish Coast, particularly in the baggy breeches and cotton shirt he wore when working. He'd been set to graduate when her mother had closed the school.

"Well, it is contained at the moment," Amélie, ever the pragmatist, reminded them all. "Russian bears lumbering along to the north. British lions roaring to the west, the Karlsruhe Confederacy breathing fire on the east."

"And to the south, the Sicilian raiders brandishing scimitars," Celeste confirmed. "If we had not discovered the lifting gas bubbling up in Bretagne, this war might have ended in our defeat years ago."

They all nodded. They'd had to learn about the event in first-year history, how the geologist Jacques Bernard had been vacationing at one of the twenty Breton spas when he'd realized the gas forcing the mineral waters from the earth was not only warm but buoyant. Now several of the spas had been converted to manufactories that produced the gas to fill military and commercial balloons. Her mother could tell which spa had produced it from one sniff.

"Bain du Loire," she'd say. "You cannot mistake that faint scent of lavender."

Now Amélie glanced around at them all. "But will it be enough, our supremacy on the sea and in the air? With the school closed, there will be no new aeronauts."

"At least ones that have been well trained," Marcel allowed dourly.

"We will prevail," Celeste told them. "We cross the Channel, bring our valiant troops to England, and it all ends. England is the glue that holds the allied forces together. We strike at the heart of England, and France is free."

"The heart of the glue?" Amélie asked with a quizzical frown, and Josie laughed.

"The heart of our enemy," Celeste amended with a smile. "The Emperor has longed to pluck it out for years, and we are going to give him that ability. That will prove the good that is taught at *l'École des Aéronautes.*"

Marcel hauled himself out of the basket to land with a thud on the scarred wood floor. "I won't mind the credit. A man has to gain the Emperor's attention somehow. A woman as well," he acknowledged with a nod to Celeste.

"And we will," Celeste assured him. "When this balloon rises over the Paris skyline, everyone will take notice."

Josie lifted her needle in salute, red thread trailing like blood. *"Vive la France! Vive l'École des Aéronautes!"*

The great bronze clock above the workshop door clicked the hour into place and tinny bells began playing. Le Sueur's *1814 Overture,* composed on the occasion of Napoleon's defeat of the Iron Duke. It was fitting, grand. A reminder of all that might be if they just persevered. But Celeste's smile lasted only until the last bell struck.

"Six!"

She whirled toward the door. "I'm late! Marcel, *vite!* Help me with the gears on the velocipede. I must reach home quickly, or *Maman* will be furious."

Amélie and Josie paled. They'd all run afoul of her mother's temper at one time or another. Sophie Blanchard's scowl alone could peel the paint from a steam boiler.

"Come on," Marcel said, heading for the door. "You can borrow mine. I learned long ago that you should not keep *La Blanchard* waiting."

CHAPTER 3

GWYNN PLACE, CORNWALL

*D*euce take it!"

A bit of raised stone caught the toe of his boot, and Arthur Trevelyan nearly fell headlong on the flagged path. Had it not been for quick reflexes, honed by the sound of propelled bullets whining past him on the Peninsula, he would have measured his length and picked up yet another bruise or scrape to add to his collection. But his crutches acted as they were meant to, giving him just enough time to get his bad leg under him and put his weight on the good one, long enough to stand upright.

If he ever recovered, he could become an acrobat and join a traveling troupe.

If he ever recovered.

But no, he must not think that way. He must look bravely into the future and see himself whole and useful once again, partnering ladies at balls instead of hiding in the card room with his leg up on a cushion, enduring the sympathetic glances of his peers.

He hated that even here in the garden, he was forced to

take steps as careful as any he had ever taken in the fields of battle, and for a much less heroic purpose. Then again, here at Gwynn Place, at least he could move without attracting the attention of an armed behemoth.

Let it always be so. Let the monsters created by that devil Bonaparte never set foot on English soil.

The garden path decanted him onto the gently sloping lawn that stretched all the way to the cliffs, giving him the most beloved view in the world. Then again, he was hopelessly biased. On his left was the wide, silvery expanse of the Carrick Roads, the deep estuary where sailing ships found safe harbor and the town of St Vivyan on the other side did a roaring trade in china clay, tin, and smuggled brandy from France. In the distance before him lay the Channel, now obscured by the haze of a warm day cooling into late afternoon. The sun lay perhaps an hour above the horizon, giving him ample time for his daily peregrination to the cliff.

The surgeon said he must have exercise, so exercise he would have—even if the pain was sometimes more than he thought he could bear. At least out here, he could be alone and no one could hear if a curse or groan broke through his self-control.

His right leg had been broken in two places when a piece of shrapnel half the size of an ox had sideswiped him in the field. The fact that he himself had given the command to the cannoneers in his unit to blow up the behemoth from which it came did not enrage him. No, it was the ridiculousness of the blasted thing exploding in such a disorganized way and taking its own back that made him furious even now, nearly six months after the fact. He ought to have foreseen the angle of the blast given the rise of the steam cannon's barrel and the arc of the ball.

But in the heat of the attack, all he had seen was the behemoth bearing down on his company like an enraged rhinoceros, its armored sides protecting its iron wheels, steam rising from its twin stacks as it gained speed. Firing that steam cannon had been the only thing on his mind.

The mighty ball had stopped it. But at the cost of two good men and his own leg—the latter an insignificant price compared to the lives of the two cannoneers. The remaining two cannoneers had draped him over the still-hot barrel and retreated with him to the next line of defense, where the army surgeon had done his best to save the leg. He had been an excellent surgeon, which was why Arthur was able to swing himself along with the benefit of both feet.

He could have come back with none—or only one.

A man in his company had had a metal appendage affixed to the stump of his left thigh, and its interior gears whined as it assisted his stride. He joked that he was one-quarter automaton. Arthur's injuries were not so severe; he had not had to be fitted for such a device, and on days like this he was almost sorry. The regimen the local surgeon had set for him demanded he make it to the cliff edge and back every day, rain or shine, no matter how much it hurt. The two bones, the surgeon assured him, had knit as well as could be expected. "The task now, Captain Trevelyan, is to convince the damaged muscles to once again take up their burden and bear your weight."

Easier said than done. But he would do it. He must, if he was to end his medical leave, rejoin his company, and recover his self-respect.

His parents and his twin sisters Cecily and Jenifer, needless to say, did not know he planned to return to France. Had they suspected, he might likely have been dispatched to some remote castle in Wales, where a distant relative would be tasked with holding him in a tower with a lot of steep stairs until the war was over.

His father's worst nightmare—losing his heir—had come true for the Penhales next door. Arthur knew it, and while he regarded his father with deep affection, he knew equally well that he had to go back. Had to keep fighting. For if good men did not stop Boney, England would wake one morning to find Fulton's submarines surfacing in the estuary and troops disembarking to form up on the golden sands of the Looe.

He did not labor all the way down here merely to appreciate the view or to obey the surgeon. No, the puzzle of the *sous-marins* propelled him to the cliffs each day, as though by keeping watch he might have first warning of their approach.

Though what he could do except fling his crutches at them was a mystery.

But something was keeping them at bay... for now. And the smugglers who plied the Cornish and French coasts knew what it was. Somehow, some way, he was going to find it out.

Arthur shook his head, lowering himself to the flat rock that served his purpose. It was still warm from the sun, penetrating his breeches as pleasantly as the fire in the parlor might if he stood in front of it. The Channel was half a mile from here, at the mouth of the Roads. Had he been in charge of a French deployment to these shores, he would have marked this place as an excellent location for a landing. The estuary cut inland all the way to Truro. Why had those wretched *sous-marins* not gained access to the very heart of the country, still submerged in deep water? Granted, they were small. But they were perfect for spying if they were not busy disrupting the movement of shipping vessels. What prevented them from attempting the obvious military maneuver?

For even an aeronaut would not detect them from his balloon. With the danger increasing from the south, there was talk from Falmouth to Marazion that Lord St Aubyn planned to allow a detachment of aeronauts to be stationed on the Mount, their balloons making regular patrols along the coast. How this was to be accomplished, Arthur and the other gentlemen of the county were not certain. Balloons were unpredictable and fragile things, more suited to the silly, circuslike public spectacles enjoyed by the French than anything that could be useful in war. Why, not so long ago, Boney's most famous aeronaut, Jean-Pierre Blanchard, had fallen out of his ridiculous contraption and plunged a thousand feet to the ground. And he an experienced pilot!

No, the Tinkering Prince and his crony St Aubyn were altogether in error with this aeronaut business. Real soldiers did not gad about the skies in brightly colored balloons. Wars were won on the ground, where a man knew what was what, not in the air where all you had to depend on was a few yards of silk that had better be applied to a fashionable woman's wardrobe.

As though his own gloomy thoughts had conjured a woman out of the air, he glanced along the cliffs to the west and saw a slender feminine figure standing on Hale Head, looking, as he had been, out to sea.

Loveday Penhale. Arthur recognized the straightness of her back and the pointed angle of her elbow, bent to hold her bonnet in place. The wind had picked up as the day cooled, and ribbons and hat pins were inadequate to their task, by all indications. She wore a dark blue spencer over a white muslin dress that bellied out like a sail in the wind.

She often came to the cliffs, he had observed, and usually at this time of day. But either she did not see him, perched upon his rock, or she did not care to acknowledge him, broken and useless as he was. They had known one another all their lives, but for some reason they did not *know* each other in the way longstanding friends did. There had been no history of playing together on the grounds of their neighboring estates; indeed, he had gone away to school at eight and returned at one and twenty, then had convinced his father to purchase a commission for him. The truth was, his sisters knew the Penhale girls better than ever he did, or likely would.

From all accounts, Loveday was an odd duck. Assisting the great Richard Trevithick at fifteen years of age? It had to be a Banbury tale. For who could have done that and maintained a respectable position in society? Frankly, Arthur pitied the poor sod the Penhales convinced to marry their peculiar daughter. He would have his hands full.

And just because he had been thinking uncharitable thoughts, she turned and saw him. They were a quarter mile or more apart, so she could not so much as shout a greeting. But she lifted her free hand and waved.

Good heavens. What had he done to deserve her notice?

But almost of its own volition, the hand that was not holding his crutches rose into the air and waved back, swiftly controlled and restored to its proper place. Never mind. He was only being civil.

Unless she developed a penchant for nursing, the likelihood of their ever being in company together, to say nothing of—heaven forfend—furthering any acquaintance, was practically nil.

~

"I SAW Captain Trevelyan from the Head just now," Loveday announced to her sisters at dinner. She seated herself in her usual place at Mama's right hand and regarded the grilled plaice with great interest. Her walks down to the Head to think always made her hungry.

"You were out on the Head?" Gwen regarded her with pity. "Never mind. I see that you were. Your hair looks like a haystack after a storm."

"Does it?" Loveday touched her braided Psyche knot, which did not seem any more out of order than usual. She had remembered to wear a bonnet.

"Be kind, Gwen," their mother said. "Loveday looks a little windblown, but it is of no consequence when we dine *en famille.* Did you note any improvement in Captain Trevelyan, dear?"

"He was sitting on a rock," Loveday said, taking her plate from Papa and helping herself with some energy to the fresh vegetables. "However, I suppose we can infer improvement since he got himself down there under his own steam."

"I wish you would not use slang," Mama complained.

"I beg your pardon, Mama," Loveday said meekly. She would have to watch the tendency to use the expressions Emory and Thomas did in the shop. Papa might wonder where she picked them up, and that would lead to his asking questions. "Anyway, he was merely watching the sea. Gazing at France, I suppose, as though it would send him back an undamaged leg."

"He is a hero," Rosalind informed her soberly, "and you are unkind to be making sport of him so."

"I am not making sport!" Loveday protested. "But he must be improving. He makes his way to the cliffs every day, that's all. As though he is expecting something."

"Boney, I suspect," their father grumbled around a succulent mouthful of plaice. "We need to see to this detachment of aeronauts at the Mount. Lord St Aubyn is no laggard. I do not understand the reason for the delay."

"Perhaps there are not enough aeronauts," Loveday suggested. "Perhaps someone ought to establish a school of flight in Cornwall, to train them. And invite women to try their hands at it as well."

Their father's eyes widened until Loveday could see the whites of them. "What?"

"Loveday would insist upon attending as a student." Gwen rolled her eyes. "And there would go all our chances of making a suitable match."

Elbowing her sister in the ribs, Rosalind said, "She is jesting, Papa. None of us have even seen an ascension. Why would Loveday have such an idea in her head?"

"I never know what Loveday has in her head," Papa said, returning to his dinner. "And for the most part, I do not wish to know."

Loveday perked up. That was something. That was very good news indeed, in fact.

She refused to look directly at Mama, but Loveday could

feel her glaring at her so pointedly that the left side of Loveday's head would surely catch fire at any second.

"Returning to more interesting subjects," Gwen said, "I wonder if Captain Trevelyan will be sufficiently recovered to attend the Midsummer Ball next month?"

"Unlikely," Papa said.

"Oh, Papa," Gwen said reproachfully. "You wound the hopes of every unattached female in the county."

"Not a one of them good enough for that lad."

"My dear Mr Penhale," exclaimed their mother, "what better wife for him than one of our own daughters? We have known him all his life, and a better friend than Mrs Trevelyan I could never hope to meet. The two of us have long harbored a cherished desire, you know, to—"

Papa lifted both fork and knife to prevent another word. "I know what you have been plotting, you two estimable women. But a man of the captain's caliber likes to choose his own wife, not have the job done for him by his mother. For all we know, he is corresponding with some likely young lady in London whom he met doing charitable work in the army hospitals." He laid his utensils down with the sound of finality. "Is there any hope of strawberry cake for dessert?"

Both Gwen and Rosalind had been stricken silent with the horror of this imagined paragon in London, so when the strawberry cake was served in the drawing room, Loveday took the opportunity to change her dress and slip out to her workshop.

She sat upon a stool and regarded the boxes of the sideboard. "What am I to do with you?" she asked them. "Here I went out to Hale Head to give you all some thought, only to be interrupted by the sight of Captain Trevelyan. One cannot think when under surveillance by a soldier. At all events, let us begin and see how much progress we make."

Tension was the guiding principle here. Tension had prevented the tiny pulleys and gears from completing their tasks, so this must be her starting point. Loveday assembled her tools and began with the bottom row of boxes, still smooth and silky to the touch despite their long journey to England and their subsequent neglect. Why, the gouge from an unfortunate slip of a tool was hardly visible—and anyway, it was in the rear.

She had adjusted the weight and tension in each end of three boxes when the door opened and Rosalind slipped in.

This was unusual, but no reason to stop one's work.

"I thought I might find you out here."

"As long as Papa or Gwen are not with you, you are most welcome." Loveday began on the remaining sides.

"Gwen does not care to know what you are doing." Rosalind leaned over to watch the proceedings. "Papa would care, however."

"Do you plan to carry tales to him?"

"Certainly not. But you must not be hard on our sister. She cannot help her views."

"Her views are those of our father, trimmed to fit." Loveday adjusted a series of pulleys, little by little. "And while I love and respect Papa, I would feel easier if his views would expand to include mine."

Rosalind stepped back to take a turn about the cramped space, lifting a tool here and a bit of wire there, moving the lamp to better illuminate Loveday's work. "I do not have much hope of that. But I did want to ask you something."

"Yes?"

"Do you not find it interesting that Captain Trevelyan is often on the cliffs when you walk down to the Head?"

Loveday lost her focus altogether at this *non sequitur* and stared at her sister. "Why should I consider such a thing? When the poor man takes his exercise is none of my business. He is a gentleman and quite free to do so without my leave."

Her sister's lips twitched. "I simply wondered if one of you had noticed the other's habits, that is all."

Loveday went back to work and did not dignify this with a reply. Honestly. One simply had enough to do during the day that the hour before dinner was convenient for a walk. That was all. She would have expected such a featherheaded connection to be made in Gwen's brain, but not Rosalind's. The latter, much to her relief, tended more to sense than nonsense.

"There," she said, laying down the tiny turnscrew. "Let us see how we do."

As before, she laid down a piece of canvas and positioned two of the boxes one on top of the other in the doorway, where the two flagged steps were shallow enough that no damage would result from a mishap.

"What are you expecting it to do?" Rosalind asked. "Why have you taken apart Mama's sideboard, anyway? Does she know?"

With a fingertip, Loveday gave the top box a push.

A whir commenced from within, and the box tumbled off its perch. But this time, when it reached the next step, the lower box responded, pulled into motion by its companion and turned upon its head. Its matched latches clicked together effortlessly, with the result that now the lower rested upon the upper, two steps down.

Loveday clapped and bounced on the balls of her feet. "Oh, well done, sideboard!" she said to the two boxes, situated rather triumphantly upon the canvas. "Well done indeed."

"Sister, dear, you are talking to the furniture," Rosalind observed.

"So I am," Loveday said, collecting the boxes and giving them an approving pat. "By midsummer, I will be able to move the sideboard anywhere in a room simply by using the power of its own motion." A happy thought occurred to her. "Perhaps I will even accompany it on walks about the estate."

"In that case, you must certainly demonstrate it to the Tinkering Prince when he comes," Rosalind said in the pleasant tone one might use to placate a person in an asylum, and departed.

CHAPTER 4

PARIS, FRANCE

*M*arcel's velocipede had the same problem with the gears—she would have to work on that soon—so it was nearly seven by the time Celeste reached her mother's house. She could not call the tall, thin house her home. *Home* had been the little gabled house near the Church of Saint Eustace, where they'd returned after every flight and where she'd nursed her father. For a while, they'd had a fine mansion nearer the Tuileries, where the Emperor could call on her mother at any time. Last year, they had been asked to move to an *arrondissement* farther out. Now, few would guess this to be the home of a famous aeronaut. It looked no different from the other two-story brick houses on the narrow street.

"Use the back stairs," their cook Madame LeGrande advised when Celeste came through the kitchen. "Dupont is waiting to help you dress for entertaining."

"Who's here?" Celeste whispered, edging for the servants' stair.

Madame LeGrande sniffed as she hitched up the soiled

apron on her broad chest. "Some fellow from the court. No one of any interest. Not like when your Papa was alive."

For once, Celeste was thankful for their lowered status. Perhaps she wouldn't have to do more than giggle at witty sayings and smile vapidly. Her mother certainly expected no more of her.

"Ballooning is dangerous, Celeste," she'd say, head cocked like a little sparrow. "I want you to live to grow old and happy."

As if she could truly be happy anywhere but in the sky.

"There you are!" Dupont hurried to meet her as Celeste slipped into the bedchamber. Iron-haired, steely-eyed, her longtime companion still managed a warm smile and fierce embrace that made Dupont feel more motherly than any other woman Celeste had met.

Celeste wrinkled her nose as she disengaged. "Sorry. Equipment problem."

Dupont was already moving behind her to begin unpinning the back of Celeste's dress. "Nothing dangerous?"

"Nothing dangerous," Celeste assured her.

Dupont had held her that dark day when Papa had fallen. She had never forgotten the perils behind their passion for ballooning. Now her capable fingers worked down Celeste's back to help her out of the dress.

"You'll find the Comte d'Angeline downstairs," Dupont told her. "I think he may be courting your mother."

"She won't have him." Celeste stepped out of the dress as it slid from her form to puddle on the thick crimson carpet. "She's still mourning Papa."

"That won't stop the Emperor from insisting on the

match," Dupont countered, seizing the evening gown she'd laid out on the bed and dropping it over Celeste's head.

Celeste wiggled it down, the rich folds of the pink satin settling about her, and Dupont began working on the fastenings.

"The pearl bandeau, my evening gloves, and the fan painted with roses," Celeste instructed her. "At least fussing with it will give me something to do if they start talking about the invasion."

Dupont finished with the gown, then hurried to the dressing table. "You could speak to that. You could recite those plans in your sleep."

"And point out the flaws we must address," Celeste agreed, tugging on the white silk long gloves her companion had offered. "But I am not to know about such things. I am a giddy debutante." She fluttered her lashes and giggled.

Dupont snorted as she went for the bandeau. "If your father were alive, he'd have something to say about that."

"If my father were alive, none of this playacting would be necessary." She wrapped the pearl-studded satin about her head and pulled a curl free here and there to complete the look. Her mother had not been amused when she'd had her dark hair trimmed into a tousled cap *à la Grèque*, but the arrangement was so much easier to manage.

Particularly where she hoped to go soon.

Dupont handed her the fan. "*Bonne chance.*"

With a smile, Celeste sallied forth.

Conversation drifted up the polished wood stairs as she descended to the ground floor. She followed the sound to the salon, where a merry fire glowed on the emerald velvet–covered settee and matching chairs, setting the gilded wood on the arms to glowing. *Maman* was in high style, her white silk gown a fitting canvas for the medals the Emperor had awarded her. The gold cross with its ruby at the center would be enough to bow most people. Not *La Blanchard*. Her dark head was high, and her gloved hands darted as quickly as birds as she emphasized a point. Celeste knew to the minute when she spotted her in the doorway, for she smiled.

Hard, brittle.

Something was wrong.

Her stomach dropped, but she sashayed into the room and dipped a curtsey. *"Milles pardons, Maman.* I did not realize we were entertaining this evening."

The gentleman on the settee heaved himself to his feet. He favored the style of the previous era, with a long, yellow velvet coat embroidered with daisies and a waistcoat with so much gold thread he glowed more than the furniture. His grey hair was parted in the middle and curled around his wide cheeks. He must spend a fortune on pomade.

"Monsieur le Comte, allow me to present my daughter Celeste," her mother said in her high, fluty voice that always sounded just the slightest bit worried. "Celeste, this is the Comte d'Angeline."

He waddled closer and swallowed her hands in his own. "My dear Mademoiselle Blanchard. You are as beautiful as your mother."

She could not doubt the statement. Too many commented on their likeness. But the compliment meant nothing. Neither she nor her mother was known for physical beauty. Theirs was a beauty of the mind. Still, she knew her response.

"You are too kind," she said. "Forgive my interruption. You were surely conversing about matters of import."

He released her hands. "Nothing so urgent. Come, sit by me. Let me look at you."

Celeste cast her mother a quick glance. *La Blanchard* made shooing motions with her hands. Not helpful. Was this a man who required charm to convince him to do something her mother wanted, or a suitor her mother wanted Celeste to frighten off?

She made herself perch on the other end of the settee from him. He beamed at her as if she had done something very clever.

"Your mother has little time to keep a home," he said, gaze dropping decidedly lower than her face.

He was ogling her! Not the sort of fellow she wanted in a stepfather. She shifted just the slightest, so the drape of her arm masked the curve of her bosom. "Alas, it is true. But I am certain the Emperor would rather she continue to use her skills on his behalf."

He shoved himself closer. "And you? Do you long to serve our great Napoleon?"

Was this a test, then? She did not dare look to her mother for confirmation. She leaned away from him and widened her eyes. "Why, of course! We must all do our duty. *Vive la France!*"

"*Vive la France,*" her mother echoed.

Now he rested his hand on her leg, as if she were a trained parrot performing for his pleasure, only no parrot had even been treated to quite so possessive a pat. "Excellent, excellent. And you understand how to direct servants, to manage a household?"

Conversing with him was like flying a balloon in a storm—

she could be sure of neither direction nor purpose. Did he expect her to stay here and manage the house while he followed her mother on her travels? Dupont had performed that function, and brilliantly, for more than a decade. That was why she had been hired—to care for Celeste, to see to their affairs, so that they need not worry about the mundane.

"Certainement," Celeste allowed. "But there are so many other things a young lady might do with her time these days."

His head bobbed in a ponderous nod. "True, true. And what interests you, Mademoiselle Blanchard? Do you sing? Play?"

And that was clearly the sum total of the abilities he was willing to ascribe to her. She kept her smile in place with difficulty. "My voice is passable, as are my skills at the pianoforte." And only because Papa had claimed her playing soothed his spirit; otherwise, she would have given up on the thing after taking it apart to see how it worked.

"Excellent," he repeated. Again he edged closer, until Celeste was pinned against the arm of the settee. Couldn't her mother see how horrid he was? Why didn't she throw him out?

"And I understand you are good with children," he said, breath fanning her face. He'd had onions, garlic, and likely red wine recently. She brought up her fan in self-defense and waved it so fast he was forced to retreat a little.

"My daughter has taught at *l'École des Aéronautes* for several years," her mother said when Celeste did not answer.

Mostly students closer to her own age. There were no little ones at the school. Why did he care about children anyway? Did he think her mother might yet bear him a son? Celeste could not imagine it. *Maman* was a wonder, a national treasure, the Emperor had said so himself. But, almost since the day Celeste had been born, her mother had wisely turned her daughter over to the keeping of others.

"Do you like children, Monsieur le Comte?" Celeste asked dutifully.

"I would like several," he allowed, flabby lips pursing. "As many as my wife and my fortune can bear." He chuckled as if he had been very witty, then turned to her mother.

"I can see the Emperor's wisdom in this choice," he said with a slow nod. "We will get on well, I think, though your daughter will need to wear a wig until her hair grows out."

Celeste pressed her teeth together to keep from saying the words that threatened to pop out.

Her mother must have seen the storm brewing, for she hopped to her feet. "Thank you for coming this evening, Monsieur le Comte. Allow me to see you to the door."

Once more, he climbed to his feet. Celeste only had a moment to catch her breath before he seized her hand and brought it to his lips for a kiss. Never had she been so glad for her gloves.

"*Au revoir*, my dear," he said with a fond smile. Her mother hurried him out the door.

Celeste rubbed her glove, but that didn't help wipe away the sensation of his touch. The front door closed, and her mother returned.

"He is an imbecile," *Maman* proclaimed, plopping down in her seat as if she was just as relieved to have him gone. "But you will accustom yourself to him."

Celeste put some distance between her body and the arm of the settee. "The question is whether you can accustom yourself to him, *Maman*. Surely you can do better."

"I would have liked the opportunity to try," she said with a shrug that set the medals on her chest to winking in the candlelight. "But the Emperor remains displeased with me. I cannot give him what he wishes most."

Celeste nodded in understanding. "The invasion of Britain. We will find a way, *Maman*."

Her mother rose and began to pace, silk skirts whispering against the carpet. "He asks the impossible. Your father, the Montgolfiers, de Rozier—none of them discovered the secret. He has given me a task that cannot be accomplished, so he demands I prove my loyalty."

"By marrying the Comte d'Angeline?" Celeste asked with a shudder.

Her mother jerked to a stop and stared at her. "*Non*. By marrying *you* to the Comte d'Angeline."

Celeste leaped to her feet. "*Maman, non*! You wouldn't. I won't."

"You must." Her mother came to take her hands and peer into her face. "He is not what I would have wished for you. I always dreamed you would find a love match, as I had with your father."

Her throat was tight. "So did I."

"But he is wealthy, and he is a friend of the Emperor," her mother persisted, giving her hands a shake. "Both facts will serve you well, particularly when Napoleon realizes I will never succeed. By marrying the *comte*, you could well keep us both safe."

"I will keep us safe, *Maman*," Celeste promised. "Give me a few days, a week at the most, and I will show Napoleon that *La Blanchard* is not a failure."

Her mother dropped Celeste's hands and cocked her head. "What have you done, my little star?"

Celeste raised her chin. "It is not what I have done but what I will do that matters. Soon, all of Paris will see what the Blanchard family and *l'École des Aéronautes* can do. When we rise, even Napoleon will bow. And I will not have to marry the Comte d'Angeline or anyone else so detestable."

CHAPTER 5

HALE HOUSE, CORNWALL

*L*oveday and her father were both early risers, so it was a surprise to see that Mama had joined them for breakfast and was already seated when Loveday came in. Loveday helped herself to a generous piece of plum cake sprinkled with nuts and selected several strawberries that had been growing in the kitchen garden not half an hour before.

"To what do we owe this pleasure, Mama? Are you going to town today?"

"As it happens, we are paying a call upon Sir Anthony and Lady Boscawen later, when the hour is more suitable."

"Is it about the detachment of aeronauts at the Mount?" Loveday asked around a delicious and generously sized strawberry. The Boscawen estate was near Marazion, and could reasonably be expected to assist with supplying such an outpost.

"Never mind that now." Papa swallowed the last of his cake and scrubbed at his lips with his napkin. "Your mother and I have something important to discuss with you."

More important than defending the Cornish coast against

the French? Loveday downed her cake and the strawberries as efficiently as possible in the unlikely event either of her parents should solicit her opinion on a subject as yet unknown.

Mama gazed at her fondly across the breakfast table. "We were heartened by your news yesterday that you had taken notice of Captain Trevelyan on the cliffs, dear."

The last bite of cake stuck in her throat and she gulped her tea. How on earth could this be more important than—

"Since your mind is clearly running in such pleasant channels," Mama went on, "we felt this would be a good time—when your sisters are not present, I mean—to tell you that contrary to what we said last evening, we do approve the match and will do everything in our power to bring it about."

Now the tea went down the wrong way, and Loveday snatched up her own napkin to cough violently. "What match?" she croaked. What madness had seized her parents? This could not be the subject of discussion. She must have missed something.

"It's time you were married, girl," Papa said gruffly. "With our Jory gone to his heavenly reward, your mother and I must look to the welfare of the land my father entrusted to me, and his to him. If you were to marry the captain, the two properties would be combined into a very pretty estate, with enough income to see to a fine dowry for each of your sisters, should I have passed by then."

"And his sisters, too, of course," Mama put in.

Loveday tried to gather her wits. "But—but I barely know Arthur Trevelyan," she stammered. "I can hardly be expected to marry the next thing to a stranger."

"You know more of him than any other gentleman in the

neighborhood," Mama said. "And the family is beyond reproach. Why, your sisters are thick as thieves with his."

"Far too many girls hereabouts of nearly marriageable age," her father grumbled. "I can't afford to take you or your sisters to Bath or London or even York to make your bows to society and capture some gentleman's eye. We must manage with what we have."

"I should not like a son-in-law from the north in any case," Mama said. "Such a distance to travel in order to visit."

Loveday felt ready to scream at this digression from their deliberate sabotage of her life. "This is your intent, then? To present me to Arthur Trevelyan as a *fait accompli?*"

"Of course not, dear," Mama said.

"That will be enough French spoken in my house," Papa said.

"Captain Trevelyan speaks French, Papa." Oh, to what depths was she sunk, to bring up such trivia at such a time. But any port in a storm.

"Captain Trevelyan assisted the Crown a full year before he was assigned the command of the battalion of cannon," her father said. "Of course he speaks French. That is beside the point. The point is that you will cease your gadding about the countryside and endless shopping trips to Truro, and apply yourself to acting like a gentlewoman."

"What does that mean?" Loveday asked in despair.

He made a gesture as though handing the discussion over to Mama.

"You know perfectly well what it means, Loveday Maria Penhale," she said. "It means paying calls upon his mother. Asking if you might accompany him on his daily walk, since he already knows you do the same yourself. Joining Rosalind and Gwen when they go into town with his sisters. And, when the captain is fully recovered from his injuries, standing up with him when he asks you to dance."

"In other words, the very life I do not enjoy," she said, with rather too much honesty for wisdom. "I shall engage in a lie in order to become engaged, is that it?"

Her father pushed away from the table. "None of your games, maidey." He must be upset, to revert to the local vernacular. "You have had twenty years of your own way. Now you will think of your family and what you owe to it."

"Captain Trevelyan is not to be sneezed at," Mama said in milder tones as Papa stalked out of the room. A moment later, the side door slammed, telling Loveday he had gone to the stables. "He is brave, of excellent character, and many believe him handsome. Even if he does not recover, all those things will still be true."

"I know, Mama," she said with a sigh. "But I had not planned to marry for some years yet. I had hoped to see success as an inventor—or even as an aeronaut."

"When I was a child, I dreamed about childish things," her mother quoted, most unfairly. "It is time to grow up, dearest, and do what you can for your family."

"But if Napoleon succeeds, my family may be in danger and the captain's good opinion will be neither here nor there."

"That is a big if." Her mother rose gracefully from the table. "The truth is, the family will be in danger if the property is not secured in the hands of a good, honorable man whom we know and respect. Captain Trevelyan is the perfect choice —we could not ask for a better, and you will not have to break my heart by moving miles away." Her mother paused. "And if I may be blunt, one woman to another, you could travel across every county on the south coast and not see such a fine figure of a man. The crutches will be no impediment in the marriage bed, my dear."

"Mother!" Loveday clapped both hands over her ears, leaped to her feet, and ran from the room.

WITH HER FATHER in the stables discussing the horses with their head groom, Loveday could not find solace in her workshop in case he should hear. But that did not prevent her from making herself invisible all morning—in the library, in the garden, and finally, in the wood growing close about Gwynn Bourne, which tumbled down the slope toward the sea.

The bourne made a soothing music in her ears as she seated herself on a handy stone on its near bank. The spreading branches of the oaks and beeches formed a cool green retreat as the sun approached the meridian.

Bring herself to the notice of Arthur Trevelyan! Give up all her dreams, her work! By rights she ought to bring herself to his notice as she really was—spotted with grease, windblown, with a turnscrew in one hand and a roll of plans in the other. How his eyes would stand out on stalks if she took the articulated sideboard along to pay a call and had it trundle into the sitting room at her side. She might allow herself to be seen at the steam works, too, hammering on the sides of the boiler, leather apron and all.

Why should she pretend to be someone she was not, simply to secure his affections? That would only prove that he cared for someone who did not exist, which was no beginning to a friendship, never mind a marriage.

Oh, she did not object to the man in general terms. On

the few occasions when they had met in company, he had been pleasant, though he always gave her the impression he was thinking about something else. Perhaps they had that in common. She was always thinking about something else. Her latest project in the workshop. Whether the steam engine would be ready by midsummer. How to cajole another book out of Emory Thorndyke. These things did not leave much mental capacity for polite conversation about the state of the roads or the likelihood of its being fair for quarter day.

But to bring herself to his attention as a possible wife?

Despite her mother's very specific list and her expectation that Loveday would follow it to the letter, she did not think she had it in her. She would be far more successful bringing herself to Napoleon's attention in a balloon.

The sound of a carriage rumbling over the arched stone bridge above on the road made her look up. It was her parents, off to pay their call upon Sir Anthony and his wife, with whom they had a lively and congenial acquaintance. The couple would, in fact, be hosting the Midsummer Ball at the local assembly rooms, and whether or not the Prince Regent actually came to join them, it would be a huge and festive undertaking, one to which her ladyship was more than equal.

Loveday leaped to her feet and ran for the stables. If her opportunities to assist at the steam works were to be curtailed even further, she must seize them where she could.

"Pascoe, will you hitch the mare to the whiskey, please?" she asked, spotting his grizzled head above one of the stall doors.

He came out, frowning. "Are you going to Truro, miss?"

What a time for him to decide to ask questions. "As it

happens, I am. I will fetch my spencer and bonnet, and be back by the time you have her ready."

"I'm afraid your father has given me instructions not to do so, miss," he said unhappily. "Any place but that, I'm told."

For the second time that day, Loveday lost her powers of speech. "He has forbidden me to drive to Truro?" she finally managed.

"Aye, miss."

"For how long?"

"He didn't say, miss, but I got the feeling it could be some time. Months, maybe."

"Good heavens!"

"I b'aint never said a word about you and the Trevithicks, miss. Nary a word."

"And I am grateful, Pascoe. I know your respect for that family and what they have done for yours over the years." Pascoe's brother and his nephew had both been employed at the steam works, and the nephew had even gone on to further his education and open his own works in Falmouth.

"So I won't say a word if you should decide to take Mrs Penhale's mare out for a ride, miss. The exercise will do her good, I say."

Loveday flung her arms about him and hugged him fiercely. "Oh, thank you, Pascoe! I shall be back directly."

The poor man was red as a beetroot as he went to saddle Mama's mare, but he was smiling.

Loveday flung on her riding habit and boots—remembered her hat and veil just in time—and within minutes after that had been boosted into the side saddle and was riding hellbent for leather along the cliff path.

It was too early in the day for Captain Trevelyan to be

taking his exercise, so she would be safe enough from view on the path rather than riding up the deeply cut wagon lane to the road to avoid the Trevelyan lands. She could not risk being caught on the road by her parents should they decide to cut their visit short. She had just reached the point where she was imagining her mother's pleasure at Loveday's generosity in exercising her mare, when she realized someone was sitting on the stone at the cliff's edge.

She brought the mare to a dancing halt, for it would not do to tear on by without a word of greeting.

"Good morning, Captain," she said as calmly as she could.

"Good morning, Miss Penhale. I trust you are well."

"I am, thank you. And you?"

His mouth twisted. "As you see." He indicated his crutches.

After all she had had to put up with this morning, the last thing she could bear was for an otherwise healthy gentleman of no uncertain fortune to feel sorry for himself.

"You do not have pneumonia? Or an ague?"

One eyebrow rose. "No, I do not."

"Then I call you very well. Your injuries, I am certain, will be of a temporary nature."

Now his gaze was decidedly cool. "You are an authority in these matters, are you?"

"Certainly not. But I see very little to complain of in your situation. You are otherwise healthy, well off, and even, so I am informed, considered the catch of the neighborhood."

"Good heavens, woman," he snapped. "I hope no one ever lets you in a sickroom. Where are you off to in such a lather, may I ask?"

Ha! She had forced him to change the subject, which meant she had got under his skin. Misery loved company. But now she must decide whether to obey her mother and say she was merely exercising the horse, or tell him the truth.

She was doing so well thus far it was a shame to stop.

"My father has forbidden me to take the whiskey to Truro, so I am riding there instead," she said.

"I see. Such a quibble makes you a good candidate for the legal profession, then, since nursing is not an option. What a pity you are a woman."

She tossed her head as gracefully as ever her mount had. "Being a female is no impediment to achievement. I am bound for the Trevithick Steam Works, where I am helping to ready the steam engine for the Prince Regent's visit. We are aiming for Midsummer's Day to have it completed and operating."

He leaned back on one hand. "You. Are working on a steam engine."

"Indeed."

"A woman of parts. And what is this engine to do?"

"Thomas Trevithick, the great man's nephew, has taken his uncle's achievements a step farther. He believes the water can be pumped out of the Wheal Morvoren mine so that it can be made productive again."

"Has he, now?" Instead of being incensed or mocking, the wretched man appeared to be interested. Blast and bebother it, she should never have stopped. "Seawater is a common difficulty, but no one has been successful yet in dealing with the thermal springs. What makes him certain that he can?"

"I do not have time to explain the engineering of it just now, but be assured his ideas are both practical and work-able," she said, gathering the reins. "I must be off. My opportunities to assist are few and far between, and I must not waste them."

"Certainly." He inclined his head, though she did not blame him for remaining seated. "Good day to you, Miss Penhale."

"Good day, Captain. My best wishes for your recovery."

She gave the mare her heels and tapped her flank with the riding crop, and the animal sprang into motion.

Loveday had a flying impression that the captain had abandoned his customary watch of the Carrick Roads and was gazing after her as though she were a new species he had never seen before.

Good. With any luck, he would tell his mother he was not at home to visitors when Loveday came to call.

CHAPTER 6

PARIS, FRANCE

*W*e must launch immediately," Celeste announced when she walked into the school the next morning. Marcel looked up from working on her velocipede, fingers thick with tallow.

Amélie frowned. "We cannot launch right now. It will take at least six hours to fill the envelope."

"Which is *fini*," Josie said, snipping off her thread.

"Why the hurry?" Marcel asked, reaching for a rag.

She was breathing as heavily as if she had run all the way from her mother's house instead of giving his velocipede an occasional push. "The Emperor doubts my mother so much that he commanded her to marry me to an old *comte* to prove her loyalty."

Josie surged to her feet, spilling fabric on to the floor. "Amélie, weather report. Marcel, inventory—gas, ropes, supplies. Celeste and I will position the envelope. *Vite!*"

As her friends burst into action, Celeste's breath came easier. Amélie lifted her muslin skirts to climb the school's observation tower, where instruments would give them an

53

indication of changing conditions. Celeste and Marcel had scaled those steps countless times—first at a plod and then at a run—as they exercised their legs to be able to work the pedals of the steering apparatus.

Now Marcel headed for the storage racks for the supplies they'd need to fill the envelope and secure the basket. Celeste helped Josie gather the yards and yards of colored silk and trundle it out into the inner courtyard of the building.

Three stories of balconies looked down on the flagstone-floored space. Once they would have been lined with students, jostling one another for a prime position to view the coming ascension. The more the Emperor had railed at her mother, the fewer the number of students who had come, until Marcel, Amélie, and Josie were all that remained. And her mother no longer had the heart to teach them.

But this—this balloon, this grand adventure—would restore the school's honor, and that of her family.

"Spread it over the frames," Josie instructed. She took one side and Celeste the other to drape the long, heavy panels over the polished trestles lined up to the north. How many times had she watched other students stretch out their envelopes while her mother looked for any imperfection?

"Reinforce that seam," she'd say. Or worse, "*Non*, take it down. You are not ready to fly."

Celeste was ready. She could feel it.

Josie stepped back to eye her work. "*Parfait*. It looks like a rainbow decided to visit."

"I don't care what color it is," Celeste said, joining her at the top of the envelope to gaze down the rippling lines of color. "So long as it carries me to England."

With a rumble of steel on stone, Marcel rolled out one of

the gas tanks and positioned it next to the steam pump in the middle of the eastern side of the square. "We have enough gas to launch, but *La Blanchard* is going to notice."

"Only after I have set out and returned," Celeste promised as he began connecting the spigot at the top of the tank with the copper piping of the low-pressure pump. "Do we have sufficient coal and water to keep the pump working for six hours?"

Marcel glanced up. "Barely. But it has been warm. We can contribute the coal for the fires."

Josie nodded. "I will gather it. Celeste, you will want to collect what you need for the trip."

"You are an angel." Celeste gave her a peck on the cheek, then headed for her workspace.

A laboratory, her father had called it, as if she mixed chemicals like Monsieur Lavoisier or conducted experiments with plants like Monsieur Thouin at the *Muséum National d'Histoire Naturelle*. An imaginarium, her mother had once said, awe tinging her voice. Ballooning had captivated them all.

Before Papa's fall. Before the Emperor's disappointment.

"We will rise," she murmured, fingers grazing the leather of her father's journals where they lay stacked on one end of her worktable. "You will see, Papa. I will make you proud."

She had thought long and hard on what to take with her on this historic journey. Most of her journals must remain here, lest she lose them at sea, so she had started a special journal for the trip. She couldn't help opening it and gazing at the proud words.

We hypothesize that it is possible to fly from France to England, using the proper application of balloon dimensions, equipment, and training. I intend to prove it by ascending from the school and descending safely in the marshes of Kent.

She'd already noted the size of the balloon and estimated the weight of it, her equipment, and her supplies for the journey. Now she noted each piece.

A portable writing desk with pencils, along with a knife to sharpen them and trim the lines if needed. Maps of England and France. Her father's brass compass for direction. A sextant to calculate elevation from known points of reference. A thermometer to tell how the temperature changed at altitude. An anemometer to determine wind speed and direction.

Celeste paused as she glanced at the explosives.

Her mother had begun crafting the deadly little balls a year ago, as a way to add more excitement to her ascensions. She would light them and toss them out at a height to brighten the night skies with bangs and booms. The dangerous practice merely showed how desperate she was to remain in the Emperor's good graces, for loud noises had always terrified her mother. Sometimes Celeste thought one of the reasons *La Blanchard* was so enamored of the sky was that she escaped the noisy world below.

Two of the charges remained from her mother's last ascension, but Celeste knew the secret of making more. Her mother might have refused to allow her to handle the various ingredients, but she'd been willing for Celeste to keep her company while she worked. Now she readily rolled the specially made gunpower and other ingredients into the paper casings with the wick so she could add two more to the stash.

Next came the spiderweb, her own invention. Her mother might shake her head over some of Celeste's ideas, but she had nodded grimly at this one. Neither of them wanted to see another fall from the sky. Josie had helped Celeste procure the spun silk to craft the bubble that would allow her to escape should the balloon become unstable. She'd only tested it once, by jumping off the top floor of the tower into the courtyard, and she'd smacked against the first-floor balcony instead of floating to the ground as she'd expected.

A chill went through her as she placed it with the rest of her equipment. She would only have to use it in an emergency.

By afternoon, she had everything ready. They all met in the courtyard, where the steadily chugging steam pump had inflated the envelope until it crouched like a rainbow-colored cloud on the trestles.

"We should reach maximum inflation in the next few hours," Marcel reported from where he perched on the end of a trestle, leg swinging in time to the engine's puff.

"No sign of leakage," Josie added as she circled the silk. "I've been watching and listening."

Amélie, hands clasped as she stood by the stairway to the tower, sighed. "I wish I had good news to share. The wind is against us. Even with your steering paddles, Celeste, it would take too long to reach the Channel. You would not have started your crossing before you began to descend."

The problem was as intractable as this war. For much of France, the prevailing winds moved from west to east. To cross the Channel, the Emperor's forces must travel in the opposite direction. So far, no one had managed it. Even her brilliant father, who had been the first to cross the Channel by balloon, had done so from England to France, and not the other way around.

"And that will never be enough for the Emperor, my little star," Papa had told her. "To serve him, we must do more."

The Emperor would never understand how hard they were trying.

"Do you see any reason to hope for a change?" Celeste pressed.

Amélie's sad face provided the answer. "I will watch."

Josie completed her circle and came to put her hand on Celeste's arm. "How late can you stay? I'm sure we can find you a bed."

Amélie blinked, hands falling. "But of course we could. You and I only take up two of the dozen beds in the girls' dormitory."

Her two friends had been enrolled in the school when they were thirteen and fourteen. Since then, they'd lost mother and father to the war. A small bequest paid for their room and board. Marcel's father was still alive, but served with the northern guard. Money for his upkeep came in fits and starts.

"*Maman* will expect me home," Celeste said. "We have the opera tonight."

Marcel shook his head. "You cannot keep pretending you care."

"I don't mind the opera," Celeste hedged. "Or the theatre."

"Admit it," he challenged. "You spend all intermission planning better ways to raise the curtains, dim the lights."

"And change the scenery." She shared a grin with him.

"You two are hopeless," Josie said. "I wouldn't mind attending balls, or going to the opera." She twirled around the envelope until she reached Marcel's side, then spread her skirts in a curtsey. "Please, sir, will you honor me with a dance?"

Marcel rose and looked down his nose at her, dark eyes hooded like a hawk's. "Girls who request dances are forward." His haughty visage cracked in another grin. "Just the way I like them."

Josie giggled.

From the tower came a clang, then a series of bonks and pings, as if something had fallen down the stairs. A ball bearing rolled out of the stairwell. Celeste and Josie frowned, but Amélie clapped her hands.

"That's it!"

"What?" Marcel asked, frowning as well.

Celeste had never seen her friend so giddy.

"I rigged a piece of tin beside the weathervane," Amélie gushed. "When the vane turned, it would knock over the tin, which would then hit a basket of bearings and send them tumbling down the stairs."

As if to prove it, a dozen more began rolling out onto the courtyard floor.

"Ingenious," Josie acknowledged. "But what exactly does it mean?"

Amélie's eyes were huge. "The wind's changed. As soon as the envelope rises, so does Celeste."

TWO HOURS LATER, Celeste was standing beside the basket, the envelope towering above her. She had changed into her flight suit. Her mother might go up in filmy muslin, but Celeste preferred something more practical. The men of the Balloon Corps wore silk trousers that fastened at the ankles. She saw no reason why she shouldn't mimic them. Josie had made hers from sea-green watered silk, and Celeste had put her serpentine redingote over the top. As she came out of her workshop, buttoning the last button over her chest, Marcel had raised a brow.

"Now I look as much like a pirate as you do," she told him.

He laughed. "So long as you fight as well as a pirate."

Celeste sobered. "I hope not to fight at all. The idea is to stay above the front."

He had nodded to the basket. "Well, you have a good chance."

She'd tried to give them every advantage. She'd borrowed not only from her father's designs, but from those of the Royal Society, whose *Philosophical Transactions* were smuggled across the Channel to France and devoured by every scientist and engineer. From them, she'd learned that England's Lord and Lady Worthington had proven the efficacy of steering paddles, made from cedar to minimize the weight. Accordingly, she'd crafted four, one for each side of the basket, and she could work one or more through levers and pedals on the floor. Bellows affixed to each corner could also help propel her in a particular direction.

It made for a rather bristling gunwale, and an even more crowded floor, with all the instruments, writing desk, her journal, food, water, ballast bags, and the explosives.

"Remember to light the fuses before you touch down in England," Josie admonished, moving around the balloon again, her critical gaze on the envelope. "That way, the smugglers will know where to retrieve you."

"I will send word to my brother, Etienne, in Calais," Marcel confirmed. "He and his ship will set out to meet you. You shouldn't have to stay in hiding more than a day or two."

That was the trickiest part of the plan. She had enough food and water to lie low a few days once she reached England. For their landing, they had chosen an area on the Kentish coastline favored by smugglers, with warrens of marshland, but she must avoid notice from the garrisons in the Martello towers at either end.

"I understand," Celeste assured her friends. "But we've planned well, prepared brilliantly. We will be victorious."

In answer, Josie saluted her.

Marcel patted the basket, as if bidding it farewell too, then stepped back. *"Bon voyage,* Celeste."

She grasped the ropes securing the basket to the balloon and swung herself inside, then took up her position among the levers and pedals. *"Au revoir, mes amis!"*

Josie waved, hand trembling in her excitement. Amélie untied the ropes on one side as Marcel did the same on the other. The balloon jolted, as it usually did—a colt free of the barn and yearning for the open fields. Then she was rising, passing the second story, the third. The doves fluttered off on the wind as if in celebration.

Her father had ascended before admiring throngs, her mother before royalty. The cheers of her friends were sweeter.

She was on her way to England and victory.

CHAPTER 7

TRURO, CORNWALL

*U*nder her riding habit Loveday wore her work dress. At her bench, she stripped out of the wool skirt and tight jacket, and put on her leather apron with a sense of relief. "Where are they, Colin? You may turn around now."

"Out in the back, miss," replied their apprentice, who had been studiously studying the equipment rack in front of him. "They're firing it up—you've come just in time."

She'd nearly missed it! Loveday ran out the back door of the workshop and into the yard in the rear, Colin hot on her heels. Here a length of greensward ran by the river, which supplied them with water for the steam engine. And there it was, its copper piping gleaming in the sun, the curve of the boiler as lovely as any sculpture she'd ever seen.

Emory and Thomas were bent to the task of shoveling in coal, and the great wheel had begun to turn, sending the pistons up and down with ponderous grace. Oh, this was a marvelous sight! Faster and faster it went, and now the steam had to be released. The prototype's relief valve had sounded a whistle they could hear in the shop. The real thing would be heard all the way down at the waterfront, she was certain of it.

The relief valve would be tripped at any second.

Emory shouted, and Thomas yelled at Colin, then leaped to grasp the backup lever that would open the relief valve if its own mechanism failed. But before he could pull it down, the boiler screamed like a species of agonized animal, and a seam separated.

The entire rear side of the boiler exploded outward with a roar, and a cascade of hot water splattered against the stone wall separating the Works from the stableyard next door. Every living thing on the wall—moss, lichen, climbing flowers, insects—was boiled alive as the cloud of steam rose into the summer sky.

Someone screamed—the high, thready scream of pain and terror.

Loveday came out of her horrified trance to see poor Colin writhing under a section of boiler. She dashed across the grass and kicked it off his leg with all the strength she possessed. It landed in the grass, where tomorrow there would surely be a burn scar as well.

"Colin—Colin—how bad is it?" She fell to her knees.

He gibbered with pain, and she could see the dreadful damage the hot metal had done.

"I will ride for the surgeon," she croaked past her fear as Thomas and Emory ran up, both apparently unharmed. "Get him into the river. Cold water. Hurry!"

Poor Colin screamed again as the two men picked him up and splashed together into the river. Loveday hauled up her skirts and ran like the wind for the stables next door, where the men had already begun to gather, asking each other what had happened and who had been hurt. Thank the good Lord they had not unsaddled the mare yet.

Heedless of her skirts, she ran to her mother's horse, used a mounting block to shove herself up into the sidesaddle, and shouted the mare into motion. The men stared at her as she pelted out of the stable.

The surgeon was several blocks away, and by a huge stroke of luck, was in his surgery treating a man for what appeared to be a severe case of gout.

"Please, Doctor Pengarry," she gasped. "There has been an explosion at the steam works. Young Colin Treloar has been badly burned. Please come at once."

"I shall come directly, miss. I must gather my salves, and we will bring him back here once I have assessed his situation."

The patient looked so relieved to have his treatment interrupted that Loveday hardly felt sorry for being the cause of it. Her fear for the possible loss of Colin's leg propelled her back to the steam works, where she threw the reins to one of the stable boys and dashed back into the rear yard.

"He's coming," she shouted. "How is Colin?"

"F-freezing," the boy said, now sitting up on the narrow bit of beach, both legs still submerged. "Didn't expect a dunking, miss," he told her reproachfully. "Though it still hurts like the devil."

She was no surgeon or apothecary, but anyone who worked with steam knew about the properties of hot water and the damage it could do to flesh. The first thing to do was to stop the burn from going deeper. The second thing was to prevent it from suppurating. The fact that Colin was sitting up and actually talking and not rigid from the shock was very good indeed.

"The surgeon will have you right as rain," she assured the boy as the man jogged across the green. "Here he comes."

EMORY KEPT his face calm as the surgeon treated Colin Treloar's leg for its burns and wrapped it in clean strips of cloth. The lad could have been killed. Emory and Trevithick might have been killed. And for nothing. The boiler was a wreck. So were his hopes of making a difference, in the war and in his family's lives.

As the owner of the steam works carried the boy to the surgery, Emory stood on the burned and gouged grass gazing at the ruin of the boiler. He didn't notice Miss Penhale was still there until she toed the piece of copper plating that had struck Treloar.

"Look. The heads of the rivets were torn right off," she said sadly. "I saw the pressure bend one whole section outward just before the entire side blew out of it."

Emory frowned, matching her memory to his. "The heads did not spread enough when struck with the peen? But we calculated it precisely."

"Precisely for an engine that will be working above the surface of the ground, perhaps," she said. "But at the depths this one could be working, it appears we must account for the greater steam pressure. No wonder the relief valve did not work. There go our hopes for a working engine to demonstrate to the prince."

Emory sighed. It wasn't just the prince. Dozens of lives

had been lost to the gas that bubbled up from the mines along with scalding water that arrived with a hiss of steam and a gush of death. The gas caused men to swoon, their limbs useless, at the first whiff of that distinctive smell. Like licorice mixed with lavender, only more toxic than any man could withstand.

"We may still show the prince the plans," he allowed.

"Or open Wheal Morvoren for the day so that he may see the scope of the project," she suggested.

She could not know what she asked. He still didn't understand why she came to the steam works, why she worked so hard. His three older sisters had no such passion beyond securing a likely husband.

He had a passion that overrode the attraction of any female he'd met thus far: the creation of a boiler and steam engine capable of removing the foul gas from the copper and tin mines, perhaps even of supporting their valiant troops on the Continent. He'd been a lad of twelve the last time the gas had claimed lives at his father's mine, Wheal Thorne. He would never forget the bleak faces of the wives, the crying of the children, when the foreman had had to announce that all men on that shift had been lost. He'd promised himself then and there he would find a way to keep the mines safe. Eleven years later, he was still trying.

"Opening Wheal Morvoren would be unwise," he said. "We can't risk that any man be harmed again."

Now she sighed. "No, of course not. At the very least, the prince may have some advice upon the subject. Everyone likes to be asked for advice. Even princes."

He felt as if the weight of the metal was perched on his

shoulders. "I doubt we should take the prince's time until we have something of merit to show him."

"Then we'll just have to persevere," she said. "This wasn't a total loss. We may be able to use the copper on other projects. I do not think it may be used a second time under such pressure without risk of its own failure."

Her practical observation soothed the frustration inside him. Emory raised his head, trying to find his own silver lining from the disaster. "And this may just be the push Trevithick needs to try the new steel they've been using in France."

She stared at him. "Are you talking about the boilers in the behemoths? I saw a drawing in a French magazine when I called upon old Madame Racine several months ago. Are you mad?"

"Not in the slightest," Emory said.

"Forgive me," she said quickly, as if she could hear the frost in his tone. "I did not mean that. I was just shocked."

Emory drew in a breath through his nose. "I don't know why you should be. Do you think me a traitor for wishing to try a technology that has been a success for our enemy?"

"No indeed," she assured him. "I am only amazed we have not thought of it before. The question is, where does one lay hands on a behemoth's boiler so that one may study it?"

"That is indeed the question," Emory said, his gaze upon the river. The river that ran into the waters of the Carrick Roads, past the village of St Vivyan, near where Barnabas Pendragon, the smuggler, was known to ply his trade. Emory's friend Arthur Trevelyan had dealings with the smuggler, secret dealings to which Emory was not entirely privy. But Arthur would know how to reach the fellow. How would the crafty smuggler deal with a request for something a little bigger than French perfume and brandy?

"Emory," Miss Penhale said, watching him, "you are not thinking of hiring a crew of pirates to bring back a boiler, surely? Why, that is sending them to certain death."

Drat the woman! He could not be so obvious. "No, of course not," he said, echoing her words of a few minutes ago. "But think of those battlefields and the debris left to lie. Even a damaged boiler would give us an idea of its design and construction. A single plate with its rivets still in place would tell us so much."

She shook her head. "You may as well attempt to extract the original plans from the manufactory at Cherbourg as scavenge parts and pieces from the battlefield. Smuggling casks of brandy is a far cry from braving the front lines to steal technology."

He eyed the bent piece of copper lying in the grass. "I suppose we must devise our own. To do that, we must begin with the raw metal. I wonder how Trevithick would feel about taking two days' journey to Portsmouth, where they are building the ironside steam ships?"

"A ship's boiler—of course!" Her grin faded as quickly as it had come. "Mr Trevithick isn't likely to allow it, but there must be plans. You must write to the Admiralty to secure them, Emory, at once."

He nodded, hope rising as surely as steam from the boiler he planned to build. "It's a start. Perhaps when Trevithick sees the plans, he will be amenable to a change in our production process. But still..." His voice trailed away.

"I know," Miss Penhale said and sighed again. "It will not be in time for the prince's visit. But it will be in support of the war effort, for tin is needed and every mine counts. If Wheal Morvoren can be opened and Thorne brought back to full production, we will have accomplished much indeed. In the meanwhile, let us clean up here as best we can. The sight of our beautiful boiler all blasted to bits makes me want to weep."

NATURALLY, by the time Loveday reached home, turned her mother's mare over to Pascoe, and reached her room without incident in order to change into a frock more suitable for tea, her parents had already heard of the explosion.

"A wretched shame, I call it," her father said when he had taken his seat on the sofa and gratefully accepted the cup from Mama. After the first gulp of his tea, he went on, "Criminal negligence at worst. Thomas Trevithick ought to be hauled up in front of the magistrate."

"Oh, surely not, Papa." Loveday must tread carefully, yet she could not allow anyone to trample upon Thomas's excellent reputation. "The Trevithick Steam Works is renowned for its business practices. From my experience there I can say—"

"Yes, Loveday, we have heard repeatedly and at great length about your experience at the steam works." Gwen reached for a savory tart from a tray laden with small cakes, slices of buttered bread and pots of jam and honey, as well as slices of cold beef and cheese. "But your information is five years old. Anything could have happened in that time."

"Sloppy practices that endanger the engineers are not among them, I assure you," she snapped. If she told her family she had actually been there and seen the dreadful event with her own eyes, that would silence Miss Gwendolyn forever on the subject. She had opened her mouth to betray herself for Thomas Trevithick's sake, when her father spoke again.

"I hear a man was injured, to boot."

"Yes, Colin Treloar was burned by a plate of flying copper," Loveday said instead, doing her best to swallow her indignation. "But he was treated promptly and is expected to make a good recovery."

Her mother put down her cup in its saucer. "Your information is better than ours," she said. "How did you come by it, Loveday? When you were exercising Iris?"

"Yes," Loveday said and took a sip of her own tea. Pascoe had clearly told her parents she had been out on the mare, but not where she had gone. "I heard of it as I was returning... from Gwynn Place."

Rosalind's cup scraped in its saucer, and even her father paused in his reach for a tart, looking astonished.

"You rode to Gwynn Place?" Mama repeated.

Had Loveday said she had met the Duke of Cornwall in the lane, she could not have had a more satisfying reaction. While her ruse had succeeded in steering them away from Thomas Trevithick and the magistrate, she would now have to navigate this new path without either raising their hopes or coming to grief herself.

"I rode along the cliffs," she said, as if this were no great matter. "And Captain Trevelyan seemed also to have deviated from his routine, for he was there, too, albeit seated upon his usual stone."

"And how does he?" Papa asked, finishing off the tart with

every indication of satisfaction, both with it and with her news.

"He seemed in good spirits," she said diplomatically. "Though of course a soldier would not admit to any discomfort in front of a lady."

"Certainly not," Papa said, nodding.

"And did you converse?" Mama asked. Oh, must she lean forward as though the fate of the House of Penhale depended on Loveday's next words?

With an inward grimace, Loveday said, "We did. He inquired after my interests."

"Did he, now?" Mama said, pleased. "I hope Iris behaved well for you."

After being ridden six miles in either direction, to say nothing of a gallop for the surgeon... "You may be assured she earned every one of the oats I asked Pascoe to give her."

Mama sat back to enjoy her tea with a smile.

"What difference does it make if Loveday converses with Captain Trevelyan or not?" Gwen complained. "He is not going to marry her. I am too young, so that leaves only Rosalind with any hope where he is concerned."

"Heavens," Ros said. "Pray do not take *my* name in vain."

"Then what is the point?" Gwen took a piece of Stilton and waved it to close the subject. "Let us talk of something more interesting. Did you find Sir Anthony and Lady Boscawen in good health?"

"We did indeed," Mama said. "And this will interest you, Gwen, if nothing else. Sir Andrew had it from Lord St Aubyn, who had it from the prince himself in a letter. It is definitely fixed that His Royal Highness will progress to the Duchy of

Cornwall and moreover that he will attend our own humble Midsummer Ball!"

Loveday's spine wilted against the upholstered back of her wing chair while Gwen and Ros squealed with delight. The prince was definitely coming, and they had nothing more than a bent and torn engine to show him. Oh, woe!

"As we know from the newspapers," Papa said, taking up the tale, "he is not seen much in company. So while he will be inspecting the shipyard at Portsmouth and conferring with his lordship about the detachment of aeronauts on the Mount, as we would expect, Lady Boscawen is quite beside herself at the honor."

"We will have to make the event one to remember," Gwen said eagerly. "Oh, Mama, please tell me Ros and I are to be presented! Please, please, please?"

Their mother looked demure, but the flush of pleasure on her cheeks gave her away. "Lady Boscawen and I spoke of that most particularly. For besides yourselves, and Isobel Boscawen, there are the Trevelyan twins, too, ready to be out in society."

"And Lady Anne St Aubyn," Rosalind said. "We must consider her to be the countess's first object."

"Of course," Mama said. "It was, of course, the countess who broached the plan to Lady Boscawen. It is far too difficult to hold such an event at their castle—one can only approach on foot at low tide, and my goodness, what if the tide were out at noon and not the hour of the ball?"

"To say nothing of people's going home," Loveday pointed out, rather sensibly, she thought. "Guests would arrive at noon on one day and be forced to stay until noon the next—

unless they wished to be conveyed to shore in a fishing boat. Which I would not mind, but—"

"You have no sense of personal dignity," Gwen informed her. "But imagine old lady Tregothnan trying to get into a boat with those big Georgian skirts."

"Quite," Papa said with a quelling glare at her disrespect of their elderly neighbor, chatelaine of the oldest estate on this part of the coast.

Gwen, thank goodness, subsided.

"The point is that you will all be presented, and my life will consequently become three times more complicated than it is already," Papa went on. "But that is the price I must pay to see you happily settled."

Mama slid a glance toward Loveday that she did her best to pretend she had not seen. Instead, she leaned forward to take a savory tart. "We must not get ahead of ourselves," Loveday said. "We have had news he is definitely coming before, and something has always prevented him."

"That was a mere rumor before," Mama said. "This time, we may place a little more stock in it, if Lord St Aubyn has had it in writing."

"But even if it is only a possibility, we must still prepare as though it were a fact," Rosalind put in. "Oh, Mama, may I not now have that beautiful blue silk in the mantua maker's window in Truro?"

Mama laughed. "Dearest, if you are to be presented, silk from Truro is not nearly good enough. The four of us will go to Exeter and have gowns made in the latest fashion."

"Exeter!" Such pandemonium reigned in the parlor that Papa snatched up a piece of cheese and fled.

But Loveday merely poured herself another cup of tea and

withdrew into the shallow protection of her chair. Exeter, piffle. If she could convince Mama that her presence was not necessary—that she might simply take along one of Loveday's dresses to use as a pattern—then she could work on the articulated sideboard undisturbed for days.

What a happy prospect.

And when her mother asked her how she liked the plan, she said with complete truth that it was the best she had heard in forever, and the day of departure could not come soon enough for her.

CHAPTER 8

PARIS, FRANCE

*C*eleste could not recall a finer evening. A warm breeze from the east tickled her curls. Moonlight gilded the rooftops and left the entrances to the gypsum mines in shadow as she skimmed the buildings at the top of Sacre Coeur. The scent of someone's dinner, tangy with peppers, floated past. A glance at her father's compass confirmed she was on the perfect heading—north by west. Ahead, she could make out the silvery thread of the Seine as it flowed out of Paris.

A stray gust plucked at the balloon, tugging it to the east. She slipped her feet into the pedals and pumped. Stronger than a bird's wing, the steering paddle flapped, and the balloon corrected itself. As easy as strolling along the Champs Élysées.

See, Papa? I knew they would work.

Her father's Channel flight had featured paddles, too. She'd seen them in his drawings and read about them in the newspaper clippings her mother had kept. Few knew the things hadn't functioned. Papa had been a visionary—Celeste was the one who had figured out how to make that vision a reality.

Of course, she had a number of challenges to overcome before she proved as much. She had to stay low until she neared the coast so that she could ride the correct air currents. She'd chosen the town of Le Tréport for her last sight of France, in part because it had a lighthouse she could use to help estimate elevation for a while at sea. But once she neared Le Tréport, she had to precisely time the dropping of her ballast bags, along with her request to pass the coastal defenses there.

After the French Navy had defeated the British Navy fourteen years ago at the Battle of Trafalgar, England had never attempted to cross the Channel directly into France. The English kept sneaking on to the Continent from Flanders in the north or Spain in the south. Still, the Emperor was taking no chances. Gun towers, some housed in monasteries and abbeys, guarded the French coastline, along with stalwart French troops.

All of whom would be swayed, she hoped, by a note from *La Blanchard*.

She cringed as guilt rode the breeze along with her. She had written the notes in her mother's name.

This is an experimental flight for the glory of France. You will allow it to pass.

   By order of Marie Madeleine-Sophie Blanchard, the Emperor's Chief Air Minister.

It truly was for the glory of France. Her mother would understand once Celeste proved it was possible to cross to

England.

And, as an experimental flight, she must record her observations. She pulled out her journal from the oilcloth bag Josie had constructed to protect it from any rain.

Wind from the southeast, steady at five knots. She looked down. There, that broad curve. *Approximately one mile from L'Île Saint-Denis.* She counted the seconds as she floated over it and toward the forest in the distance. With a nod, she noted the pace. *Traveling at approximately five miles per hour. Temperature falling as the night lengthens. Sextant calculations indicate approximately one thousand feet above ground.*

She shifted to better position her journal, and her foot bumped the package of the spiderweb, also encased on oilcloth. With any luck, she would not have to use it. Once she brought the balloon down in the Kentish marshes, she would return with it in Etienne's ship. Marcel's older brother was one of hundreds of smugglers the Emperor had in his employ all along the coast of England.

Thinking of Etienne and his merry band of thieves reminded her of the explosives. She moved over to touch the top of them, more to assure herself they were well secured than to count them. How the crowds adored her mother's displays, oohing and ahhing at the bursts of yellow and white light. They could not know the danger. Throw too lightly, at the wrong angle, or into the wind, and the things could explode too close to the balloon, potentially setting the basket ablaze. And should one ignite the great gas envelope...

Celeste tugged her redingote closer. She was not her mother. She would only use these explosives to mark her descent and show Etienne and his crew where to find her.

She continued her observations as the balloon drifted over

a series of fields and forests, dark and mysterious in the moonlight. It was still night by the time she reached Le Tréport. The moon had set, but the tall steel pillar of the lighthouse flashed its warning over the coast and far out to sea. By it, she made out the gun towers near the old abbey overlooking the harbor. She'd already secured her notes to the sand-filled canvas ballast bags.

"It is a matter of height, speed of the balloon, and strength and direction of the wind," Amélie had explained when she'd handed her the calculations. "That should allow you to drop your bags right into the guard's square."

"And a guard's lap," Josie had added with a laugh.

She couldn't make out a soldier from this height in the dark, but she heaved up the bag, counted off the seconds, and let fly one, then two. She thought she heard a whistle as they fell. Then she was past the tower and headed out to sea.

Darkness engulfed her. The envelope even blocked out the stars. If she squinted, she could make out a haze of spangled brightness in the distance.

England.

Something whizzed by, close enough that the balloon swayed with its passing. She glanced back. Lights blazed from the tower now, and tiny figures swarmed the rampart. She heard the boom just as another cannonbomb roared past her, only to drop into the waves below before it exploded.

"*Imbéciles!*" she cried. "I'm on your side! Can't you read?"

She dashed to crank the bellows to the north, then rushed to the pedals and pumped. The balloon veered south, fighting against the wind. Another ball whizzed past, too close to where she had been.

She jumped off the pedals and bent to heave up another of

the ballast bags. The moment it went over the side, the balloon edged higher. The next ball must have clipped the basket, because it began to swing, tumbling her against the side. Righting herself, she grabbed another bag and wrestled it over too. Once more, the balloon climbed.

But now she was moving backward, closer to France. *Non, non, non!* She hopped on the pedals and pumped for all she was worth. Slowly, struggling, the balloon continued toward the west.

She kept pedaling until her legs shook and her breath came in gulps. When she finally stopped, she heard no more cannonbombs. She must be out of range. Glancing back, she saw only a flash from the lighthouse.

And the glow of the sunrise in the east, a fiery red.

Celeste sank onto the floor of the basket and took a deep breath, then stretched out her legs as much as she could in the cramped space. She was free of France. Free of anyone's dictates, actually. She ought to dance, to sing. But she just wanted to put her head down and sleep. By Amélie's calculation, it would take six hours to reach the marshes from here. Perhaps she had time for a nap. She leaned back against the side. Just a short time. Then she would start making observations again. It would be good to see the strength of the wind at this height. Perhaps…

She blinked, and light met her gaze. At least, as much light as could be found on such a dreary day. Thick grey clouds covered what she could see of the sky under the envelope.

Climbing to her feet, she looked around and down. Below was only water, a deep blue-grey. Her father's compass suggested she was slightly off course, headed more west than north. Best to correct that. She climbed on the pedals, and her legs protested. *Tant pis.* She had to make up for lost time.

She managed to steer the balloon back on a north-by-west heading. When she peered out, she spotted a line of darker grey along the northern horizon.

England!

She sagged against the rim, drew in a deep breath. She was going to do this.

Perhaps some bread to celebrate. She released the gunwale to bend for the sack Josie had sent with her. Oh, how kind to pack some of the good baguette! Even a night in a cloth sack had not ruined the crisp, buttery crust, the soft interior. Celeste sighed, content.

But not for long. She'd missed a great deal as she'd slumbered. She pulled out a pencil and began making notes in her journal.

Fitful west wind, sailing approximately... She peered over the side at the choppy waves below. Close enough that she did not have to use the sextant to calculate, even if she'd had a clear line of sight to a known elevation. *One thousand feet above the water. Each five minutes of pedaling causes the balloon to veer approximately five degrees in the proper direction. Clear skies to the west and south...*

But not to the northeast, where the Channel led into the North Sea. Black clouds boiled through the narrow neck between Calais and Dover, and she caught the flash of lightning. That could not be allowed to catch her.

She packed away her journal, the pencil, and the food, then positioned herself on the pedals, legs pumping. Even her growing fear could not seem to fuel her leaden muscles. They trembled with each stroke. Every look to the northeast revealed the storm gaining ground. Already, contrary winds buffeted the balloon, knocking it south—east—south again.

She would never outrun it. She could not survive it. One bolt of lightning, and the balloon would go up in flames before plummeting to the icy seas below.

Her mind clicked through options, odds. She was closer to England than France now. The storm was eclipsing the light as it advanced, but it had seemed as if she had no more than an hour before landing. Could she ride the wind in to shore?

Lightning flashed, close enough that the hair tingled on her body. That was her answer. No way to save the balloon. She had to jump.

As the rain began to fall, she pulled out the spiderweb and slipped her arms through the leather straps, then tucked her father's compass deep inside her redingote. Her stomach sank as she gazed at the oilcloth package that held her journal. She could not hope to carry it and swim. Whatever record she'd made of her passage would be lost, unless the basket somehow survived.

The wind was strong enough to swing it now, knocking her up against the side. One of the bellows broke free and fell into the churning sea. Righting herself, she grasped the rain-slick ropes and pulled herself up onto the gunwale. Lightning flashed white, blinding her a moment. When she blinked hard, she saw that the waves were closer now. Either they had risen, or the balloon had sunk, or both.

Please, Lord, help me reach land.

She pushed off.

The wind rushed past her face as she fell. Her skin pressed against her cheekbones. Her fingers felt thick, but she tugged on the tie that would release the spiderweb. For one terrifying moment, it refused to give. Then—

Snap!

Up she went, caught on the air currents. The inflated silk bubble floated a moment, like a dandelion seed on the wind, sheltering her from the rain. She drifted toward shore, closer, closer…

Her feet hit the water, and the waves sucked at her greedily, tugging her down. Cold covered her a moment before the spiderweb floated over her to veil her head. The waves consumed the silk, pulling her under. She couldn't breathe.

Non!

Thrashing, she broke free of the silk and wiggled out of the spiderweb's straps. Arms flailing, she popped up to the surface and gasped in a mouthful that was still more water than air. Her silk trousers were like ice against her legs. Where was she? Where was England?

There! As one wave crested over her, she sighted the mass ahead. She struck out for it, her legs nearly useless now. Her last thought was that there was a reason everyone complained about the English weather.

Then, everything went dark.

CHAPTER 9

HALE HOUSE, CORNWALL

*P*apa had occasion more than once to flee the distaff side of his household and the mounting excitement over the trip to Exeter. Yesterday evening they had all been confined indoors due to an appalling storm swooping in from the northeast, and he had taken refuge in a thick and intimidating book entitled *Drainage and Water Management*. This morning he had escaped to the stables, where much to Loveday's disappointment, he had not had the carriage horses harnessed. If he had, she might again have taken Mama's mare and gone to Truro, this time to give all the assistance of which she was capable to Thomas and Emory in cleaning up after the boiler disaster. Instead, Papa had decided that he and Pascoe must take inventory of the carriages, particularly the older ones left by previous generations of the family.

Papa did not like to dispose of anything that was still useful, even if the oldest might have seen its heyday when old Lady Tregothnan was a bride. Had Loveday been in charge, the old relics would have gone to a local farmer for drayage. But Loveday, as was evident to all, was not in charge.

She bid farewell to a few stolen hours in her workshop and wandered disconsolately back through the kitchen garden, then out by the orchard gate. The apple trees had lost their blossoms a few weeks ago, and now tiny round fruit had appeared on the branches. The harvest would be a good one by summer's end. She touched the trunks of her favorites as she passed—the Beauty of Bath, the Pippin—and let herself out the ivy-covered gate on to the side lawn.

She could not go back inside and be dragooned into looking at back issues of *La Belle Assemblée*. It was simply too much to face. Cecily and Jenifer Trevelyan had called, and five women exclaiming over patterns was infinitely worse than only three. She would take a walk instead, bonnetless and out of sorts as she was. The activity would do her good, and the sunshine would improve her mood enough that she would not deal the cut direct to the first person who asked where she had been.

Loveday set out for the cliffs, wondering if she and Papa had more in common than she had ever suspected.

After the storm, the sea was still restless, heaving in toward shore with a hollow thump of waves and a drag and clatter of stones. She would not look to the east to see if anyone occupied the flat observation rock on the cliff. She would simply walk out to Hale Head as usual and enjoy the freshness of the breeze—all right, the strength of the wind. Fortunately the sun was warm, for she wore no spencer, either.

Someone shouted, too far away to make out words. She glanced behind her to see whether she'd been caught trying to escape, but the lawns were empty. Another shout, and she saw a figure on the cliffs in the direction she had been determined not to look, but nowhere near the flat stone. He appeared to be waving a crutch at her.

Goodness, Arthur Trevelyan was hurt!

She picked up her skirts and ran along the cliff path, dodging tussocks of grass and exposed stones as skillfully as ever Iris had on her gallop a few days ago. She ran up to him and stopped short, panting with the sudden exertion. "Are you all right? Can I be of assistance?"

"Did you not see it? I was pointing straight at it!"

"See what? Have you fallen?"

"Of course I haven't fallen. But someone has—look!"

With one hand, he seized her by the shoulder and turned her so that she faced west again, looking at Hale Head. "Captain!"

He removed his hand as though her sleeve had burned him. "On the beach. Do you see? A body."

This time when she sucked in a breath, it was from shock. "Was there a wreck? We did not see a signal fire."

"They must have gone overboard. There may yet be life— you must go down and see. I will fetch help."

She, go down and see if someone were *dead?* "But—"

"At once, Miss Penhale! They may be taking their last breath while you stand here dithering!"

The sheer injustice of this galvanized her into action. She snatched up her skirts and left him there to devise how he was going to fetch help at this distance from any house. The path down to the beach from Hale Head was tricky, full of switch-backs and crumbling earth and sharp rocks, but she had been climbing it all her life. She bundled her skirts over one arm— it was too far for anyone but an eagle to see details of leg and ankle—and took the path at as fast a walk as she dared. The last few feet had weathered since the last time she had been down here, but her boots were up to it as she slid to the shingle in a shower of gravel.

The tide was coming in. She must be quick. If there was no life on the beach besides herself, that would mean one course of action. If there were... well, she would deal with it when she knew for certain.

It looked less like a person than a bundle of clothes. She approached closer. Clothes of some quality. Silk.

Good heavens—it was a woman!

Dead or alive?

The woman lay on her stomach with her face turned to one side, white as the stones. Her hair was brown and cropped short. Had she been ill? Oh goodness, had she died aboard ship and her body consigned to the waves?

She must not be a coward or let her imagination run away with her. Loveday dropped to her knees and touched her hand.

The hand was cold—so cold. But did she yet breathe? Loveday grasped her shoulders and turned her over, and as she did, seawater gushed out of her mouth. The sensible thing to do was as she'd seen them do when the lifeboats went out— turn her on her side, grasp her, and put pressure on her lungs to squeeze out any remaining water.

A great rush of it came out, and the woman coughed.

"Blessed Saint Piran, you're alive!"

She groaned, and tried to curl away from Loveday's grip.

"No, you must get all the water out. Please forgive me." She squeezed her again, and what seemed to be the last of it dribbled down the woman's chin and into the gravel. A bout of coughing finished the job, and her half-dead patient was at last able to open her eyes.

"An—Angle—England?" she croaked, clearly having difficulty forming the word.

"Yes, you are in England. My house is just above." She indicated the cliffs with a lift of her chin. "Someone has gone to get help, but we must get you higher up the beach. The tide is coming in."

"England," the girl repeated, as though confirming the salient point in all this information.

Perhaps she spoke a different tongue. "Yes," she said. *"Ja. Si. Oui."*

With a sigh, the girl went limp, and Loveday realized she had fainted.

"Oh, dear." She got her feet under her and her hands under the girl's armpits. "What a lovely redingote," she told her unconscious companion. "This may not be very comfortable, but I am sure the last thing you wish is to be submerged again. Come."

Loveday hauled her up the beach to where the path had decanted her into the pebbles. There was nothing for it now but to wait and hope that Captain Trevelyan had succeeded in finding help long before he was in need of it himself.

OF ALL THE times for his body to betray him!

Arthur Trevelyan struggled up the slope toward Hale House, which lay far closer than his own, cursing with each painful step. Finally by sheer chance he discovered that if he swung himself off both feet in a regular rhythm, he could cover the ground much faster than taking one hop-and-step at a time. The only thing he must watch for was—

"Arghh!" One crutch went into a rabbit hole and wrenched itself out from under him. He went down—turned himself to land on his good side—and clocked his head on a tussock of grass that was nowhere near as soft as it looked.

"Arthur!" His sister Cecily screamed his name, and now practically the whole Penhale household came streaming down the lawn to witness his ungainly struggle to his feet.

Thank heaven. The situation was too urgent for pride.

"Arthur, are you all right?" His sister was as white as her own sprigged frock.

"Yes, I'm fine. Cecily, you must fetch Mr Penhale and some of his men. There is a body on the beach on the east side of the Head, cast up by the storm."

Cecily gasped and clapped a hand to her mouth. Then she whirled and practically ran into Mrs Penhale. "Arthur says there is a body on the beach. The tide is coming in—we must organize the men to bring it up."

"The person may yet be alive," he called as the tide of females turned to ebb back up the lawn. "Miss Penhale has gone down to see."

"Loveday!" Mrs Penhale gawked at him. "Gone to see if they are dead or alive? Captain, how could you have let her?"

"Someone had to go, ma'am." It had not until this moment occurred to him that there was something improper about seeing whether or not someone was alive. On the battlefield, proof of life was essential when one's comrades were under enemy fire. As a general rule, though, perhaps he ought not to have demanded such a task from a young lady of gentle breeding.

Never mind, he thought in the next moment. It was Loveday.

Mr Penhale, one of his grooms, and Cowan from their own home farm came around the side of the sturdy stone manor house at a jog. The groom carried what appeared to be one half of a door from an ancient carriage under his arm with which to transport the body up the cliff.

"Do come inside, Captain." Mrs Penhale urged him. "There is nothing more you can do but wait until they come back."

The truth, no matter how irritating, must be acknowledged gracefully. "Thank you." But he could not keep from lagging behind, his gaze drawn to the line of the cliffs where surely they must appear.

"Perhaps a restorative cup of tea on the terrace might help while we wait." Mrs Penhale wasted no time in ordering it, and soon his sisters and the Penhale girls were seated about the small terrace like so many drifts of snow in their white dresses. He himself could not sit. So he balanced his cup and saucer on the wall and acted as watchman. Superfluous, really, as every one of his companions were doing the same. But it was all he could do.

An agonizing half hour passed before his sharp eyes spotted movement on the cliff. "They are coming," he said tersely, and on one crutch, hobbled down the three flagstone steps.

A single figure in a white dress materialized as she climbed the last of the path and set off toward them across the lawns at a rapid walk. When she was within hailing distance, Loveday called, "She is alive! They are bringing her directly. Mama, we must prepare a room for her at once."

"Good heavens!" Mrs Penhale said blankly. "The dead body is a woman? Alive?"

Some terrible tension within him relaxed. Alive!

Miss Rosalind tossed her tea in the rosebushes. "Cecily, come with me. We will make up the guest room."

Mrs Penhale recovered herself. "Jenifer, dear, if you would run down to the kitchen and ask Mrs Kerrow to start some kettles of water boiling, our guest may wish a bath. If she is injured, we may need water for that, too."

"What can I do?" Miss Gwendolyn asked.

By this time Loveday had arrived and absently drained the teacup Arthur had left sitting on the wall. "She appears to be about your size, Gwen. You could choose a dress for her, and some small clothes. She has nothing but what is on her back, and after goodness knows how many hours in the sea, that may not be salvageable."

Her youngest sister whirled and disappeared into the house after the other girls.

Loveday looked about her at the empty terrace. Then her knees appeared to collapse, and she sank into a chair. "You look as though you need another cup of tea," Arthur suggested. He offered his empty cup, and she poured some for herself.

"Thank you." She downed half of it and then looked up at him, still standing so uselessly on the steps. "If you had not seen her, she would have gone out with the tide, likely still unconscious." Her voice was hoarse from all her efforts.

The image chilled him. "Did she regain consciousness? Is she hurt?"

"She has no visible injuries," Loveday said. "She awakened just long enough to ask me if this was England."

He tilted his head. "Curious. Would a person not say, 'Where am I?'"

"I have not been nearly drowned, so I cannot say. But if such a question indicates that her mind has not been disordered, then I am glad. She cannot be much older than I."

From the corner of his eye, he again caught movement on the cliffs. "Here they come."

Loveday went to the terrace doors. "Mama!" she called into the house. "They have reached the top of the cliff. They will be here in moments."

Arthur could not hear the reply, but above, under the gables of the roof, a window was thrown open and he could hear his sister Cecily excitedly giving Miss Rosalind the report of the men's progress. And likely completely forgetting she was supposed to be making up a bed.

Loveday stood, too, marking her father's steps as he accompanied the other men, one on each end of the carriage door. "At least that old coach has been put to some use today," she murmured. "Even if there are no horses involved."

His lips twitched in a smile, and then both their attention was completely absorbed by the limp figure upon its makeshift bier. He had a brief impression of pale skin and dark hair rimed with salt as it dried, and a strange garment sticking to her limbs that resembled breeches reaching all the way to the ankle.

And then she was lowered to the flagstones and the groom instructed to lift her and take her upstairs.

"Thank you, Captain, and you, Loveday," Mr Penhale said. "You have saved a life today. The tide line was within a foot when we reached them," he added for Arthur's benefit.

"A higher power was watching out for the young lady," he

said soberly. Time and chance bringing both himself and Loveday to the cliff's edge were all that had saved her. In a strange way, it gave him a bond with Loveday Penhale, odd as she was, that he was not entirely comfortable with. "You will send someone with a message later, to let us know how she does?"

"Of course," Mr Penhale said. "And now I will send your sisters down to you, so that you may escort them home. Allow me to order the carriage brought around for you."

"Absolutely not, sir," Arthur said. "It is an easy enough walk now that the emergency is past."

It would not be easy. But not for worlds would he admit it. He would be forced to take to his bed tomorrow, but he was happy to pay that price.

It was clear that Mrs Penhale and her daughters had everything well in hand. So Jenifer and Cecily walked home along the cliff path with him, slowing their own more lively paces to his awkward one. As his sisters hopped across the flat stones forming a path over Gwynn Bourne, he looked back over his shoulder.

A slender figure in white raised her hand in farewell. Then she turned and went into the house.

CHAPTER 10

*L*ight.

Sound.

Celeste strained to focus on something solid in the murk surrounding her. Everything felt stiff, weighted. Was that a voice? Yes, a woman, talking. She could not make out the words, as if they were in a foreign tongue.

"Amélie?"

The voice stopped. Why were her eyelids as heavy as the ballast bags?

Ballast bags.

The balloon.

The storm.

Celeste bolted upright, eyes flying open. She was lying in a bed in an airy room with light-colored walls. The delicate furnishings were lacquered in white with gilded edges, while paintings of the sea hung on the walls.

Beside the bed, a young woman with blond hair pulled back in a knot sat properly on a wooden chair and stared at her.

Celeste blinked.

"You're awake." The woman sounded excessively relieved, but that was... English?

Of course it was English. Did she think she'd gone down just short of her goal and somehow reappeared in Paris? Thank the good Lord her father has insisted she learn the language, if only to read the scientific treatises coming out of the country. England might be the enemy, but her scientists and engineers did have an occasional good idea.

"I believe I am awake," Celeste said, voice coming out raspy. "Where am I? Who are you?"

"This is Hale House," the young woman said, rising and setting aside the volume she'd been reading. "I am Miss Loveday Penhale, and I am under strictest orders to bring my mother to you the moment you wake. If you'll bear with me." She hurried from the room.

Hale House. Celeste had never heard of it, but that meant nothing. What had meaning was that Miss Penhale's family home had a name. That spoke of position. And Miss Penhale had been dressed in white muslin, not as fussy as some of the latest fashions, and bearing a slight stain at the hem. On Amélie or Josephine, she would have known it to be grease. Surely not on the lovely Miss Penhale. Did that mean she had no servants to aid in cleaning and laundry?

Celeste peered over the edge of the bed. Aubusson carpet. No mistaking that weave. Everyone in France wanted the rugs that resembled those in the Emperor's palace. No, Miss Penhale likely had plenty of servants and pretty dresses. Wherever Celeste had landed, it was into wealth. And in England, like France, wealth meant power.

She shivered. They could not be allowed to know all, or she'd end up in a prison, not this charming bedchamber.

So, how easy would it be to escape? Gingerly, she pulled back the thick covers. All her limbs appeared to be intact, for her toes wiggled nicely. She patted along the pretty pink flannel of the nightgown and felt no bulges of bandages or splints. What had they done with her clothing?

The door opened, and Miss Penhale returned with three other women, each showing a differing degree of calm and decorum. The oldest, and most serene, was clearly *Maman*. She bore a decided resemblance to Miss Penhale, as did the two younger women crowding behind her, the younger eager, the elder wary. All wore fashionable white muslin with delicate embroidery Josie would admire along the hem and modest necklines. They were followed by a stern-faced fellow in a country tweed coat and chamois trousers. Those narrowed eyes under his thatch of greying hair said he'd be the one to watch.

"How lovely to see you awake," the mother said in perfectly polished tones as Celeste modestly pulled up the covers in the presence of a man. "Can you tell us your name, dear? We would like to notify your family that you are safe. They must be so worried."

If she thought of her family—Marcel, Amélie, Josie, yes, even her mother—she would start to cry. How she had failed them! But she couldn't reveal her heritage. Even here, the name of Blanchard might have meaning.

"Celeste Aventure," she temporized, knowing Amélie and Josie would smile to hear her claim kinship. "But I fear you will not be able to contact my family. We were exiled from

France to Portugal, and I ran away on a ship bound for England."

"Ran away?" The lady exchanged glances with her husband before frowning at Celeste. "Why would you do something so disobedient?"

Disobedience was apparently a hanging offense in this family, for Miss Penhale winced and her sisters nudged each other as if anticipating a scene.

Celeste dropped her gaze. "It was not disobedience. My mother is being pressured to accept an offer for my hand from a man we cannot admire. He wanted only the considerable dowry I will bring to a marriage. It was her wish that I escape to the country that honors its ladies."

"Quite right," the father said.

Celeste dared a glance up and saw a smile hovering on the lady's face as well.

"And how did you come to wash up on our beach?" the father asked.

She heard no censure, only curiosity. Had they found the balloon? Her journal?

"Was no one and nothing else found with me?" she asked. It wasn't hard to sound plaintive.

"No," Miss Penhale volunteered. "You were all we found. We feared there had been a wreck. Were others washed overboard in that storm, too?"

Relief was quickly followed by despair. Then she really was lost here.

They were all watching her, waiting for her to tell them her sorry tale. Celeste took a deep breath and set out to weave one as colorful as the carpet on the floor.

"I was strolling on the deck, enjoying some fresh air, when

the storm, as you say, blew in. It came so quickly, I could not reach the stairs before I was washed overboard. I do not know what became of the ship."

"Such storms have taken many a ship along this coast," the father lamented.

They all looked sorrowful for the other souls that must have gone down to the depths. She was simply thankful they did not ask her the name of the ship. Did they name sailing vessels after people in Portugal? Places? What if she accidentally used the name of a real ship, with a real captain who could confirm no Celeste Aventure, heiress or otherwise, had sailed with him, much less been washed overboard? Oh, but this lying was difficult!

"Well, you are safe now," the lady said, reaching out to tuck the covers closer. "The doctor says you should recover fully in a few days."

Mrs Penhale seemed so kind. Tears gathered anew. Was it possible that she had washed up on the beach of one of the few helpful English families? The Paris papers were always describing the treachery, the cruelty of the English. Did she dare to take them at their word and trust them?

"Where had you been heading, dear?" her hostess asked as she stepped back.

Might as well stick as close to her plans as she dared. "I had hoped to make my home among the émigré community in Kent, though we know no one there. Are they nearby?"

Once again, the parents exchanged glances. The younger two daughters shook their heads as if she ought to have known better. Miss Penhale looked contrite.

"I'm afraid Kent is quite far," their father explained. "Days away. You had the good fortune to wash up in Cornwall."

Cornwall!

She nearly yelped the word aloud. How had she veered so far off course? She must consider her last readings, see if the family knew anything about the course and ferocity of the storm. Then she could—

Her journal noting her last readings likely lay at the bottom of the Channel.

This time, she let the tears fall.

"There, now, you've upset her," the mother admonished. "You have no need for concern, Mademoiselle Aventure. You are welcome to stay with us as long as you like. My daughter Loveday will have the care of you." Her look to her oldest daughter warned her not to disagree.

"Happy to be of assistance," she said, pasting a smile on her face.

"Rosalind and Gwendolyn will be busy with other activities," her mother clarified. "But I'm sure they'll look in on you as well, and you may ask them for anything you need."

The simpering smiles belied her statement, and she felt some sympathy for Miss Penhale.

"Now," her mother said, stepping back. "We must let you rest."

"But Mama," one of the younger sisters objected, "you said we might ask her about her clothing."

"It was rather daring," the other agreed with a look toward the wardrobe on the far wall.

At least now she knew where to find her things. "My mother insists I wear the latest fashion from Paris," Celeste explained. "Empress Maria has several outfits like that. You would look well in the silk trousers, I think."

One of the younger sisters preened, while the other gaped. She thought Loveday hid a smile.

"We can discuss that later," her mother said in a tone that told her daughters they certainly would not. "Sleep well, Mademoiselle Aventure. When Loveday is not available, you need only ring the bell on the bedside table, and a maid will see to your needs. Come, girls." She sailed from the room, and the others followed. Only Loveday looked back, a puzzled frown on her face.

She could be no more puzzled than Celeste. How could she send word to Marcel and the others that she was safe? How could she return home?

And how could she trust that the members of this English family were as pleasant as they seemed? Was this kindness, this charity all a ruse to force her to spill her secrets? Surely they were hiding something.

But what?

CHAPTER 11

*S*he was trapped in an invisible prison of kindness.

Loveday paused on the stairs with the break-fast tray for Celeste, feeling as though her heart would burst from her chest. She had just had a note from Emory that he was on his way to Portsmouth to tour one of the steam ships and obtain schematics of the boiler design in person. There was no time to wait for the Admiralty Office. Now that the Prince Regent had said he was definitely coming by midsummer, it was more urgent than ever that they redesign and complete the new boiler with a foolproof adaptation of a working design—and foolproof rivets. Loveday needed to return to the steam works—needed to join Thomas and Emory, for they would require every hand.

And what was she doing instead?

Taking coddled eggs and toast to an invalid.

With a mighty effort, she resisted the urge to fling the tray over the banister just for the satisfaction of hearing it crash in the flagged entry hall. But that would net her nothing but a mop and bucket and at least a year of recriminations from everyone in the household.

She drew a calming breath and proceeded up the stairs.

Celeste was sitting up when she knocked and came in, evincing enough interest in the tray that it appeared her appetite, at least, might be fully recovered, if nothing else.

"You are too kind," the young woman said, taking the tray and picking up the spoon. "I hope I will not inconvenience you for long."

"Doctor Pengarry will return in three days to pronounce sentence."

The spoon froze halfway to her mouth. *"Pardon?"*

Loveday smiled. "Forgive me. My family does not appreciate my sense of humor, either. He will tell us then if you are able to leave the sickroom and perhaps take some exercise."

"Ah." The coddled eggs vanished and the toast, too. Loveday ought to have brought some strawberries and possibly a whole boiled codfish. "Was it your good mama who bathed me after I was rescued from the sea?"

"Yes, she and Morwen, the maid. Having sea-bathed myself, I know what happens to skin and hair when the salt is not cleaned out of it. Mama was glad to see that you sustained no external injuries. And from your appetite, I hazard a guess there might not have been internal ones."

"I do not feel injured. Only very, very tired. Every muscle aches."

"I expect it does, if you had to somehow stay afloat." She poured a cup of chocolate for each of them.

"Thank you. *Chocolat.* It is my favorite."

"Can you swim?"

Celeste nodded. "Can you? You must, if you sea-bathe."

"Enough to swim out to the rocks and back, and only at low tide, when we may touch the bottom. I can't imagine how terrible it must have been to be swept overboard. To not know whether you were going to live or die."

"It was indeed." She sipped at her chocolate. "I cannot bear to speak of it."

Loveday could not blame her. "Did you like living in Portugal?"

"It was... hot. But my family had no other choice. My parents had been disgraced in the Emperor's eyes, and once that happens..." She gave a very Gallic shrug.

Loveday did not know what the consequences of disgrace would be, but Boney had such an evil reputation—had been the cause of so many deaths—that she could imagine a family's choosing exile rather than waiting to be sentenced at the Emperor's pleasure.

"Let us talk of other things," she suggested, taking the empty tray and putting it on the chest at the end of the bed. "If you will tell me what you like to read, I will see if our small library has anything that will interest you."

Celeste laughed. "I doubt it will contain what interests me."

"We have a few things from the circulating library, too," Loveday said, wondering what she could mean. Surely she did not mean to offend. "*Camille* has just come, and something called *Emma*, by the author of *Pride and Prejudice*. Mama disapproves of the author, because she thinks she is a bad influence on my sister Gwen, but I quite like her."

"Then by all means, we must have this *Emma*," Celeste said with a smile. "Do you not find that a bad influence is, at least, an interesting one?"

Loveday was too honest to offer a proper young lady's argument. It was difficult to argue when part of you agreed. Mama certainly thought Loveday a bad influence on her sisters, when she meant no harm at all.

It took them two days to read aloud the first volume of *Emma*, chapter by chapter. Two days for Loveday to speculate with increasing anxiety about Emory's journey to Portsmouth and how soon he might return. Two days for both of them to become so fidgety and restless—despite their both being excessively entertained by *Emma*—that Celeste could no longer stay in bed. They read the final pages of the volume while strolling the upstairs hall from one end to the other.

"I think that tomorrow, we might anticipate the doctor's orders just a trifle by allowing the two of you out on the terrace," Mama said, upon discovering them. "I am pleased to see that Gwen's yellow batiste fits you well enough, Celeste."

"I am grateful to her." Celeste swished the skirts. "Someday I hope to repay you for your care of me."

Personally, Loveday thought the yellow that looked so wonderful on Gwen rather unflattering on poor Celeste— with her dark hair and eyes it made her look sallow—but Rosalind's frocks would be too long, and her own too badly treated to offer to a guest without insult. Why, this one had a grease spot near the hem that not even Morwen's skilled ministrations could lift. It had become a house dress, or at most a walking dress, never to be seen in company.

She had made the mistake of wearing it into her workshop last evening after Celeste was asleep and stained it again in the same place. But the remaining sections of the articulated sideboard now operated properly, and she had actually got it to walk across her workshop and down the steps into the yard. And she hadn't even told it to—simply set it in motion and watched to see how far it would go. That was worth the sacrifice of a bit of sprigged muslin from two springs ago.

On the third day, out on the terrace, Celeste was content to converse rather than to read. Loveday could have insisted that Rosalind or Gwen sit with their patient, but the truth was that she and Captain Trevelyan had saved the girl's life. Did that not make her at least partly responsible for her welfare? Besides, every now and again, little things that Celeste said made her curious. "The wind speed is dropping," she'd said just now, when anyone else might have said, "Not so strong a breeze today."

So instead of volume two of *Emma*, Loveday fetched one of her own prizes from the circulating library. An illustrated treatise on the steam-powered wagons proposed by Mr Robert Stephenson for the mining industry. She began to read with a lively interest—an interest so consuming that she reached the second section before she raised her fascinated gaze to her guest.

Who was sound asleep on the chaise longue.

Rosalind bumped open the French door to the terrace with one hip and brought the tea tray out. "The doctor is come. Put that treatise away—Mama will be out to fetch Celeste directly."

Celeste woke with a gasp at the sound of her name, but before Ros had even set down the tray on the low table, Celeste had recovered from whatever had ailed her. "I do apologize, Loveday," she said. "I seem to have fallen asleep."

"I'm sure it was what you needed," she said mildly. *And Stephenson was exactly what I needed.*

Mama came out and ushered Celeste into the parlor for

her conference with Doctor Pengarry. But in less than ten minutes, all three had returned, Celeste wreathed in smiles. "She has a clean bill of health," Mama said as she seated herself to pour the doctor's tea. "I am so glad."

"And no restrictions?" Loveday asked. "You are free to go about as you please?"

"Within reason, for a stranger to our shores," Doctor Pengarry said. "But yes. I believe that Miss Aventure may share in any activity you young ladies enjoy, from reading to dancing."

"What good news!" Mama said. "Now we have nothing to wait for but the Prince Regent's visit and the Midsummer Ball."

AT LAST! The past three days had been torture worse than what was rumored to happen in the Emperor's dungeons. Every moment Celeste had feared they suspected, they knew. She wasn't sure what she'd said, what she'd done, to give away the game, but their behavior now was highly suspicious.

First, they'd brought out a chaise longue for her should she desire to rest on the lawns overlooking the sea, as if taunting her. So close to freedom, yet no way to escape, especially with Loveday hovering over her like the mother hens Celeste could see through the open gate in the wall to the orchard.

Then Loveday spent even more time reading to her from engineering papers. Celeste had absorbed every word of Stephenson while pretending to be asleep. What fashionable young lady in England read engineering papers? Few young ladies in France read them. She, Amélie, and Josie had lamented the fact often enough.

"Ah, here's one from Lady Worthington," Loveday had said only this afternoon as she'd turned the page on *Philosophical Transactions.* "Of course her husband gets the authorial credit, but I recognize her theory on propulsion. The Royal Society of Engineers still refuses to publish papers by women. Philistines."

Celeste willed herself not to react, even though every fiber of her being longed to learn what the famed lady aeronaut had written. She covered her hand with her mouth and pretended to yawn.

"Have you no copies of *La Belle Assemblée?*" she asked. "We have heard that is your ladies' magazine. It would be amusing to see what passes for fashion in your little country."

Loveday's jaw hardened as she glued her eyes to the page. "I'll have to ask my sisters. They are devotees. I believe they plan to ask you for permission to sketch your clothing so they can request copies from our modiste."

That could lead to trouble. The Penhales might not recognize the design for what it was, but any former military man might have seen its like on a French aeronaut.

Right before a bomb dropped nearby.

"Oh, my modiste would not allow it," Celeste said airily. "She is very protective of her designs." Inspiration struck. "But if you gave me pen and paper, I could write to her for permission—that is, if you know a way to send a letter to France."

Loveday met her gaze, head cocked so that the breeze tugged a strand of uncurled hair out of her knot. "But I thought you had been living in Portugal."

Celeste's gut twisted. Why was she such a terrible liar?

She'd learned to spin a spiderweb out of silk to protect herself should she fall from the sky. She ought to be able to spin a tale to satisfy Loveday.

"Yes, that is where I was living with my family," she assured her. "But the outfit was made before we left Paris. That is where I must write to my modiste."

"Ah." She straightened. "Well, there may be an opportunity. I understand we have smugglers in the area. They might be able to take it, assuming we can find a way to make their acquaintance."

Oh, but she would find a way! She allowed some of her delight to leak through. "Smugglers! How intriguing. But I would not want you to jeopardize your reputation by approaching them. Perhaps if you tell me their direction, I could request the favor myself."

Loveday regarded her a moment, and Celeste feared she'd gone too far. But the Englishwoman shook her head. "I'm afraid I don't know their direction. I may, however, know someone who does. Captain Trevelyan, the one who first sighted you on the beach."

"A sea captain?" Celeste asked on a sudden spurt of hope.

"No, a former officer for England and the oldest son of our neighbor. He watches the sea often enough. He may have noticed a smuggler's craft."

Her tone had cooled, her face tightened.

"You do not like him," Celeste surmised.

Loveday started, then shook her head. "You're very observant. It isn't that I dislike him, precisely. I've been all but ordered to marry him. Unlike you, I have no fortune to rely on without marrying. And no other source of income should my father pass. My only brother was killed in the war."

Guilt poked at her. Silly. She hadn't shot the fellow. "I am sorry for your loss," she murmured.

She nodded. "We all are. Jory would have been the one to inherit. My sisters and I cannot. Suffice it to say, unless I marry—and Arthur is my parents' choice—my father's estate will go to a stranger."

She sounded so sad. Celeste felt for her. "And he is fat and ugly, this Arthur?"

Her brows shot up. "No, not at all. He was accorded quite the Corinthian before he was injured in the war."

"Ah, then he is of low character—consorting with smugglers, gamblers."

That made her laugh. "Arthur Trevelyan, a gambler? I assure you, he is the least likely sort to take chances. He is entirely a traditionalist, like many in the neighborhood."

Her tone had darkened again. Celeste thought she understood at last. Her hands pressed down on the soft cambric of the gown they had given her to wear.

"After the French Revolution, my *maman* told me, many women rose to new heights—officers in the Army and Aeronautical Corps, physicians, advisors to the Emperor. Some men feel this was a mistake, that liberty and equality are only for those of the fraternity. Is the latter the same here?"

She sighed. "All too often."

The injustice of it stiffened her spine. Celeste waved a hand. "*Fah* on them! We will prove our worth."

Loveday smiled. "Indeed we will. Some already have, I hear. Didn't your Emperor make a woman the head of his aeronauts? Madame Blanchard?"

Why would she bring that up? Celeste could not have blundered so badly. Keeping her smile in place made her mouth ache. "Why, yes. And she is a fire-breathing dragon. My mother insists that I emulate her, but me? I prefer fashion to flying. Now, let us talk of more pleasant matters. Have you good society here in Cornwall, soirees, balls? I understand you English love to dance."

"It is a healthful exercise," Loveday said primly, pulling *Philosophical Transactions* closer once more. "Sir Anthony and Lady Boscawen host the Midsummer Ball every year. My sisters will be making their bows, so you and I will be expected to attend."

Unless she found a way to escape before then.

"*Magnifique*," she'd said, leaning back on the chaise. "For now, I tire. Please feel free to read to me what this Lady Worthington has to say."

THANK *le bon Dieu* the doctor had said Celeste could rise, walk about the house and gardens, resume her life.

As if he had any idea of the life she'd led.

Neither did Mrs Penhale, of course. She was pleased to pour tea that afternoon in the withdrawing room off the entry hall, with her daughters and Celeste. It was a pleasant enough room with a cozy fire, but she felt as if the paneled walls were closing in.

"I'm delighted you could join us at last, Mademoiselle Aventure," her hostess said, handing Celeste a fine bone china cup with a pattern of roses along the silver-edged rim. "We must make you known to our friends and acquaintances in the neighborhood."

For a moment, she wondered about the smugglers, but

Mrs Penhale would surely not know how to reach them. Only this captain, it seemed, could point out their direction.

"That would be delightful," she assured the lady, balancing the cup neatly over the white lawn gown. She suspected this one had been Loveday's, as it smelled faintly of lubricating oil. She still wasn't sure how the Englishwoman came into contact with such things. Perhaps it had something to do with Arthur Trevelyan.

"I understand your neighbors are quite interesting," she ventured. "The Trevelyans, I believe?"

Gwendolyn and Rosalind shared a giggle. A look from Loveday silenced them.

"They are good neighbors," Mrs Penhale agreed. "In fact, we have been invited to dine with them this very evening. Do you think you would feel well enough to join us? I'm sure Mrs Trevelyan won't mind another at table."

Loveday glanced at her imploringly, as if willing her to agree. So tempting. Yet, if the family were all out, would this not be her opportunity to escape? She could find the smugglers, or, failing that, at least locate a bolt hole along the shore where she could keep watch for the movements of their vessels.

She allowed her hand to tremble just the slightest. "Alas, I do not believe I have recovered enough for such an occasion. *Merci* all the same."

Loveday looked even more disappointed than her mother.

Celeste was careful to stay in her room until she heard the carriage leave and the maid had carried off her dinner tray. Then she slipped out of the nightgown and into her flight suit. At least her corset fastened in the front. The maid had goggled at its brass fittings when she'd helped

Celeste into the day dresses the daughters had loaned her. She slipped her fingers into the inside pocket of the redingote and sighed in relief at the feel of the smooth brass compass. No one had laundered the garment, and, since the wool had been milled, it had not shrunk after its time in the sea.

Now, to see if she could locate these smugglers herself.

She cracked open the door of her room and glanced up and down the carpeted corridor. From her movements indoors and out, she knew the basic plan of the house and the number of the Penhale servants. This floor held mostly bedchambers. No, no one moved, not even Morwen, the maid. No voices murmured in the distance. Hugging the wall, she crept to the stairway and started down, listening for any presence. Something thumped, as though dropped from a height. She froze.

Silence.

Perhaps a servant preparing the dining room for breakfast. All she had to do was move swiftly, quietly. Drawing a breath, she managed to reach the entry hall. A few more steps, and she'd be out the door and headed toward freedom and home.

Clump, clump, clump.

She whirled, expecting to see a dozen servants marching toward her. Instead, an ungainly piece of furniture that seemed to be made up of boxes stood in the corridor behind her.

Celeste leaned to one side to catch sight of the servant who must have set it there. The corridor was empty. Nothing moved.

She turned back toward the door. Took one step.

Clump.

She whirled. The piece of furniture now blocked the doorway to the corridor itself.

Celeste wondered for a moment if she was dreaming. She gave her head a shake. A servant had to be cleaning the piece, kneeling behind it, out of her sight. She must go before she was seen.

Another step, and with a racket of clanks and clumps, the boxes tumbled past her. She leaped out of the way, dodging for the door, and it contorted to stack itself against the panel, blocking her escape. As she backed away, a box tumbled off the top, setting the whole thing in motion again. It clipped the tall Chinese vase by the stairs, which teetered and crashed on the flagstones with a high-pitched tinkle of breaking porcelain.

Celeste turned and pelted up the stairs. Darting into her room, she slammed the door and pressed her back against it, heart pounding.

Was she dreaming?

Was she mad?

What was going on?

CHAPTER 12

"What is the meaning of this?" Papa roared.

Mama, Loveday, and her sisters piled up in the doorway behind him, leaning this way and that around his stocky form to see what was the matter. Finally Loveday extricated herself from her sisters' dinner dresses and cloaks and stood aghast at the mess in the entry hall.

"George, your grandfather's vase!" Mama wailed. It lay in a thousand pieces all over the flagstones and not standing at the bottom of the staircase where they had all been so used to its presence that they barely saw it anymore. "It has been in the family for over a century!" Then her tone changed as she reared back. "What is that thing doing here?"

The articulated sideboard stood defiantly at the foot of the staircase, for all the world as though guarding the castle gates from a pack of marauders.

Loveday struggled to find her tongue. Words flapped uselessly in her brain, but none of them seemed remotely adequate to the situation.

"Loveday, isn't that the old sideboard that was out in the tack room?"

Oh, Rosalind. But her sister would not consciously have given her away. She was simply seeking information.

"Yes," she sighed.

"Someone fetch Morwen," Mama said. "This must be cleaned up immediately before one of you cuts your feet. Loveday, you will please explain what you know of this?"

"I—I cannot." She felt strangely short of breath. For she had left the sideboard in the workshop. How had it crossed the yard, come in through the back door, and stationed itself here? Their land did not slope in this direction, so it had not rolled or fallen. No one would have carried it into the house, especially not from the stables.

Then how on earth…?

"Is it gone?" A tremulous voice came from the landing above.

"Mademoiselle Aventure?" Gwen called. "Is that you?"

"Yes." A slender figure in a pink night dress peeped out of the shadows. She caught sight of the sideboard gleaming in the light of the lamps that had been lit in anticipation of the family's return, gasped, and whirled, her footsteps fading along the corridor in retreat.

A door slammed.

"I *will* have an explanation," Papa said in the tone that meant *immediately.*

"I will, too," Mama added grimly. "I ordered that wretched sideboard taken away months and months ago. What is it doing back in my house? Did someone move it in here as a joke, and tipped over your great-grandfather's Chinese vase in the process?"

"Loveday?" Rosalind unfastened her cloak and laid it over her arm. "Why did she say that? Is what gone?"

"Intruders!" Gwen squeaked, pressing against her mother's side.

"She said 'it,' not 'they,' you goose," Rosalind said.

"She clearly meant the sideboard." Loveday sighed again. "I believe this is my fault."

"I am waiting," Papa said.

Wordlessly, Loveday picked her way across the hall to the foot of the stairs. Better to demonstrate than attempt to explain. "Come along," she told the sideboard. "Back to the workshop."

She pushed one of the boxes on the end closest to the corridor, and to the accompaniment of gasps and exclamations from her family, the sideboard tumbled along after her in its higgledy-piggledy fashion. Down the corridor they went, past the little room where Papa did the accounts, and out the open back door into the yard.

"We are in such trouble," she told it. "What possessed you to come into the house? Were you just out for a bit of exercise?"

But the sideboard, sadly, had no answer for her. As it assembled itself with painful neatness into a highboy against the side wall of the workshop, she had the distinct impression it was trying to get back into her good graces.

She laid an affectionate hand on its topmost surface, gleaming in the moonlight that came in through the dusty window above. "It's all right. I'll find out from Celeste what happened—you must have given her an awful fright. But you mustn't come in the house, you know. Mama is liable to take the fireplace poker to you, and that would be a shame now that you've come so far."

With a final pat, she made certain the workshop door was firmly latched, then walked back into the house to face her parents.

She found them in the drawing room, with Morwen just placing a tea tray on the table. "I'll have the hall cleaned up in a trice," she assured Mama. "I'm that sorry about the vase, ma'am."

"I'm not," Gwen muttered. "Awful, ugly old thing."

It was fortunate for Gwen that Papa had been distracted by Loveday's appearance in the doorway. "Are you responsible for that mechanical... automaton... thing?" he demanded, chomping into a biscuit.

There was no getting out of it now. "I am," she confessed. "I rescued it when I saw it in pieces in the cart. When I looked closely, I realized that it was not merely a storage chest. Half its pulleys had rotted away, and its gears had rusted. It had never been put to its original use."

"Which was?" Rosalind asked.

"As a chest of drawers or a sideboard, I suppose," Loveday said, "but it is perambulatory by design. Whoever made it was a mechanical genius."

Mama sniffed. Apparently geniuses and suspected pirates ranked the same in her view. Guilt by association.

"At any rate, I promise it will not come into the house again. I shall be making use of it in my workshop."

"What workshop?" Papa demanded. "I am not going to countenance any more of your nonsense about the steam works, maidey."

"I meant my workshop in the old tack room, Papa," she

said, carefully evading any reference to the forbidden subject of the steam works. "My books and papers and drawings are out there, so they do not incommode anyone in the house."

"And so they should be," he grumbled, taking another biscuit from the plate Mama offered him. "It is a disgrace, a young lady messing about with mechanical nonsense. As bad as the French."

"Mr Penhale!" Mama said in a low tone. "Remember Miss Aventure is French, though of course she is no loyalist to Bonaparte."

"And so fashionable," Gwen said. "Mama, may I have my hair cut in the Titus style? It is as straight as a stick, not curly like Miss Aventure's, but—"

"Absolutely not!" Papa said, his voice rising again.

Thank you, Gwen, for the distraction, Loveday thought with some relief.

"Not so fast, maidey," Papa said, catching Loveday sidling toward the door.

"Yes, Papa?" She did her best to look chastened.

"That workshop of yours is off limits until we discover the whereabouts of Miss Aventure's family and see her returned to them. No more dodging your duty, miss, and messing about with pulleys and such. You are to be a friend to that poor young woman and, if we and the gentlemen of the neighborhood are lucky, mayhap some of her feminine graces will rub off on you."

Her shoulders sagged. "Yes, Papa."

When she was released a few minutes later, she hurried up the stairs to Celeste's room and knocked upon the door.

"Come in." Celeste was in bed, the blankets pulled up over her chest. "How was your dinner?"

"Uneventful."

"And the captain?"

"Pleasant enough." Loveday seated herself in the chair that had become hers by default. "He does not yet dare to venture out to dinner elsewhere."

"And…?"

Loveday frowned. "I hardly know. He has not been what I expected."

"And what was that?"

"I did not come to talk about Captain Trevelyan." She looked the girl in the eye. "I need to know what happened this evening."

"What happened?" Again, she had that curious sense that Celeste had gone still, as though caught in the act of something that society would not approve. But that could not be so.

"Yes, with the sideboard." At the incomprehension on her face, Loveday elaborated. "The chest of drawers. *Le buffet.*"

Celeste's face relaxed, and hot color bloomed in her cheeks. "I am sorry to be such a coward. But the… *le buffet*… it sneaked up on me. Frightened me."

"We found it at the bottom of the staircase," Loveday said. "What do you mean, it sneaked up on you?"

"I wanted to go out for—for a breath of air. Into the garden, to smell the lavender and think of home. And there it was, blocking the way. I do not understand. It moved. All of itself. How is that possible?"

Loveday dared to smile, even to show a glimmer of pride. "It is nothing to be afraid of. It is a project I have been working on, restoring a mechanical chest to good working order. It was designed to be perambulatory—to move on its own."

"But why should anyone design their furniture to walk about the house?" Celeste sounded perplexed even as her eyes were bright with interest.

"Do you think furniture, like women, ought to be decorative and nothing else?" If her tone were slightly bitter, could she be blamed?

"*Certainement pas,*" Celeste said, an odd note in her voice. "Women are capable of every achievement men have won, even going to war, whether on the sea, the land, or the air." She caught her breath, as though she realized she had become carried away by her feelings. "Though I must confess I should not actually like to fight on the land or the sea."

"Yes, though we stay at home, women are at war, too, aren't they?"

Celeste nodded. "Helping as best we can from behind the scenes—feeding the children of soldiers, clothing refugees, even rolling bandages for the hospitals and saving silk for—" Her throat closed, and she stopped.

"I had hoped to do something to help the war effort, but it seems I must stay at home." Loveday did not want to betray her discontent to this poor girl, who had nothing to content herself with but what others gave her. She made herself smile and hoped it looked sincere in the semidarkness of the room. "And be a good friend to you."

A few seconds of silence ticked by. "I should like that. My friends are all so far away."

Her voice trembled, and impulsively, Loveday took her hand and squeezed it. "Then we are agreed. Good night."

"Good night, my friend."

And as Loveday made her way to her own room, she reflected that it could have been worse. She had begun a friendship, strangely enough, thanks to the articulated sideboard. And at least Papa had not forbidden her to leave the estate.

"YOU ARE NOT to leave the estate," Papa said firmly to her the next day at lunch, as he sliced into the chicken and leek pie that stood a proud eight inches tall on its platter.

"Mr Penhale!" Mama remonstrated. "Loveday is perfectly capable of getting herself into a scrape whether she is on the property or not."

"Are you telling me you do not wish her to bear the consequences of breaking Grandfather's vase?" He laid a generous slice of the pie on Mama's plate.

"I am telling you that Doctor Pengarry said that Miss Aventure was to be out in the fresh air and taking active exercise."

"What does this have to do with Loveday?"

Meekly, Loveday took the slice of pie, and helped herself to the salad of lettuces. If she kept quiet, Mama might fight for her freedom without Loveday having to say a word.

"Because Loveday must be able to go about with her. In the whiskey, walking over to *Gwynn Place*—" She eyed Papa meaningfully, her brows raised. "Celeste has yet to call to thank Captain Trevelyan herself, and of course Loveday must accompany her."

"And I," Gwen said.

"And I," Rosalind echoed. "We must confer further with the twins. Not one of us has decided on patterns for our gowns."

Papa finished carving the pie for his family and subsided into his chair with his own. "Very well. Perhaps I have been too hasty. But you are not to drive to Truro." He glared at Loveday.

"No, Papa." Her father would be utterly to blame if she went mad with anxiety about the steam works. But there was nothing for it. He was her father, and he must be obeyed. She could still take the whiskey out. She still had her freedom. She ought to be grateful for small mercies.

After lunch, she picked a bouquet of lavender and sweet pink rosebuds, and placed the vase on Mama's writing desk, where she was writing out a list of the things they must take with them to Exeter. She dropped a kiss on her mother's hair. "Thank you, Mama, for forestalling my no doubt grim punishment."

"I am still most displeased about the vase, but as you were half a mile away at the time, it seems unfair that you should be blamed entirely for the mishap."

"May we have the whiskey to go into St Mawes? I have had a note that a book I have ordered is in, and Celeste has expressed a wish to go with me."

"I will not ask about the content of such a book, for I fear it is neither cookery nor a treatise of the enlightening sort."

"I can promise it will be both enlightening and a feast for the mind, Mama."

"Oh, go on with you both, and drive safely." Her mother gave her an affectionate nudge, and Loveday practically danced from the room.

The day seemed to be made for a drive, with the skies a shining blue dotted with clouds and a pleasant breeze blowing over the burgeoning fields. Loveday's green linen spencer was almost too warm, but the straw bonnet she had trimmed with silk daisies and matching green watered silk ribbons was so becoming that it was a sacrifice she was willing to make. One did not give up one's small advantages so easily.

"I am so grateful to your mother for giving me this rose-colored twill for a spencer. It is very pretty." Celeste smoothed the fabric of the sleeves with pleasure.

"I agree." Loveday guided Rhea to the left for the road down to St Mawes. "We might buy you a length of ribbon at the milliner's to trim that bonnet, too, don't you think?"

But her primary objective was the bookshop, and the treasure she found waiting for her there: *The Voyage of the Minerva: Being a True and Scientific Account of the Flight from London to Edinburgh in Despite of Its Detractors.*

"I know you do not care for scientific works, but I have been waiting for this one for months," she said as the two climbed back into the whiskey, treasure safely in hand. She unwrapped the parcel and gazed upon it with awe that it was hers at last.

Celeste gasped. "You have the account of Etienne-Gaspard Robert? Can it truly be? Oh, how long have I wanted to read it!"

"But— I thought— What?" Loveday stared at her, feeling rather as though the earth had cracked open and shown her something astonishing.

The color drained from Celeste's face. For a moment, she looked as though she might leap from the whiskey and run. But then she seemed to shake herself, or say something silently to herself. She took the parcel and held it protectively as Loveday turned the horse back on to the main road. "A woman may enjoy both fashion and science, as you do."

"But—"

"I am afraid I have made you think I care more about the former than the latter. In truth, it is the reverse. *Minerva's* voyage was to prove the advantages of powered flight." Her voice sounded almost reverent. "None of your clumsy steam boilers and behemoths and *sous-marins. Powered flight.*"

Trying to recover from her surprise, Loveday flapped the reins and they continued down the hill toward the milliner's. "I am glad you appreciate his work. I was convinced you were the sort who would advocate for a cookbook or… *La Belle Assemblée.*"

Her companion colored a little. "Each of those has its own time and season." Celeste touched the red cloth cover with reverence. "It is forbidden to read him in the Empire, you know. Since he took the plans for *Minerva* to England, he has been in disgrace—more even than my father. He is *sous paine de mort.* What is that in English?"

"Under pain of death… for not handing his plans over to Boney?"

Celeste's eyebrows rose. "Boney?"

"It's what we call him. It is an English habit—we call our own Prince Regent *Prinny*, but with much more affection. *Boney* is not a term you would call anyone you liked. But Celeste, truly? Pain of death? Like your parents?"

She nodded sadly. "It is similar, though in our case with the possibility merely of imprisonment. But let us not talk of that. Let us read together."

"And so we shall, once we are home. So you have been hiding behind a mask, have you?"

Again that peculiar stillness. Only for a moment, but long

enough for Loveday to wonder what had frightened her this time.

"What mask is this?" Celeste asked.

"Why, the one I wear." Loveday tossed a smile at her. "The mask of a well-brought-up young lady, when underneath I am... an engineer."

Celeste gazed at her. "Is it true? Where did you study?"

Loveday felt heat flood her cheeks. "I have no training but that which our local school may offer, and after that, my own reading and experimentation."

"Can your parents not afford to send you? Are there schools of engineering here?"

"Well, yes, in London. But a woman would never be allowed to attend." She snorted. "Or so Emory Thorndyke has taken care to tell me while he questions every little thing I do at the steam works. Or worse, while he adapts my ideas to his own work and takes all the credit. Honestly, do men truly think our brains are smaller or softer or less able to retain information? It is both ridiculous and maddening and there is not a thing we can do about it."

Celeste was silent, her face a study in pity and surprise.

"You cannot tell me *you* have been to a school of science," Loveday said, nettled.

"Not exactly."

"Well, then. It is our lot to stand at the doors of higher learning with no one to hear our knock, I suppose. But at what a cost! At least I have been able to help a little. And there are my own studies and experiments."

"Ah. Like *le buffet.*"

Loveday drew up outside the milliner's. The shop fronted on the harbor, but some distance away from the docks where the fishing boats and Channel trade tied up. Here, there were shops, a bakery, and even a tea shop where one could taste the latest imports… if one could afford it.

"I may not have attended a school of engineering in London," Celeste said, again touching the cover of the book, "but I know in my heart that they are wrong, those who say that powered flight is a less likely means of defense than that carried out on land or sea."

"I agree with you," Loveday said. "Why, the very sea birds teach us that an attack from the air is at once the most efficient and the most difficult to counteract."

"Precisely." Celeste smiled at her.

How had she ever thought that her companion was a featherhead, only interested in trivial pursuits? *Minerva* had torn the mask away and revealed her as she was, it seemed.

"I think we are going to be better friends than ever," Loveday told her impulsively. "Come, let us find you a rose-colored ribbon and then hurry home to taste the delights of Monsieur Robert and his *Minerva*."

CHAPTER 13

So, this was why Loveday read engineering treatises for fun! How wonderful to find someone who understood, even so far from home. A shame Marcel wasn't here. He would have been more than happy to talk to Loveday about nuts and bolts, gears and pulleys. And they could all read *Minerva* and talk long into the night about the sheer possibilities of powered flight.

Just the thought of Marcel's swarthy face made her smile slip as Loveday turned the cane whiskey into the lane leading to Hale House. As pleasant as Celeste's sojourn with the Penhales had been, their kindness held her captive. She had no idea how to reach the smugglers or whether they'd be willing to help her by carrying a note—much less her person—to France. Much as she felt an affinity for Loveday at that moment, she was still alone.

"Who could that be?" Loveday asked.

Celeste frowned at the hooded landau waiting on the drive, its coachman out checking the horses. "You do not recognize it?"

"No." She pulled Rhea to a halt, and a groom came running to take charge of the whiskey.

Mrs Kerrow, the Penhale housekeeper, met them in the entry hall. "There's a lady here to see Miss Aventure." She eyed Celeste as if none too sure of this new development.

Loveday untied the bow under her chin and handed her bonnet to the housekeeper, but her gaze was on Celeste. "I wasn't aware you knew anyone else in the area."

She sounded a bit affronted by the idea.

"I wasn't aware I did, either," Celeste assured her as she removed her bonnet as well. She accompanied Loveday to the withdrawing room.

Mrs Penhale was entertaining a woman who was small of stature and quick of movement. Celeste could only see the back of their visitor, but her heart leaped. *Maman? Here?* She rushed around the sofa. A stranger gazed back at her, grey eyes bright in a lined face. Up close, it was clear that her dark hair had gone more salt than pepper.

Mrs Penhale smiled. "Madame Racine, allow me to present our guest, Mademoiselle Aventure. Celeste, this dear lady is an émigré of some standing in our area. She has tutored many of our young gentlemen in your language."

Celeste bobbed a curtsey. *"Enchantée, Madame."*

"Et moi aussi," she responded, hands clasped over the head of an ebony walking stick. "But let us speak English. This is my home now. I understand it is to be yours as well."

Not if she could help it.

But Mrs Penhale was nodding, so Celeste took her seat beside the lady on the sofa even as Loveday perched in the wing chair she favored nearby. How tempting to pour her heart out to another Frenchwoman, but not with an audience.

And Madame Racine had made it sound as if she had already decided never to return to France.

"Mrs Penhale and her family have been so kind to allow me to stay," she told the lady. "I know I cannot impose much longer."

"You are welcome for as long as you like," Loveday's mother promised her. "I would hope for the same treatment if my daughters were lost in a foreign country."

"But you are not lost, are you, Mademoiselle Aventure?" the Frenchwoman asked with a knowing smile.

Her stomach plummeted. What had she done now to give herself away?

"Not with such friends beside me," she hedged with a smile all around.

Madam Racine beamed. "But of course. You will find the English to be an intelligent, compassionate people, not at all what the Emperor would have us believe. You have met the Emperor?"

As Celeste Blanchard, daughter to the famous Sophie, the answer was *too often for comfort*. He also had sharp eyes like this woman, as if he could see inside one. But would Celeste Aventure, the heiress, have met him?

"Before we fled France for Portugal, my mother was required to present me at court," she allowed. "I did not enjoy the experience."

"Such presentations are not the most pleasing in England, either, I hear," Mrs Penhale said, nose up. "His Royal Highness keeps delegating them to the Queen Mother so he can spend more time with his silly contraptions. And as for the Princess of Wales taking on such a duty—*pfft!*"

"The prince's inventions may yet prove to be the turning point in this war," Loveday insisted loyally.

"And yours as well, Mademoiselle Penhale?" Madame Racine asked.

When Loveday gaped, speechless, the Frenchwoman tutted. "I see you on the road to Truro. The engineers at the steam works are handsome, *non?*"

"Non," Loveday said emphatically even as the housekeeper appeared in the doorway.

"Forgive the interruption, ma'am, but a Mr Thorndyke is here to see Miss Penhale, and he did not seem inclined to leave his card."

Loveday leaped to her feet, then seemed to control herself by smoothing her skirts. "I'll speak to him. I'm sure it will only take a moment." She hurried from the room.

"Please excuse her," Mrs Penhale told their guest. "I fear you are right about the attraction of the steam works. Mr Richard Trevithick showed an interest in Loveday's aptitude for such things when she was younger. We indulged the pastime. It seemed harmless enough, and it furthered her education. But she seems to have taken an unnatural interest in mechanics."

Celeste had to bite the inside of her cheek to keep from responding. Loveday was very clever. She had ideas beyond what others considered. Her mother should be proud!

"Perhaps she has found her calling," Madame Racine said. "Her purpose. It is what we all seek. Do you not agree, mademoiselle?"

"I do indeed," Celeste said. "There can be nothing finer than knowing you are making a difference, whether that is in a steam works or in a sailing ship or in a drawing room."

Madame Racine nodded. "And you? How will you make a difference?"

Oh, but her smile was slipping now. She'd had such dreams! All her plans, for naught. No way to salvage her equipment. All that silk, wasted! Who knew where it had ultimately come down after she'd jumped. But to give up on everything, settle herself in England?

Non, non, non. The Penhales could not possibly allow her to stay here forever. If they insisted that Loveday marry, how much more would they expect it of her—for a letter to her imaginary parents in Portugal would never see a reply. Both of the women were eyeing her, as if measuring her for a wedding gown already. Had they picked out the groom as well? Someone old, established, who would think a woman only as good as her dowry?

Her fabricated, nonexistent dowry?

Celeste popped to her feet. "Thank you for reminding me, Madame Racine. My purpose is to show gratitude to this family for taking me in. I must see to Miss Penhale, who ought not to entertain a gentleman alone. Excuse me."

She picked up her skirts and dashed from the room, feeling as if the Comte d'Angeline howled at her heels. She barreled into the entry hall and smacked into a tall, muscled frame.

Large hands reached out to steady her. "Pardon me, miss."

She looked up at the gentleman. He had short, sandy hair swept back from a lean face. Amélie would have admired the chiseled line of his cheekbones, the cleft in his formidable chin. Josie would have gazed into the sea-green eyes and ordered a skein of silken thread in the color. At the moment,

Celeste was more aware of a *tap-tap-tap*, as if her heart raced, its sound audible in her ears.

Then Loveday shifted, and she realized it had been the sound of her friend's foot against the flagged floor.

"Mademoiselle Aventure," she said, one hand wrapped around a roll of parchment, "allow me to present Mr Emory Thorndyke."

This was the man who had so incensed Loveday, the one who challenged her every move at her beloved steam works? Celeste stepped back, and his hands fell from her shoulders.

He gave her a short bow. "Miss Aventure, a pleasure."

Oh, but it was hard to remember her role and not give him a dressing down. She fluttered her lashes. *"Bonjour,* Monsieur Thorndyke. *Comment allez vous?"*

His smile apologized. "I never learned French, I fear."

"So he is as dense as you claimed?" she asked Loveday in French.

"Mais oui," Loveday responded with a smile. Then she switched to English. "Mr Thorndyke came to tell me that thanks to his information from Portsmouth, he's developed a new boiler design and would like me to look at it." Her hand tightened on the parchment.

He shifted on his feet, setting all six feet of him to swaying. "It was Mr Trevithick's idea."

"Then we must thank Monsieur Trevithick," Celeste said brightly. "And we must thank you, Monsieur Thorndyke, for coming such a distance. We should not keep you further. *Bon voyage."*

"I hadn't planned on taking a voyage," he protested, but Celeste wiggled her fingers at him. Given no choice this side of propriety, he bowed to her and Loveday and departed.

"That was brilliant," Loveday said as the door closed behind him. "Thank you."

Celeste curtsied. "What are friends for?"

"May I impose further?" she asked, head cocked.

"I have certainly imposed on you enough," Celeste said. "What would you have me do?"

"Come out to my workshop, and we will have a look at these." She waggled the roll.

There was no resisting such a temptation.

WITH EVERYONE in the household occupied elsewhere, and Papa having made himself scarce with his steward upon the arrival of Madame Racine, whom he did not like, Loveday felt no compunction at all about taking refuge out in her workshop.

Celeste sidled in, eyeing the sideboard, which had not moved from its position against the wall. "Is it still… active?" she asked in a low voice.

"It is being very well behaved," Loveday assured her. "Sideboard, this is Celeste Aventure. She means you no harm and is my friend."

The sideboard did not move, which Loveday took to mean acceptance.

She unrolled Emory's drawing and weighted its corners with whatever came to hand—an iron nail, a bell with no clapper, two cogs. Then she and Celeste bent over them.

He had changed the shape of the boiler and made it sleeker, with components that she suspected were directly out of Portsmouth. Here was the release valve, here the fire door. It was unobjectionable in every way.

"It is not very interesting," Celeste finally said. "For this he had to ride six miles?"

"We both peeked at the sketches for *Minerva*'s boiler," Loveday said. "We have been spoiled."

"And yet..." Celeste indicated a line here, a curve there. "If these were adapted more closely to Monsieur Robert's ideas, rather than that of a steam ship, think how much more efficient the pressure would be, even if it is not at altitude."

"I hope you will not be offended if I say the likelihood of Thomas Trevithick adopting the ideas of a French engineer are as good as his adopting mine." Loveday sighed. "He allows me to suggest small changes, and improvements to the process, but Emory and he are in charge of design exclusively."

"Hmph. Let us exchange this so dull design for Monsieur Robert's. I will be in a much better temper afterward."

Loveday opened the book to the center illustration of the ship's design, which could be removed entirely and spread out upon the bench. She moved the lamps closer.

"You see, of course, why the ship went down," Celeste said soberly.

"It was not for the reasons the newspapers gave, certainly." She pointed. "It was this."

Minerva had gone down just outside Edinburgh, with the scandal sheets and the military band and a crowd of a thousand horrified people to witness it. Monsieur Robert had built in failsafes so that the ship would not plummet or burn, but glide in an arc to the ground. Still, his career had not survived the public humiliation when everyone had expected a triumph.

He had installed a prototype high-pressure boiler just like theirs, with components that could not withstand what was being asked of them.

"If only I had seen this before we began the build," Loveday said.

"Would they have listened to you?"

"No," she admitted. "But at least I could have tried, and resisted the urge to say, 'I told you so' afterward."

"I wonder if one could build a much smaller version out of different materials," Celeste mused. "Just enough to power, say, a touring balloon."

"I suppose one could, if one had a good design and could lay hands on materials."

Celeste held her gaze.

"No," Loveday said. Her heart had begun to pound for no reason at all. "It is impossible. Even if I could scare up some scrap metal at the steam works, I am forbidden to go to Truro."

"But I am not," Celeste said.

The two young ladies stared at each other.

Nothing moved—not even the sideboard. And when Rosalind called, "Loveday!" from the kitchen garden, both of them jumped as if they had been doing something not only unsuitable, but illegal to boot.

"Loveday!" Rosalind's voice was closer. "Madame Racine is leaving, and Mama says you must come."

"She is not calling upon me," Loveday muttered. She rolled up Emory's design and laid it with Monsieur Robert's book in the topmost compartment of the sideboard, to be collected later.

They gathered in the drive as Madame Racine was handed into the landau by her coachman. "I hope the two of you know you will be most welcome, should you wish to call," the older lady said to Loveday and Celeste.

"Why, how kind." Mama stared, as though she had never seen Loveday smile before. "We should be delighted."

Madame Racine knocked on the door and sat back, and the landau rolled away up the gravel drive.

Mama waited for Loveday to take her place at her side to proceed into the house. "Since when, my dear, are you so pleased to call upon a lady who has not had the pleasure of your company above twice a year?"

"Since Celeste has come to stay," Loveday said with a glance over her shoulder at her, walking beside Rosalind and leaving Gwen, as the youngest, to bring up the rear. "Do you not agree that opportunities to speak her own language in comfort and safety would make her stay more pleasant?"

"And are you sure that there is no other motive for traveling to Truro to pay these calls?"

"No indeed, Mama. Though I must tell you that we are obliged to go to the steam works tomorrow, to return Mr Thorndyke's design. He was courteous enough to solicit my opinion, so I must be prompt in its return."

"Of course you should. Celeste shall go with you."

"I was hoping so, Mama."

Her mother turned at the door of the drawing room while her sisters scattered to their rooms and Celeste hovered in the background. "I must thank you, Celeste, for the beneficial effect you are having upon my daughter. She has become positively amiable lately."

"I am certain it is your own tutelage and upbringing that is the cause, Madame."

Mama gave a snort and proceeded into the drawing room, leaving Celeste to raise her eyebrows and Loveday to cover her mouth, lest a peal of sudden, imprudent laughter spoil everything.

CHAPTER 14

TRURO, CORNWALL

*W*hat was he to do with the pair of them? Emory watched as Miss Penhale led her new friend around the Trevithick Steam Works as if they were on their first outing to the British Museum. Everyone else had stopped work to watch, as if the sway of their skirts was mesmerizing.

Which it rather was.

He snapped his gaze back to the plans laid out on the drafting table, plans that now bore a number of arrows, suggestions, and amendments. Why anyone thought it wise to consult the cosseted daughter of landed gentry about anything as intricate as a high-pressure steam engine still continued to elude him. He'd attended Eton and Oxford. She'd had, what—a governess, Richard Trevithick's patronage notwithstanding? His sisters had had a governess. They visited the steam works on occasion too. Much as he loved them, he would never have let them through the door.

"Half-inch steel rivets," he muttered, trying to decipher her writing. "Why on earth... Oh, I see."

Well, maybe not all her ideas were rubbish. A broken clock was still right twice a day, as his father liked to say.

His grip tightened on the pencil, and he made his fingers relax. Was it any wonder he was tense after his conversation with his father over breakfast that morning?

"You've spent enough time fooling with that boiler," his father had railed, grey hair sticking out around his ears as if he'd been tugging at it. "I need you at Wheal Thorne. The thrice-cursed gas is keeping us from sending the men down and every day, we lose money."

"We continue to progress at the steam works," he'd told his father. "It's only a matter of time before we solve the problem."

"I'm not getting any younger, you know," his father had complained. "I want to be confident you can manage the place when I'm gone, with a wife at your side to cheer you."

As if he had time for a wife when the mine was in danger and the future of the empire might rest on this boiler.

For some reason, his gaze was drawn to Miss Aventure again. Few would accord her a great beauty, particularly when she was standing next to Loveday Penhale. If she had been an automaton, he could have listed her flaws—eyes too big, nose too pointed, mouth too small, body too short and slender.

But she wasn't an automaton. When he stood near her, he was acutely aware that she was a lady. There was a light in her brown eyes, an elegance to her movements, that pulled him closer. And those unruly curls looked soft enough to caress.

The drawing. He was studying the drawing.

"She's something, isn't she, that Miss Penhale?"

He refused to share Rudolph Clement's grin. The other engineer his age often worked a different shift and so didn't interact with Miss Penhale a great deal. Now Rudy wore a look so besotted Emory was tempted to toss the pencil at his bulbous nose.

"Yes," he said. "She's something."

"So's Miss Aventure," Rudy added. "Whoever knew a lady so interested?"

Who indeed? Miss Aventure asked too many questions for his peace of mind. Even Miss Penhale was looking at her askance as the Frenchwoman quizzed Mr Trevithick about a set of gears. Gears! The poor fellow was turning redder than his hair as he rapped out answers.

Emory frowned. Why *did* she ask so many questions? Was there a purpose other than curiosity? They were years ahead of the French in perfecting a high-pressure boiler, were they not? Could their enemy have sent a spy?

She laughed in delight at something the older engineer had said, and Emory's mouth turned up in answer before he thought better of it. No, surely he was worried for no reason. Not even the French would send a woman to spy on an engineering manufactory.

THE AFTERNOON WAS FAR ADVANCED, the sun heading toward the west, when they started for Hale House. Celeste leaned back against the seat and imagined all the wonders that might be accomplished with the application of a high-pressure steam boiler. Marshes pumped for new farmland. Houses warmed and cooled. Steam carriages! Powered flight!

But the farther they traveled from the marvelous steam works, the more Loveday's body tightened. Her fingers must have tightened as well, for the horse fretted in the traces. Celeste had been scolded by her mother often enough for monopolizing the conversation about engineering matters. She knew she could be overly enthusiastic. She hadn't thought Loveday would mind.

"Pardon me if I chatter," she said, attempting greater civility. "It was such a delight to see so much progress."

Loveday raised her chin, as if she'd made a decision, then drew the whiskey to the side of the road and reined in. She turned to Celeste, face set in firm lines.

"And how, exactly, did you know it was progress?" she demanded.

Celeste's mouth went dry. "You told me it was."

"I spoke about our work and what we were trying to achieve," Loveday insisted. "Your questions today displayed an interest and knowledge far beyond that. As did your observations last night. Even Emory Thorndyke noticed. I saw him watching us."

So had she, and something had zinged through her, like gears suddenly meshing with perfection. Had he only been watching because she'd asked too many questions? Why did that disappoint her so?

She dropped her gaze to the lap of her muslin gown. "You must forgive me if I embarrassed you in front of your colleagues."

Loveday blew out a breath. "I wasn't embarrassed. It was rather gratifying to see them realize more than one lady takes an interest in such matters. Sometimes I feel like an anomaly. But you puzzle me, Celeste. How do you know so much about steam boilers and gears and—and Monsieur Robert?"

Celeste dared a glance up. Those blue eyes were so earnest.

Why shouldn't she tell Loveday the truth, at least the part that did not betray her country? She could not bring herself to confide the Emperor's plans to invade. They would likely come to nothing anyway with the loss of her balloon. Her mother was so despondent that she would not believe Marcel, Amélie, and Josie if they asked for more funding to recreate everything.

"I have not told you all," she began. "Please understand that I did nothing to harm you or your family. I did not know you when I woke in your home. You could have been the sort to turn me over to the authorities."

"The authorities," Loveday repeated, the color fading from her face. "Celeste, what have you done?"

"Nothing," Celeste promised. "But I am not a French heiress, though I am running away from an unwanted marriage. I grew up all over Europe, following my parents as they traveled. For the last ten years, I have been living in Paris. For the last four, I have been an instructor at *l'École des Aéronautes*."

Loveday stared at her. Her mouth opened. Closed. Then— "In France they let women our age teach the art of ballooning?"

"The *science* of ballooning," Celeste corrected her. "And yes, they let someone my age teach when that someone is the daughter of Jean-Pierre and Sophie Blanchard."

Loveday's lips formed a perfect circle before she snapped them shut and shook her head. "It won't wash. No one's ever mentioned Madame Blanchard having a daughter."

Celeste's fingers were tangling in the folds of the dress as if they were ropes anchoring her to a balloon. "When my mother performs, all the focus is on her. And she does not approve of my following her in her profession. What I know of ballooning, I learned from my father. He was brilliant, but he found it difficult to concentrate on anyone or anything, especially after his accident. Still, I am their daughter. Ask me anything about balloons—their construction, their capacity for flight, the duration they can sustain themselves—and I will answer."

"What circumference is needed to support two people?" Loveday asked.

"Approximately thirty, figuring thirteen feet per person and factoring in the combined weight of the basket and ropes."

Loveday cocked a brow. Was she impressed or skeptical? "How long to fill that size balloon?"

That was more Marcel's area of expertise than hers. Celeste screwed up her face, thinking. "Nine hours, perhaps a little less on a warm day when the gas expands."

Now Loveday's eyes narrowed. "How do you generate such gas?"

That was a state secret she was not at liberty to share. Her mother claimed the English still relied on hot air or manufactured hydrogen, the latter of which was generated through a messy, dangerous process involving metal filings and acid. Perhaps another half-truth was warranted.

"The gas is provided to the school in metal kegs," she allowed. "We connect them to a low-pressure steam pump and hoses to fill the balloon. A shame we do not have your knowledge. Can you imagine what we could achieve with a high-pressure steam engine?"

A light came to her companion's eyes. "Yes, I think I can. It's not just the filling that would advance." She bit her lip, then blurted, "I will tell you a secret. Our prince has offered a prize for anyone who can produce an air ship."

Celeste stared at her. "*C'est vrai?* Oh, but I would like to see the results."

"So would I. Perhaps we'll have the chance, with you making your home in England now. And speaking of home…" Loveday gathered up the reins and clucked to the horse, which obligingly set out at a trot once more.

Celeste leaned back against the seat and let a sigh escape. That hadn't been so bad. Perhaps she and Loveday could still be friends. She'd always wanted a sister, someone to share ideas with, to encourage, to commiserate with. At times, she envied Amélie and Josie. But, somehow, she didn't think sisters withheld secrets from each other. Then again, with her balloon at the bottom of the Channel, she had no need to explain her original purpose in coming to England.

Even if a part of her warned it would be better to tell Loveday everything.

LOVEDAY HAD BECOME VERY good at escaping the house in favor of her workshop, but now her sanctum was open to Celeste and was no longer quite hers. However, this afternoon Celeste had been drawn into a discussion of a new evening frock and this irresistible subject had freed Loveday to find her own solitude.

The sideboard was still immobile against the wall.

"We are not going to punish you, you know," she said to it when she slipped inside and latched the door. "Or send you away, or take an axe to you. You are quite safe here, should you feel the need to change position occasionally."

It did not move, but Loveday spotted something under it that she was quite certain had not been there when she and Celeste had left at Rosalind's call yesterday.

A piece of wrapping paper. Likely from the bookshop.

"Were you hiding this, or preserving it?" She pulled it out from under the lowest box and spread it on the bench. She found a pencil, but it dangled loosely in her fingers as the astonishment washed over her again, though this time it didn't render her speechless. "I cannot believe we have been harboring none other than the daughter of Jean-Pierre and Sophie Blanchard under our roof."

For of course she knew of Sophie Blanchard, Boney's own Chief Air Minister. The woman who knew more about balloons than anyone on earth. The news that she had a daughter no one had ever heard of was scarcely more believable than their pulling said daughter out of the sea last week. If Portugal was a hum, but the unwelcome marriage was not, then what about the ship and the washing overboard? Would the daughter of two famous balloonists, who taught in a school for aeronauts no less, do anything so prosaic as book passage on an ordinary sailing ship?

She tried to put herself in Celeste's position. Unwelcome marriage... a school possibly full of airworthy balloons... a key to which she had access...

The impossible—a flight from France to England—was just possible.

Could have happened.

She turned to the piece of wrapping paper, her fingers trembling around the pencil. Celeste might be the key to the

Tinkering Prince's prize. For surely someone as knowledge-able about balloons and as passionate about powered flight as Loveday was herself would make the best possible partner in such an endeavor?

She had to put the pencil down to breathe.

They must simply master the physics of weight. None of your heavy steam boilers and wooden gondolas built to mimic sailing ships. Monsieur Robert's mistake was in attempting to make *Minerva* all things to everyone. A floating household, in fact. No, an air ship—even a small, two-person shallop of a ship—ought not to have a basket, like a touring balloon, but a gondola, made of sturdier stuff but built for one purpose. A cane whiskey, as everyone knew, was built for a different purpose than a family carriage, and was therefore smaller and lighter.

She snatched up the pencil and drew the arc of Madame Racine's landau. The pilot and co-pilot would sit here—she sketched in a seat—and the engine, oh yes, the engine, as small and light as the gondola itself, would go back here, where the luggage rack was. Instead of running the steam engine constantly to keep the air hot, could they not somehow lay hands on a barrel of that lifting gas Celeste had spoken of? For if the envelope were permanently inflated, then the power of the steam engine could all be directed to propulsion and steering.

The drawing she produced was nothing short of a flight of fancy. Even she had to smile at it as she laid her pencil down.

They might as well tie a bed sheet to Grandpapa's old carriage back there, and hope the wind would catch it.

Hmm.

"I'll be back in a moment," she told the sideboard. "I want to look at something."

It was midafternoon, but the carriage house tended to be dark, so she lit a lamp and carried it across the yard.

"Miss?" Pascoe said, coming out of the stables. "Would you like to take the whiskey out?"

"No, thank you." She smiled at him. "Is my father still planning to get rid of the old carriage?"

Pascoe huffed air from his nose. "Aye, miss. Poor old thing would never survive a journey. It would let in all the rain if it didn't shake to pieces first."

"I'd like to have a look at it, Pascoe."

"As you like, miss."

He led her into the carriage house, lit his own lantern, and walked over to the far corner where the old coach reposed.

"She were a goer in her day," he said. "Modern lines for the time, and suspension had just been invented."

"It is curved on the bottom," Loveday noted. "Somehow I remember it as square, but it is not, is it?"

"This were considered a fine town coach," he said. "But the leather straps are eaten through, and one shove would take the body right off, I suspect. Missing a wheel, too. I've got her up on a sawhorse on the far side."

"Pascoe, what would it take to remove all the wheels and suspension, leaving only the rack and the sword case?"

He eyed her. "That'd be the work of a morning. What's in that mind of yours, miss?"

"I wonder if the old girl could be put to a different use. How heavy is that body?"

"Not so very heavy. If you take out the upholstery and the squabs, that'd lighten her up considerable."

"Enough so that two people could pick it up and carry it?"

He waggled his head from side to side as though to say maybe.

"Papa has said he wants it gone," she told him, "but I have a project in mind for it. Could you do all that and have two of the grooms carry it into my workshop?"

"Aye, miss, if you don't mind us opening up the old stock door in the back."

"I don't mind. In fact, do that first."

"As you like, miss. Is Mr Penhale going to approve of your helping yourself to his grandfather's carriage?"

She knew perfectly well he would not. "You know my father, Pascoe. He hates to see anything go to waste."

CHAPTER 15

TRURO, CORNWALL

*S*uch a fascinating place. The smell of lubricating oil and hot metal, the sound of pistons pumping. Celeste watched as Loveday took tongs and dipped the sheet of copper for the redesigned boiler into a vat of water to harden it, heedless of the steam that had made her hair crimp around her face. Perhaps when she returned to France, she could interest Marcel in visiting the Emperor's steam works.

She dropped her gaze. Why did she persist in thinking about home? She would not be returning any time soon. She'd found no way to contact the smugglers.

"I'd be happy to explain the process, Miss Aventure," Emory said beside her.

Loveday cast her an arch look. She knew Celeste had no need for tutoring, but Emory didn't. Celeste brightened her smile and put her hand on his arm. "But of course, Monsieur Thorndyke. I am always delighted to learn more."

Red climbed onto those sculpted cheeks, and he stood a little taller. "Steam from the boiler moves into this cylinder and causes the piston there to reciprocate."

"Reciprocate," Celeste said. "As a lady might reciprocate a gentleman's regard?"

Loveday started laughing and turned the sound into a cough as she pulled the metal out of the water and set it dripping on the worktable.

Emory smiled at Celeste. "Not exactly. By reciprocating, I mean it moves up and down in a pumping action."

"Fascinating," Celeste said. "And have you applied this principle to pumping lifting gas, perhaps?"

Loveday eyed her. Emory blinked. "Do you mean hydrogen? Certainly not. Associating a flammable gas with a heat source could be dangerous."

"Non, non," Celeste insisted. "Not if the fire is placed securely inside a firebox and surrounded by an insulator—say, lambswool."

He frowned. "You may have something there."

Celeste laughed. "But of course I do. Did you not just instruct me in the matter?"

Loveday snorted, then smacked her hammer down on the metal as if to hide the noise.

He regarded Celeste. "I begin to believe you have no need of instruction, Miss Aventure. Is your father an engineer?"

"Really, Mr Thorndyke," Loveday said, bringing up her hammer and thrusting it at him. "If you insist on hovering about, make yourself useful."

"Happy to be of service," he said, accepting the tool. Celeste met Loveday's gaze and nodded her thanks.

But Emory remained standing beside them, turning the hammer back and forth in his hand. "You didn't answer my question."

Like a dog with a bone, this one. Still, she couldn't help

admiring his tenacity, or the way the muscles bunched under his sleeve as he brought the hammer down at last with a clang that made Loveday wince.

"My father passed away a few years ago after being paralyzed in a fall," Celeste explained as he paused expectantly. "He taught me a great many things as I nursed him. One was to be thankful for today, as we are not promised tomorrow."

"Very wise." He gave the metal another bang. "And forgive me for bringing up what is obviously a distressing subject."

Celeste had no trouble manufacturing a sniff. "I miss him terribly. But being here, among so many clever gentlemen I know he would admire, helps."

"Doing it too brown," Loveday muttered under cover of reaching past her for a turnscrew.

"You are always welcome here," Mr Trevithick offered with a fatherly smile as he passed on his way to the boiler.

"*Merci beaucoup, monsieur*," Celeste said with a dip of a curtsey. "Alas, I should spend no more time in your delightful company this morning. I promised Miss Penhale's *chère maman* I would deliver a request to Madame Racine. I will hope for a moment with you all when I return."

"We will await you eagerly," Emory assured her.

Loveday rolled her eyes.

Celeste smiled and excused herself.

Mrs Penhale would likely have protested had she known that Celeste intended to walk from the steam works to the émigré's home, but it proved to be but a short distance in the bustling town. She should have known Madame Racine would not live in the grand houses on Lemon Street or near the assembly rooms. The émigré's comfortable little house was situated on a bluff overlooking the harbor. If Celeste craned her neck, she could see the slate roof of the steam works below.

A maid answered her knock and escorted her to a pleasing withdrawing room at the back of the house.

"Mademoiselle Aventure," the older woman greeted her, rising to kiss Celeste on each cheek. "How delightful you would come to call on me."

"I was in Truro, visiting the steam works with Miss Penhale," Celeste explained, reaching into the little bag Rosalind had loaned her—a reticule? silly name—and handing the lady the note. "Mrs Penhale asked me to deliver this."

Madame Racine accepted it eagerly and took it to the window, angling it to the light as she opened it. "She invites me to join them at the next assembly. How kind." She refolded the note and looked up. "It will be probably more than I can manage, but you will be attending, I'm sure."

"Very likely," Celeste said. It wasn't as if she was going anywhere else.

Madame Racine returned to the chintz-covered armchair and spread her skirts to sit. "But the Trevithick Steam Works, how exciting. I have heard it spoken of many times, but I do not understand what they do there."

"All kinds of wonders," Celeste assured her. "They hope to build a high-pressure steam engine that could help our lives in so many ways. Why, you'd never have to build a fire again with warm steam wafting through pipes in the walls."

The old lady clapped her hands, then paused. "Oh, but they must have been teasing you. No one could do such a thing."

"They will," Celeste predicted. "They are determined. And this steam engine will do more too. Pumps to keep the sea from flooding the mines. Steam carriages that can carry us all over the country."

She clasped her hands together. "Amazing! Perhaps I should request a tour."

Celeste smiled at her excitement. "I'm sure they would be happy to oblige."

"And you?" she asked, lowering her hands. "Are you feeling more settled in your new home?"

Celeste shifted on the chair. "In truth, I still think about France. But I know of no way to return."

"Those who flee France seldom go back," Madame Racine acknowledged with a commiserating smile. "And you are making friends here. They are not so different, these English."

"Not so different at all. I find them easier to like than I expected." Why did Emory Thorndyke's face come to mind?

"And your *maman?*" she asked politely. "Have you found a way to tell her you are safe, with friends?"

Celeste shook her head. "No. As tight as the French defenses are now, I don't know if any correspondence can get through."

Madame Racine folded her hands in her lap. "Some of the émigrés have found ways to alert family, friends. If you give me your mother's direction, I might be able to send word to her."

She could not know the gift she offered or the danger it presented to them both. Celeste didn't dare tell her the truth. Only Loveday knew her mother's true name.

Yet Madame Racine was watching, eyes bright with hope.

"I cannot be certain of my mother's location," Celeste told her. "She travels, you see. But her niece, my cousin, works at *l'École des Aéronautes* in Paris. If you address the note to Amélie Aventure, it will reach her."

"I will see to it this very day," the old lady vowed. Then she leaned forward. "Now, tell me more about your trip to the steam works and why it put such a gleam in your eyes."

LOVEDAY SPENT two blessed hours at the steam works, then collected Celeste at Madame Racine's cottage, where she changed out of her old, stained frock and back into the muslin in which she'd left home.

"I feel uncomfortable deceiving Papa," she confessed as they climbed into the whiskey. She took up the reins and flapped them over Rhea's back, and they bowled off down the street. "Even though I may truthfully say we have been visiting Madame Racine, it is only a half truth."

"Perhaps I ought to coach you in French on the way home," Celeste suggested. "Would your parents believe you have been taking French lessons?"

"They are more likely to believe I had taken up fencing," Loveday said. "Oh, dear. Brace yourself. Here is a contingent of the coastal militia."

But their experience this time was very different. Clearly the presence of two young ladies, dressed in summer colors, their bonnet ribbons snapping in the breeze, was enough to produce an abundance of politeness in the men. All six pulled their horses to a halt. Six caps with gold braid and plumes were swept from six heads. And murmurs of "Good afternoon, ladies," followed them as they passed.

Clearly this was not the same company that had nearly run

her off the road two weeks ago. Perhaps those ones had been sent to watch a lighthouse in Wales.

"How charming they were," Celeste said, still smiling. "I wonder if they will attend this Midsummer Ball that Gwen never stops talking of?"

"It is likely. If you listen closely—which I never do—you will hear her likewise lamenting the shortage of gentlemen in the neighborhood. I suspect that Lady Boscawen has been thoroughly briefed on the necessity of inviting them."

The journey home was a pleasure. Celeste was such good company, with a wicked sense of humor that gleamed out at unexpected moments. When they handed the whiskey over to Pascoe, she touched her companion's arm before she crossed the yard into the house.

"Celeste, I must show you something. I was working on it yesterday and I should like your opinion before we go in."

Obligingly, Celeste followed her into the workshop, then stopped short on the threshold. *"Qu'est-ce que c'est?"*

The old carriage had been disassembled and now took up most of the space in the workshop, reposing on the curve of its belly. The doors on both sides were open, stripped of their velvet padding and brocade shades, and all the upholstery had been torn out of the walls and ceiling, leaving only a thin layer of padding on the seats. Ragged bits of blue velvet hung dispiritedly from nails that had been overlooked.

Loveday clapped her hands. "Excellent! How quick they have been."

Her companion turned, disbelief in every line of her face. "You wanted this? It is not a joke?"

"I did, and no, indeed. Come. I will show you."

The sideboard had moved to the wall next to the door, for

all the world like someone backing away from a large and most unwelcome house guest.

"It is all right, sideboard. The carriage is going to be the basis for an experiment. We will take it outside again as soon as may be."

The sideboard did not look convinced.

"Loveday," Celeste said, "it is disturbing that you speak to the furniture in that manner."

"At least it never argues with me." She opened its topmost box. "That's odd. I put it right here." She let down the fronts of the other boxes, and finally located the piece of wrapping paper with her drawing in the second row from the bottom. "Of course," she said. "It moved, so it has reconfigured itself. I shall have to remember that in future."

"Instruct it to keep things where you put them," Celeste said dryly.

"That is a good idea. Sideboard," she said to it, "I shall keep things only in the topmost right box if you endeavor to present them to me the same way." She glanced at Celeste. "If I find a use for all the boxes and fill them, we shall be in complete confusion. But that is a puzzle for another day." She spread the wrapping paper on the bench. "Here is what prompted the disassembly of Grandpapa's carriage."

Celeste bent over the drawing, her intent gaze tracking from one end to the other. Finally she turned to what was left of the carriage. "And this is to be your gondola."

"If somehow we can come by some of that lifting gas you mentioned, we will not have to use the steam engine to heat it. The engine can go where the luggage rack is, and you and I will have the controls at our fingertips."

"You and I?" Celeste echoed. "You wish me to assist you? To make an ascent in this—this—"

"Air coach. Ship. It must be in working order to compete for the prince's prize."

Celeste caught her breath. "You do not do things by halves, do you? But look. Do you mean to operate the steering paddles manually?"

"Not paddles. Vanes, with sails like the windmills in Norfolk. They will extend and retract using a lever."

"We must have additional steering," Celeste said with the authority of someone who had flown and discovered this herself. "Vanes in the stern, like the rudder of a ship."

"Yes, indeed." Loveday sketched them in, along with the ones on the sides.

"I take it there is enough of the carriage remaining to provide the pilots shelter from weather?"

"Yes. We will sit in one half, and the other half will contain the controls for the engine and steering. And there are the windows, particularly in the rear, for easy access to the engine."

"It could almost work," Celeste breathed. "Except for one thing."

"The gas." Loveday's good spirits deflated. "I cannot solve that. I thought you might."

Celeste passed her fingers over her lips, deep in thought. Then she shook her head. "I do not know how one could obtain it in England. And even if one could, I do not think purchasing a barrel would be as simple as your subscription schemes here, for balls and libraries and such."

"Nor do I. But until we do obtain one, this design is useless. We will be forced back to the old way, with the steam engine used to produce hot air. Two engines, plus water and coal for both, will make the air ship too heavy to lift."

"Perhaps Mr Thorndyke might shed some light upon the problem."

"Emory?" Loveday shook her head. "I'm not going to bring him in on this. You know how men are—always so anxious to take the credit for what a woman has done. Here, anyway," she said hastily. "It seems to be different in France."

"Not so different," Celeste admitted. "But some skills are—"

"Miss Penhale," Pascoe called. "You're wanted up at the house."

"Ohhhh, bother," Loveday said to Celeste. "What is it, Pascoe?"

"The mistress and your sisters are out and you have a caller, Mrs Kerrow says."

Loveday groaned. "I suppose I must do the honors. Let us hope it is not Lady Tregothnan."

She put the drawings back in the topmost right box of the sideboard, and Celeste followed her out. A yellow and black curricle she did not recognize stood in the sweep, looking practically new. Mrs Kerrow met them at the door.

"I'm ever so glad you're back, miss," she said. "I've put Captain Trevelyan in the drawing room. I'm so glad he hasn't come all this way for nothing."

Captain Trevelyan? Calling upon them when it was they who ought to have called upon him long before this? She and Celeste exchanged a guilty glance.

"Thank you, Mrs Kerrow. Would you bring some tea, please?"

"Aye, miss, straight away."

They found Captain Trevelyan by the doors to the terrace, looking down the lawns as though remembering the pain they had caused him. He held no cane, only a parcel wrapped in oilcloth in one hand.

"Good afternoon, Captain," Loveday said, curtseying. Celeste did the same, her attention on the parcel.

"Good afternoon, Miss Penhale, Miss Aventure."

"Won't you sit down? Mrs Kerrow will bring some tea, and some cakes, I hope." Loveday was suddenly hungry.

She and Celeste sank on to the sofa, while the captain took Papa's chair, declining to rest his leg on the ottoman in front of it.

"You are making progress, I hope?" Loveday ventured. "It seems you may find walking less uncomfortable?"

"I brought my curricle, as you no doubt saw. I find that driving gives me no discomfort. When I am able to ride, I shall consider myself recovered. But strangely, all my urgent movement across the lawns the day we rescued Miss Aventure seems to have set me ahead instead of back. Doctor Pengarry is quite perplexed."

"This is good news," Loveday said. "I am glad."

"I may not be much good for dancing, but at least I may walk into a house like a gentleman," he said. "Speaking of rescue, I have brought a curiosity that washed up on the beach below Gwynn Place."

"A creature?" Celeste had barely taken her gaze from the parcel enough to exchange pleasantries.

"No. Something much more strange and unusual."

From the oilcloth pouch, he slid a slender, leather-bound book, sea-stained around the edges but otherwise unharmed.

Celeste drew in a breath so quick it was almost a gasp. She

wrapped her arms around herself as if she were cold, though the room was pleasant.

"Our groundskeeper's daughter was down on the beach hunting for mussels and found it cast up by the tide. Heaven knows how long it has lain there. We are only fortunate it was not taken out again. She brought it to her father, who brought it to me. Look."

He opened the book on the low table between them and turned it toward Loveday and Celeste.

Directional headings. Wind speed. Temperature. Landmarks.

Paging farther back, Loveday saw sketches. Drawings of balloons in close-up, technical drawings of engines that showed size and weight of parts to the last detail.

Estimations of silk needed to construct an envelope, with lengths and weights.

Paddles that could be controlled with the feet to adjust course.

Paddles.

Not ten minutes ago, Celeste had mentioned steering paddles.

She sat back. Gazed at Celeste, whose face was as white as her frock, eyes swimming with tears.

"I am no expert, but in my work for the army, I have had some experience in staving off invasions," Captain Trevelyan said into the silence in a conversational tone. "If I were to venture an opinion, I would say that someone has been trying to determine the feasibility of invading England by air." He closed the book and returned it to its oilcloth pouch. "Would you not agree, Miss Aventure?"

CHAPTER 16

HALE HOUSE, CORNWALL

*C*eleste's body felt as if were crumpling like paper stuffed in a shoe. She knew to the moment when Loveday realized the truth. Her friend's shoulders stiffened, her eyes narrowed to slits of ice. And her head turned, slowly —agonizingly slowly—toward where Celeste was shrinking into the fabric of the sofa.

"This is yours," she said, and there was no doubt in the accusation.

There was also nowhere to hide, no way to pretend. Her balloon may have gone down, but she was the one plummeting.

"*C'est vrai*," Celeste said. "It is mine."

Captain Trevelyan placed the journal in his lap. "I believe, Miss Aventure, that you owe us an explanation."

"Mademoiselle Blanchard," Loveday corrected him, body so still she might have been made of stone. "She is Madame Blanchard's daughter."

He too stiffened. Oh, this was worse and worse!

"My mother is Sophie Blanchard," Celeste admitted. "The

Emperor's Chief Air Minister. My father was Jean-Pierre Blanchard."

"The man who first crossed the Channel by balloon," the captain said. "From England to France."

Celeste nodded. "The Emperor has challenged my mother to do the same, but from France to England. She has not been able to achieve it."

He thawed as only a superior-minded Englishman could do. "Small wonder. The prevailing winds blow up the Channel and toward France. The Channel squalls have prevented the French navy from crossing. I can't imagine a balloon would get far."

Now came the hardest part. Celeste moistened her lips. "This is about more than a single balloon. The Emperor has in mind a *Grand Armée*, an invasion of England from the skies."

Captain Trevelyan dropped the journal on the table with a thud, as though he could no longer touch it, and Loveday sucked in a breath.

"Is it possible?" she demanded of Celeste. "These drawings, your presence here—you managed it, didn't you?"

"Not quite, or you would not have discovered me," Celeste reminded her. "I had intended to land in the marshes of Kent, where smugglers would have ferried me and my balloon home in triumph. But one of your squalls blew me off course and downed my balloon. I would have died had you not rescued me."

Loveday's face softened just the slightest. "Be that as it may, you found a way from France to England by balloon. Others could do the same."

"Not without my journals," Celeste told them. *"L'École des Aéronautes* has all except this one, but the students will get nowhere without my mother's support, and she has stopped trying. It was no lie that she plans to marry me to an elderly man. The most despicable Comte d'Angeline. This is how the Emperor wants her to prove her loyalty. He is the only one who believes crossing to England is possible, and I think even he has begun to doubt."

"Then he cannot gain access to this journal," the captain said. He rose, scooped up the journal, and tucked it under his arm, as though it had become a state secret to be held rather than a betrayal to be flung away.

Celeste surged to her feet. "No! Please! That is all I have of my life's work, my father's dream."

He stepped back, as if determined to keep a distance between them. "A dream that could threaten every man, woman, and child in England. I cannot allow that."

Loveday was frowning at him, but Celeste felt as though he was stealing her very breath. To think her work had survived the crash, that it was within reach! Oh, what she and Loveday could do with that information! And he would not give it to her.

With every ounce of will, she put on a contrite smile and resumed her seat, dropping her gaze to her lap. "Oh, but Captain Trevelyan, I will show it to no one. You know I have no way to communicate with France."

"There are ways," he said cryptically.

She looked up, but he had turned to Loveday. "I don't believe Miss Blanchard meant you or your family any harm, Miss Penhale, but if you would prefer to withdraw your hospitality, I will understand."

Withdraw her hospitality? Throw Celeste out of Hale

House? Was she never to share scientific secrets with Loveday again? How could she bear it?

Loveday regarded her a moment, and Celeste held her breath.

"That shouldn't be necessary, Captain," she said at last. "I believe it best if we keep all this quiet. No need to inform my mother or father of Miss Blanchard's true identity."

He frowned. "Surely your father—"

"Needs nothing more to concern him," she snapped. "I must insist on this, sir. You may protect the journal. I must protect my family."

He nodded slowly. "Very well. But if I learn Mademoiselle Blanchard is still lying and more treachery is afoot, I will speak to your father."

"If Mademoiselle Blanchard is lying, you may well have to speak to the War Office," she retorted. "Now, thank you for calling, but you must go. My family will return shortly, and the less said, the better."

He bowed, and it was all Celeste could do not to rush him and snatch back her journal.

"Good day, then, Miss Penhale. Please know that if you need anything, you have only to send word." He regarded Celeste as if she were a burr he'd found under his horse's saddle, an annoyance easily tossed aside. Then he left them.

Mrs Kerrow, coming in with the tea tray, made a sound of distress that their guest was leaving so soon.

"It is all right, Mrs Kerrow. Miss Bl—Aventure and I will have our tea here."

"Tell me now," Loveday commanded the moment the housekeeper was out the door. "Were you lying? Should Papa be escorting our family to London for safety?"

"You are safer here," Celeste murmured. "The soldiers would land near Dover and march to London to capture your prince."

Loveday paled. "How could you turn your science to such an end?"

Celeste threw up her hands. "It was a challenge! A way to see my mother returned to her former glory. He has her perform at events like a trained monkey. The famed aeronaut, Marie Madeleine-Sophie Blanchard, reduced to throwing out explosives to captivate the crowds. The school she and my father started, now holding less than a handful of students with nowhere else to go. What did I care about a nation that has done nothing but trap us, bait us, squeeze us ever tighter? I never knew there were kind, clever English until I met you and your family."

Her chest was rising and falling at an alarming rate. Had she been a steam engine, Celeste would have tripped the relief valve already.

"I have heard little good of your Emperor," Loveday said, "but I have admired his stance on science and his willingness to allow women positions of power. I certainly never thought everyone in France was the same sort of arrogant windbag."

Her mouth twitched, despite herself. "Windbag?"

"Yes, you know—one who speaks far too much and believes every word to be priceless."

The smile won. "I would almost think you know our Emperor."

Loveday's smile broke free as well. "I may not have been properly introduced, but I've met enough fellows like him." As quickly as her amusement had come, it faded. "I will have your word, Celeste. If you are to stay in England, and continue associating with my family, you must disavow support to Napoleon, in all of his causes."

Celeste raised her chin, stood at attention like the aeronauts her mother had trained. "I do. I promise. England must be my home now. I see that. I will protect her with my life."

"Let's hope it doesn't come to that," Loveday said.

WORDS. They could not be trusted. Even good drawings could not be trusted until they were proved by action and turned into reality.

And Celeste had seen Loveday's drawings.

Celeste had gone to her room, her face bearing the tracks of tears, and Loveday had taken refuge in the orchard with the sunshine and the chickens. Mrs Kerrow's hens hunted in the grass beneath the trees, ever hopeful that a windfall might have come down in the night. Somehow their busy industry comforted her. She sat upon the bench under the old Beauty of Bath, and before long one of the hens came to loll in the sun at her feet.

Already, not fifteen minutes after Arthur Trevelyan's abrupt departure, she was having second thoughts about swearing both him and herself to silence.

She had known of Sophie Blanchard in the sense of knowing *about* her, from the broadsheets and even the caricatures in the scandal sheets. But she and Arthur were the only ones in the country who knew about her falling star in the Emperor's sky, the subsequent heartless exchange of a daughter's body for the mother's loyalty.

Loveday shuddered. Had she been in Celeste's position,

with a balloon and all her skills, she would certainly have done the same. But she was not in Celeste's position. Had she not used the very words, "return in triumph"? Had Celeste succeeded—landed unharmed in Kent and been ferried back by the French smugglers—England would now be in the greatest danger it had ever faced. And the Prince Regent, the government—not one of them would have known about it until the blue, white, and red striped balloons of the invading aeronauts appeared in the clouds, innumerable and unstoppable.

Loveday had no doubt at all that the same vision had been in Celeste's mind. A vision of triumph, not terror. She could have done it and seen her beloved mother reinstated to all her former glory as Chief Air Minister, no doubt sailing at the head of the invasion.

Loveday choked and buried her face in her hands. The hen looked up, searching the sky for what had disturbed her, then moved under the bench just to be prudent.

What was she to do now?

Celeste knew all the details of Loveday's plans for the air ship. For the prince's prize. How quickly she had fallen in with them! How delightful it had been to bounce ideas off her keen brain, making the project even more possible. How wonderful it had been to have a friend with the same tastes and even greater knowledge than she had been able to gather in the whole of her life.

And therein lay the rub. She had had a friend half an hour ago, and now she did not.

Celeste had vowed loyalty to England, it was true. But had Loveday been marooned in France, she would have been quick to do the same and not meant a word of it. But the other option did not bear thinking of—the option Papa would surely insist upon if he knew. If Celeste were taken up by the coastal militia as a spy, there would be a businesslike hanging and no more said about it.

Of course Celeste had vowed her loyalty.

But only time would prove whether she meant to keep that vow.

ARTHUR TREVELYAN WALKED SLOWLY down to the flat stone on the cliffs, deep in thought. Or rather, his thoughts had taken wing out over the Channel, as he attempted to apprehend the sheer scope of Bonaparte's plans. The audacity of it! Had Celeste Blanchard succeeded, the Prince Regent and his government might even now be in mortal danger.

He knew, of course, of Sophie Blanchard's reputation and the esteem in which Napoleon had once held her. The fact that the Chief Air Minister had a daughter whose skill and determination were at least her equal was an utter surprise to him—he, who had once been one of the best informed spies in the Walsingham Office. What terrible luck had washed her up at the foot of Hale Head, where a tinkering girl resided! The question was, did the French have an equivalent branch of government named for a famous spymaster? Would Bonaparte have been informed of Celeste's activities? Had it been his plan all along to insert a French aeronaut along their coast? If so, why had she said she didn't know how to communicate with France?

Outside of asking Celeste directly, he supposed, there was no way to know. She must be living in a constant state of fear.

Had he been captured in France and was facing a military tribunal, he would have gone to his death still loyal to his own country and his mouth firmly closed. But then, he had spent some years in His Majesty's service and was not a terrified girl.

A terrified girl. Was he asking the wrong questions in this case? Could Celeste really be just a girl using the skills she possessed—changing the world of technology in the process —in order to escape an arranged marriage?

Sometimes the smallest things—the most intense emotions—provoked the greatest advances in history.

Look at Leonardo da Vinci, the Architect of Venice, and all the inventions with which he was credited. Necessity might be the mother of invention, but intense emotion could certainly be its other parent. It was a historical fact that the Doge of Venice had been so afraid of being found and assassinated by his enemies that he had commissioned da Vinci to put the entire city on a massive gearworks rather than the pilings of logs the city fathers had proposed. Arthur had read many a treatise on the engineering triumph, so far ahead of its time that it seemed miraculous even in this enlightened age. Twice a day, the church bells rang, the bridges rose, and each neighborhood turned into a different position. The terrified Doge had been dead four hundred years, and still his legacy lived on.

Would the contents of that journal do the same, penned by a frightened but determined girl?

Awkwardly, Arthur got to his feet, thankful that for once he had not been too proud to bring along his cane. When he reached the house some minutes later, he labored up the stairs to his room, where the oilcloth pouch containing Celeste's journal lay in his desk drawer. At the very least, withholding these drawings could mean the downfall of Bonaparte's plans for good. They must be preserved somewhere safe. It was fortunate this old farmhouse had a few secrets left to which he and his father were privy. He pressed a rosette on the carved mantel of the fireplace, and a panel snapped outward. He slipped the pouch into the cavity behind it, then pressed it closed.

At least now the upstairs maid would not carry Celeste's journal away thinking it was good only to be thrown out. Or worse, that its pages might be torn out and used to write letters on.

With the journal secure, what ought he to do now?

Arthur needed to talk his thoughts through with someone who was not only dependable, but also sensible and fiercely intelligent. He could not keep this solely to himself, not when he was barely able to walk about the estate. In a pinch, it would be better if someone else knew the facts of the matter. Not the coastal militia, with whom, as an Army man, he was barely on speaking terms. But someone he had trusted since they were boys. Someone who knew engineering better than nearly anyone in Truro.

His friend Emory Thorndyke.

CHAPTER 17

The tavern that Emory had always considered a friendly place for a pint seemed to be collapsing around him, the wood-paneled walls narrowing, the scarred plank floor tilting.

"Celeste *Blanchard?*" He pressed Arthur for confirmation, praying he'd misheard. "Surely you are mistaken."

"I wish I were," Arthur said, hands cradling his tankard. "But I heard it from her own lips. I simply don't know what to do about it."

Neither did he. As it was, his mind moved faster than a well-oiled piston. "You cannot think her a spy."

Arthur regarded him. "You're certain she isn't?"

"Yes," Emory said. "Oh, she's clever enough, and she's quite capable of twisting a fellow around her little finger, and I grant you she has an astonishingly good grasp of engineering principles, but—"

Arthur raised an eloquent brow.

"But I cannot have been so taken in," Emory finished lamely.

Arthur shook his head. "That is the *role* of a spy, Thorndyke—to take us in, to convince us to confide our deepest secrets."

His sisters called him the most pig-headed of men. Perhaps they were right, because Arthur's impeccable logic made no dent in his own certainty.

"No," Emory insisted. "I won't believe it. What's more, I'll prove it to you."

Arthur leaned back in the chair. "How?"

Emory straightened. "I'll speak to her myself."

"No offense, my friend," Arthur said with a chuckle, "but you aren't exactly known for subtlety."

"Which is all to the good in this instance," Emory assured him. "You can be certain of my veracity. I will let you know what I discover."

WHAT A DIFFICULT EVENING! Sitting at the dining room table, listening to the conversation among Loveday and her family, Celeste had been acutely aware that she was the visitor, the stranger, and that her right to remain might be taken away at any moment.

At least Loveday had been willing to give her a second chance. The two had reached a *rapprochement* and spent the latter part of the afternoon discussing plans, but some of the zest was gone. Every once in a while, Loveday would look at her out of the corners of her eyes, and Celeste would know she was wondering.

Had Celeste finally told her everything?

Was an aeronaut force on its way to England?

Were they in danger?

She did her best to pretend all was well. She smiled, conversed, suggested ideas for the air ship Loveday was designing. She even accompanied her friend to the henhouse in the orchard the next morning, even if she could not quite fathom why Loveday found the birds so fascinating.

"They are not noted for their ability to fly, *n'est-ce pas?*" she asked as Loveday bent to pick up one of the hens.

"Not at all," Loveday confirmed, stroking the speckled feathers. More of the hens clustered around her muslin skirts, clucking softly. "But they are excellent listeners."

Celeste studied the hen's reddish head. "I see no ears."

Loveday smiled fondly down at the bird. "Penny keeps her ears concealed, don't you, my sweet? You could tell our friend Celeste many secrets after hearing me expound on my dilemmas over the years."

The hen cocked her head and regarded Celeste with bright brown eyes, as if she knew exactly what was going on in Celeste's mind.

"Pardon me, miss."

Celeste and Loveday looked up to find Morwen, the Penhale maid, standing in the doorway of the garden wall.

"Mr Thorndyke is here again," she said with some asperity.

Loveday set the hen on the ground. "I'll see him."

Morwen's gaze swung to Celeste. "He spoke with your father, miss, then asked to speak to Miss Aventure. Privately."

Privately? Celeste and Loveday exchanged glances.

Loveday clasped her hands behind her back. "Tell Mr Thorndyke that Miss Aventure will meet him on the rear lawns. I'll take a walk along the cliff. I'll be in full view at all times. Celeste can call if she needs me."

The maid hurried off. Celeste sent her friend a grateful smile, and the two headed out onto the lawns. As Emory came around the house along the walk through the shrubbery, Celeste put her hand on Loveday's arm.

"Slowly, now. We must not appear eager."

"I'm not in the least eager," Loveday assured her. "But I admit to some curiosity. It would seem too early for declarations, but I suspect, traditionalist that he is, he'd likely seek permission from my father first."

This was *not* what Celeste had been expecting. The man had come bearing designs the last time. She dropped her hand. "Permission from your father? As in a marriage proposal?" Her feet froze in the grass.

"Yes, just so. I don't know what else he might have to say to Father before seeing you." Loveday took a couple more steps before apparently noticing Celeste had not followed. She glanced back. "Celeste?"

Celeste swallowed. She had not really expected her second worst fear to be realized quite so soon. "Coming."

They met Emory partway across the lawns. With the back of the house framing his dark coat and trousers, he looked tall, formal. He snatched the low-crowned hat off his sandy hair and bowed to them both.

"Miss Penhale, Miss Aventure. Thank you for agreeing to see me."

"I must determine the wind's direction," Loveday announced and promptly marched toward the cliff.

Emory watched her go. "Kind of her."

"How might I be of assistance, Monsieur Thorndyke?" Celeste asked.

He brought his gaze back to her. "Straight to the point. I

admire that. Allow me to do the same. It may have come to your attention that I hold you in the highest regard."

Explosives like the ones her mother tossed out seemed to sparkle around him. She thought she might be going to faint. This could not be. Not now. *She* did not know who she was anymore. How could he know her well enough to admire her?

Deep breaths. When she felt less lightheaded, she spoke. "And I am impressed by the work you do," she countered. "Such clever innovations. Tell me, have you solved the problem with the timing of the piston?"

"I believe I have. It may be a matter of the thrust to weight ratio. If we were to adjust..." He trailed off, and some of the animation leaked from his face like steam through a faulty valve. "That is, we are working on the matter." He glanced to where Loveday had paused beside a fat shrub that bore an uncanny resemblance to the Comte d'Angeline.

Emory offered his arm. "Would you walk with me?"

"Certainly." She put her hand on his arm but made sure to angle them across the lawn on a heading that would keep Loveday in sight.

He was silent a moment, gaze going out over the sea, sparkling blue-green below.

"Is something troubling you, Monsieur Thorndyke?" she felt compelled to ask.

"Yes," he admitted. "I had a conversation with Arthur Trevelyan yesterday."

Her breath caught, but she kept her tone light. "Oh? I did not know the two of you were acquainted."

"Since we were boys," he explained. "I've always considered him a friend."

A friend who shared secrets? Oh, please, *non!* "And did you find him well?" Celeste asked politely.

"Yes, yes, quite well. It was the topic of his conversation that concerned me." He dropped his voice as if he, too, thought the chickens in the orchard might listen. "I understand you are the daughter of France's chief aeronaut."

She could claim surprise or deny it, but she was so tired of pretending. "I am, but I must ask you not to shout that about. Not everyone will be as understanding as Captain Trevelyan and Mademoiselle Penhale."

He glanced to where Loveday was striding back and forth along the cliff, arms swinging as if she were exercising. "She knows, then."

"She does, but her family does not. We thought to spare them… concern."

"Understandable," he said. "I'm struggling to take it in myself. You could likely do old Boney a great service by revealing what you know about our high-pressure steam engine."

The unkind nickname did not bother her as much as it had only a few days ago. "Perhaps. But I no longer have any interest in serving Napoleon, in any capacity. My life is in England now."

She felt the tension leave his arm. "Good. Excellent. I shall take you at your word."

Celeste gazed up at him. His brow had cleared, his smile was satisfied. He would accept what she said—no posturing, no questions. He was either an innocent fool or the most forthright man she'd ever met.

"Thank you," she said.

His smile broadened, and the day felt warmer, brighter. He

stopped in the middle of the lawn. "Will you be attending the Midsummer Ball?"

Celeste blinked at the *non sequitur*. At the abrupt removal of both her fears. "Yes, I believe so."

"Might I request the first two dances?"

Like a hummingbird, joy zinged past her. "I will save them just for you."

"Excellent." He took her hand and bowed over it. "I will anticipate the evening. Until then, Miss… Aventure."

Celeste curtsied, and he released her to stride from the grounds. She couldn't seem to move as Loveday hurried to join her.

"So?" she asked.

"He knows. Your Arthur told him."

She stared after Emory. "And?"

"And he wants the first two dances at the Midsummer Ball."

Loveday reared back. "Well. Not quite a declaration, but a statement nonetheless. A gentleman does not request two dances unless he is smitten."

That hummingbird was looping around her heart now. "Perhaps he is only being kind. He understands I know few people here."

Loveday shook her head. "Dancing the minuet with your great aunt Hornpraddle is kind. Importuning a lady for the first two dances is something else entirely. You have made a conquest, Celeste."

The hummingbird dove for her stomach. "Perhaps, but that only raises a matter of greater concern." She turned to face Loveday. "How do you dance in England?"

THE CLOSER THE Midsummer Ball approached, the more excited and shrill and unbearable Loveday's sisters became. All she heard from dawn until dusk was *debut* and *ballgown* and *lead off the set*. She was of half a mind to tell the whole family about Celeste's mission and the incredible danger the nation had missed because of a squall in the Channel—the verbal equivalent of a good shaking.

But of course she could not. For imagine if there had been no ball to look forward to, only day after day of normal existence, and her knowledge pressing upon her mind like a storm front. She ought to be grateful that such a burden had been taken from her. She had not even the relief of the trip to Exeter, for it had been canceled when no further information about the prince's plans had come.

She would very much like to talk it all over with Captain Trevelyan. She walked on the cliffs at least once a day, but inexplicably she did not see him sitting upon his stone. Did he now believe there to be no danger from the south? Or was his household in as much of an uproar as her own?

When the ball was three days away, her parents invited the Trevelyans to dine. Loveday and Celeste had been in Truro, ostensibly to call upon Madame Racine, but really to see for themselves that young Colin was on the road to recovery, and from him to discover that the new boiler had been ready to test. In the excitement of seeing the pressure gauges swing to the right and the relief valve behave as it should—only to have disaster strike *again*—both she and Celeste had completely forgotten the hour. What had possessed Rudy Clement to bolt tin to the copper? They'd be picking up pieces days from now.

When the bells of the church pealed three times, Loveday and Celeste had gasped and practically winded poor Rhea getting home in time to wash and change for dinner.

Luckily Mama seemed to think that her flushed face was the product of some kind of suppressed emotion at seeing Captain Trevelyan seated at their table. It did feel rather strange to be beside him rather than in her usual place.

Very strange, indeed.

Or perhaps it was simply that her new dinner dress was slightly lower in the neckline than she was used to. It was a soft green silk, embroidered with lilies about the neckline and hem rather than the heavy-looking puffs and vandykes so popular this season. Less decoration was better, in her opinion, and she tried not to wonder if he thought she looked well.

"Have you heard the news, Mr Penhale?" Mr Trevelyan said when the fish was brought in. "His Royal Highness has been spotted incognito in Lyme Regis, visiting an engineer that my son tells me is famous for some invention or other."

Excited babble broke out around the table.

"Can it really be?" Mama said. "He has actually left London and is halfway here?"

"What I would like to know is how it is possible for him to travel incognito," Cecily Trevelyan wondered aloud. "Everyone in the country knows what he looks like if they have ever opened a newspaper."

"But an engraved drawing may not be a good likeness," her mother reminded her. "Besides, sometimes we do not believe the evidence of our own eyes. Why, remember the time I saw Lady Boscawen in Bristol? I nearly walked past her without so much a bow because she was not in her proper place. Thank goodness her husband crossed the street just then and called her by name. So one's surroundings become part of one, do they not?"

"So true," Captain Trevelyan said. "Why, should any of Miss Aventure's acquaintance travel here from France—"

"Or Portugal," Gwen put in.

"Gwen, dear, I hope you do not plan to interrupt the gentlemen in this way at the ball," Mama said severely.

"She might not be recognized at all, simply because she is not in her usual context," the captain concluded. "However, as a former member of the Walsingham Office, I must say we could never depend on something so ephemeral as context. We always assumed we would be recognized at any moment."

"Quite so," his father said.

"Indeed," Celeste murmured and addressed herself to her asparagus.

"Well," Gwen said a little defiantly, "the only context in which I should like to see the Tinkering Prince is our own. Oh, Papa, Lyme Regis is not so far away that he could not journey here in three days, is it? Please say it is not."

But Papa shook his head. "It is well over a hundred miles."

"Probably nearer one hundred fifty," Mr Trevelyan said. "Fifty miles a day is quite impossible unless he takes to the air like a crow."

Gwen's shoulders slumped in disappointment.

Celeste and Loveday slid twinkling glances at one another. If the air ship drawings became a reality, the prince might indeed fly!

"If he is visiting an engineer," Loveday said, "he might not be prepared to attend a ball. Why, he might have only chambray shirts and doeskin breeches in a single valise, and a pair of trunks filled with nothing but engine parts."

Celeste laughed, and even Captain Trevelyan smiled at her whimsy.

Gwen was not smiling. Neither were Rosalind, Cecily, or Jenifer. "I shall never be presented, shall I?" Gwen moaned. "How am I to make my bows if there is no one to bow to?"

"The same way I or Mrs Trevelyan made ours, Gwendolyn. There isn't a girl in Cornwall who has had to be presented to a prince or a queen in order to come out."

Mrs Trevelyan nodded. "One simply takes one's place in company at a ball like this, or one given by your family, and gets on with the business."

"But imagine being noticed by His Royal Highness," Jenifer sighed dreamily. "One could take precedence over every girl in the room then, could not one?"

"That's not likely to happen to you," her sister informed her.

"Girls," Mrs Trevelyan said in a warning tone, and they subsided into discussions of evening frocks and silk and arrangements of the hair.

"It is quite certain, then, that the prince will not be able to attend?" Loveday asked Captain Trevelyan under cover of the chatter.

"At least you need not be concerned about your come-out," he said with a smile, "and may concern yourself with other matters."

"I have been out in company these two years already," she said. She enjoyed balls and assemblies, as long as they did not interfere with her work. "As far as other matters, I do think he ought to be informed that—" She lowered her voice. "— Napoleon is rather more serious about an air invasion than we had thought."

"Our mutual friend said he was not. That he had almost given it up."

"But if not for a squall that would no longer be true. Indeed, one might come this close—" She held her fingers a quarter inch apart. "—to reciting Queen Elizabeth's 'heart and stomach of a king' speech when the wind comes up again."

His shoulders shook with a chuckle before he sobered. "The trouble is, we cannot make him or anyone outside our own circle aware of the circumstances without naming names. And neither of us, I think, is prepared to do so."

"No, indeed. I cannot bear to lose my friend in such a fashion. I would rather be wrong about her than betray her."

"She has not given us reason to do any such thing as yet," he reminded her. "Emory agrees with you. He believes her to be true."

"I should think so. He has asked her for the first two dances at the ball," she blurted, swinging from affairs of state to affairs of the heart like a silly coracle in the waves. He would think her a complete ninny, unable to keep her mind in serious channels.

"Has he, indeed?" Captain Trevelyan asked in surprised tones. "Well, I had best not be a laggard, then. I must follow his excellent example. Miss Penhale, will you honor me with the second country dance? Only the one, I am afraid, and that only if it is a slow one. I do not think my leg will bear quick movements."

Her jaw sagged as she stared at him in astonishment. Here were singular events afoot, with invasions being scotched by fits of bad weather, the Prince Regent paddling about in plain clothes in Lyme, and captains of the army asking for dances when they'd barely been able to walk scant weeks ago.

"Miss Penhale? Have I spoken amiss?"

"No," she managed. "I mean, yes. I mean, yes, I will be honored to accept."

If it were to be announced that the moon was expected to fall out of the sky three nights hence, she might almost believe it.

But she hoped it would not. Every ball must have a moon.

CHAPTER 18

$\mathcal{T}$hank you, Monsieur Thorndyke, for allowing me to sit out the first dance," Celeste said as they perched along the assembly room wall, dowagers eyeing them on either side from their scroll-back chairs. "I merely wished to see how things are done here so I would not disgrace you."

"Perfectly understandable," he assured her. "Though I doubt you could ever disgrace me."

He was certainly no disgrace. The black evening coat, the breeches buckled at his knees, and that perfectly tied cravat would have been applauded even in the Emperor's court. She was very glad for the blue silk gown Gwen had so kindly lent her, for all it reminded her of the last gown she'd had fitted. The dress with its tiny capped sleeves and graceful drape might have been borrowed finery, but it looked well on her.

Sir Anthony and Lady Boscawen had turned the assembly rooms into a fairyland fit for a midsummer's night. And, Celeste thought, just in case the Prince Regent should make an appearance against all odds. There were candles in all the sconces and no fewer than three chandeliers, their mirrored drops throwing light in every direction. Garlands and boughs tied up with silver ribbon suggested an enchanted forest, and she had no doubt that when the supper was laid out, every morsel would be judged delicious by Titania herself.

"Are things so different here than in France?" he asked.

"Perhaps not," she said, watching Loveday skip down the center of the line of couples, her hand in that of a gangly young man with a face red enough at the moment to hide his freckles. The dance, inexplicably, was called "Black Nag." Sometimes she thought she would never understand the English. "The Emperor occasionally allows a minuet or a gavotte, but he favors the waltz. I am told that is not approved of here."

"I haven't even heard of it," he admitted. "Perhaps you could teach it to me."

The thought of being held in his arms, whirling around the floor together, sent a flush of warmth through her. "Perhaps another time." She changed the topic. "I regret I have not had a moment to visit the steam works. How are things progressing?"

"Agonizingly slow. Mr Clement insisted on using tin on certain aspects to save costs. I advised him that might not go well once the boiler was heated. Well, you were there. You saw him ducking as the pieces popped off and shot around the room."

Celeste nodded, listening, but she kept an eye on the dancers. That sideways hop—yes, and that *chassé*. It was not so different from what she'd learned from the court dance master at her mother's insistence. She'd joked with Josie that perhaps she would be able to dance from one side of the basket to the other with grace when the wind shifted.

A wave of homesickness swept over her, made of equal parts longing and loneliness. Would she ever see Amélie, Josie, and Marcel again? At least whatever word Madame Racine had been able to send might ease their minds. Maybe they would write back to let her know they were safe, as well. And *Maman*, and Dupont.

"Miss Aventure—Celeste—are you all right?"

She blinked and felt the moisture on her cheeks. She wiped away the tears with her gloved fingers. "Forgive me, Monsieur Thorndyke. I find myself overcome."

The alarmed look on his face melted into compassion. "It is quite the spectacle, isn't it? Perhaps you miss similar events at home. Well, wait until you see the Twelfth Night Ball. It's a masquerade. Some of the costumes are highly original."

The music ended. Gentlemen bowed, and ladies curtsied. Emory offered her his arm. "Are you ready to enter the lists, Celeste?"

That was twice he'd used her first name. She would not protest. "Delighted, Emory." She set her hand on his. His smile lit the room.

He executed the steps of the country dance with precision, never missing his mark, always ready to catch her, guide her. She was as buoyant as her balloon, riding the breeze. Ah, but she should not have hesitated earlier!

It wasn't until they stood out at the end of the set that she noticed the gazes being directed her way. And not only those of Loveday and Captain Trevelyan, who were leading off the set. Three women, two with sandy hair the color of Emory's and one with darker hair and his chiseled chin, were frowning at her from along the nearest wall as though she were an unusual specimen of mushroom clinging to the assembly room floor.

"Do you know those ladies?" she whispered to Emory with a tip of her head in their direction.

He glanced that way, then stood taller, impressive chin up as if he faced the guillotine. "Yes, to my sorrow at moments like these. They are my older sisters. Henrietta in particular likes to concern herself with my wellbeing. Our mother died when I was a lad, and Henri all but raised me."

Celeste pasted on her best smile and met them look for look. The younger two found other things to fascinate them. The oldest, this Henri, narrowed her eyes further.

"You are fortunate to have sisters," Celeste told him. "My mother never wanted more than one child. I'm not sure she even wanted the one."

His kind eyes searched hers. "I'm very sorry to hear that. She should be proud to have such a clever daughter."

She was glad they had to return to the dance then, so she was spared a response. It would only have turned her into a watering-pot once again.

The younger two sisters descended on them the moment Emory led her from the floor.

"You must make us known to your new friend, brother," one simpered. A shame she had crimped her sandy hair in curls around her face. The arrangement only emphasized the length of her cheeks.

"Emory is forever forgetting the niceties," the other complained, darker haired and heavy chinned, as she fussed with the pink satin ribbons on her puffed sleeve.

"Miss Aventure, allow me to present my sisters, Miss Thomasina Thorndyke and Miss Georgiana Thorndyke."

Celeste curtsied. *"Mesdemoiselles, enchantée."*

Miss Thomasina Thorndyke, the one with the curls, wrinkled her nose. "Is that French?"

"Father doesn't hold with speaking the language of the enemy," Miss Georgiana informed Celeste.

Their father probably wouldn't hold with his son consorting with the enemy either, but she would not allow that thought to linger.

"If you don't speak your enemy's language, understand how she thinks, how can you hope to defeat her?" Celeste asked, widening her eyes innocently.

Thomasina put her nose in the air. "Through good English ingenuity and hard work."

"Indeed," Emory said, taking a step closer to his sisters as if to warn them to behave. "Miss Aventure values such things highly. That's why she has made England her home."

Not exactly, but she would not correct him. "I admire England above all things," she said, fluttering her lashes at him. "Your brother is the perfect example of all that is right and good in your fair land."

He reddened again. "I cannot lay claim to that."

"And why not?" Thomasina demanded, drawing herself up. "I quite agree with Miss Aventure's assessment."

"And may I say how refreshing it is to find a lady with such excellent taste," Georgiana agreed with a smile to Celeste. "You have obviously helped shape her thoughts, Emory, as a gentleman should."

"Oh, is that the next set?" Celeste turned to look at the floor and bit her lip to keep from responding to the ridiculous statement. Emory shaping *her* thoughts? *Non, non,* it was the other way around.

"No," Georgiana answered her. "We have time to chat. The musicians appear to be taking a moment to refresh themselves." Celeste turned back in time to see Emory's sister fanning herself with her hand. "And why not? It's stifling in here."

Thomasina smiled up at Emory. "Be a dear, brother, and bring us some punch."

Emory glanced between his sisters and then at Celeste. She could see the gears meshing in his mind—he wasn't about to leave her to the mercies of these two.

"Perhaps I could prevail upon you to help me carry the glasses, Miss Aventure," he said.

"Don't be silly," Thomasina said, linking arms with Celeste before she could respond. "You can make more than one trip."

"Regardless," Celeste said, removing her arm, "I must leave your company. I believe Miss Penhale is looking for me. I hope to see you later, Mr Thorndyke, for our second dance."

Both his sisters stared at her, but Celeste turned and swept across the room to where Loveday and her family were gathered.

Mrs Penhale was instructing Rosalind and Gwendolyn on the finer points of conversation while her husband surveyed the room as if looking for likely gentlemen.

As Celeste came in next to Loveday, her friend tilted her blonde head closer. "I see you met the Thorndyke ladies."

"Two of them, in any event," she murmured back.

"And that was quite enough, I'm sure."

Celeste couldn't help glancing toward the refreshment table, where Emory was now in conversation with his oldest sister. Henri Thorndyke's face was pinched, as if his behavior had truly worried her. She put a hand on his arm and looked up at him beseechingly.

"I don't know," she admitted to Loveday. "They are narrow-minded, but they clearly adore their brother. They can be excused for wanting the best for him."

"Certainly," Loveday said, "so long as they acknowledge that he could do no better than you."

Emory bowed to his sister, then abandoned the punch bowl and strode their way. Celeste's pulse quickened.

"Pardon me," he said to Loveday's parents before turning to Celeste. "Forgive me, Miss Aventure. I will have to rescind my offer of a dance. It seems I am urgently needed. I expect I will see you and Miss Penhale at the steam works."

As Loveday's father started and scowled at the mention of the manufactory, Emory bowed, then turned and hurried off.

And Celeste could only wonder what his sister had said to him that could have made him run from her side.

LOVEDAY WATCHED Emory walk out of the ballroom and could have felt Celeste's dismay from ten feet away. Strange how the evening had begun with such promise for both of them and practically at the same moment had ended with disappointment.

For Captain Trevelyan seemed to have overestimated the strength of his healing leg. They had barely reached the bottom of the set—a fairly sedate dance without many sudden turns—when his clenched jaw and pale face gave her a few seconds' warning.

"I am very sorry, Miss Penhale. I cannot continue. Pray excuse me."

And he had turned and left the ball.

Sir Anthony's insufferable heir, his nephew Christopher, promptly swept in to take her back up the set, far too pleased with his own gallantry to even notice her distress. Unhappily, she couldn't very well plead a headache in the middle of the set when she had been perfectly well with a different partner.

"I suppose you have heard that the Prince Regent is in Lyme," he said, quite unnecessarily pointing a toe in the *balance*. They pressed hands and separated.

"I had, in fact. We had hoped he might appear this evening."

"Every gentleman here has a wager on whether he comes, but I doubt he will."

"My father does not. We heard three days ago, and even had he left then on a fast horse it would not be possible."

"I should have managed it in my high flyer."

Loveday tried not to roll her eyes.

"We are racing on Friday at Torquay. You must come, Miss Penhale. You would enjoy it above all things."

"I think not." If her tone were a shower of rain, it could not have been colder or more intended as a wet blanket. "I am designing something for the prince's prize, which I believe might contribute to the war effort. I have no time for such entertainments."

He actually laughed. "You are so droll, Miss Penhale. You ought to have said you were entering one of Boney's behemoths in the race. I might have believed you, then."

Did Sir Anthony have another son? Because the temptation to throttle this one was overwhelming. The end of the dance could not come soon enough.

Apparently some mischievous pisky was up to its tricks this evening, for there seemed no interval when she was without a partner. And the wretched part was, she could not refuse any without refusing all and going to sit with the drooping young ladies over there on the wall. At last she asked her partner for a glass of lemonade and wound through the crush toward the long windows to catch a breath of air while he went into the next room to fetch it.

Her father came up beside her. "Here you are, Loveday. Are you enjoying yourself?"

"As much as can be expected."

"I was delighted to see you dancing with young Mr Boscawen. You could do far worse, you know. He is—"

"Yes, Papa, I know. Boscawen's heir and will come into Rosehill Park with three thousand a year."

"I am glad you listen to some of the things I say."

"I listen to everything you say, Papa," she told him, turning to smile and making a tiny adjustment to his snowy cravat. "Some of it does not apply to me, that is all."

"I should like you to apply yourself to charming Christopher Boscawen," he said. "Get ahead of the field."

"I thought you wanted me to apply myself to charming Captain Trevelyan."

"I do. There is no harm in allowing a gentleman to think he has competition. All the better, I say. Shame about Trevelyan."

"Yes," she agreed. "He could not finish the country dance with me."

"Thorndyke has taken him home."

Good heavens. "Surely it is not as bad as that? I thought he went to find a chair in the card room. I had no idea." He must have been in far more pain than he had let on if he had to leave altogether.

"Apparently he has overdone it. Ah, here comes your latest partner. A gentleman, Loveday, but don't encourage him. I hear he is quite the spendthrift. No daughter of mine is going to spend her life wondering where her next meal is coming from." He bowed as briefly as possible to the approaching gentleman and departed.

Loveday wished she could do the same. Instead, she smiled and thanked the young man, and found the first possible excuse to return to Celeste.

Christopher Boscawen had just escorted Celeste from the floor, bowed, and departed.

"Odious French minx," someone said from behind a carefully constructed bower.

Shocked, Loveday looked about her, but could not see the speaker. Celeste's face had gone pale.

"I hope she has not set her cap for Christopher Boscawen," another young woman said. "She may be an elegant dancer, but imagine presenting a baby with those raisin eyes to the heir to Rosehill Park!"

Her companion squealed. "Shocking! You must not say such things."

"She had best return to France and leave our gentlemen alone," the first girl said. "For all we know, she could be a spy. I should like to turn her over to the coastal militia myself. Oh, speaking of, did you see Lieutenant Osgood in his regimentals? Is he not the most handsome man of your acquaintance?"

Loveday took Celeste's elbow. "Let us take the air."

Celeste moved like an automaton, her arm looped in that of Loveday. "She didn't mean it, did she?" She choked. "About turning me over?"

"Certainly not. I am nearly certain that was one of the Tregothnan nieces, and they are a spiteful lot. Always counting to the last farthing what is due them."

"And she believes that gentleman to be her due?"

"If she does, I am sorry for her. She will have Christopher Boscawen's full attention on only two occasions in her life. When he puts the ring on her finger and when she puts his heir into his arms. The rest of the time he will forget she exists."

"His raisin-eyed heir," Celeste said with a sigh.

Loveday pulled her into the entry hall, where people stood visiting and where it was noticeably cooler. "You do not have raisin eyes. Your eyes are lovely and sparkling with wit and intelligence, which I doubt I could say of that young lady. And best of all, Emory Thorndyke enjoys gazing into them."

Celeste squeezed her hand. "You are a good friend. Always building people up, not tearing them down."

"We are builders," Loveday said gaily. "It is what we do, whether people or machines."

"I would rather be with the machines. Even your so odd friend the sideboard would make a better partner than Monsieur Boscawen, despite his elegance of manner."

Loveday had to smile at the vision this presented to her imagination. "How maddening it is that we women, who have so much to offer the world of science and technology, must be reduced to—as Papa says—applying ourselves merely to securing a good marriage. How many mathematical minds have had to make do with multiplying teaspoons of baking ingredients? How many chemists found their only exercise in compounding elderberry syrup for coughs?"

"If you think that way, you will drive yourself mad," Celeste told her. "Have you had your breath of air?"

"Yes." Loveday resigned herself to returning to the ballroom. "They are right to call this the longest night of the year. Come on. Once more into the breach."

CHAPTER 19

*C*eleste followed Loveday and her family into Hale House. Several other gentlemen had requested her hand to dance, but none had been quite so satisfying a partner as Emory. And more than one had had family or friends regard her with suspicion. They might not have known her true origins, or thought she had eyes like raisins, but she was still French and therefore not one of them.

Would she ever be?

She was beginning to think she wanted to be.

"Rosalind, Gwendolyn, help each other out of your gowns and stays," Mrs Penhale instructed her daughters. "Morwen will start with me, and then Loveday. Celeste, I will ask you to wait."

"Of course, Madame," Celeste said.

Loveday walked beside her up the stairs and down the corridor. "What a night."

"Indeed," Celeste said. "I'm sorry your prince did not make an appearance."

Loveday shook her head. "So am I. Am I never to meet him? Think of the opportunities lost."

"We will find a way," Celeste promised. "First, we must finish this marvelous air ship you have devised."

Loveday smiled. "Let's see what progress we can make in the morning."

"Bonne nuit," Celeste said.

"Good night." Loveday entered her room.

Celeste continued toward the guest chamber door, then paused. It could be an hour or more before the maid came to help her out of her evening clothes. Why wait until tomorrow to make progress? She could fetch the plans up to her room and look for opportunities now. She turned and hurried back down the stairs and headed for the rear door out into the yard.

Moonlight brightened the space sufficiently that she could pick her way across to the workshop. A low murmur from the chicken house told her Loveday's hens had heard her and were inquiring as to her intentions. Even the sideboard looked drowsy as she entered the workshop, a sliver of moonlight just brightening the long room and casting impenetrable shadows behind the wheel-less carriage. Celeste went straight to the worktable, which looked unusually empty.

She frowned. Perhaps her eyes deceived her in the dim light. She reached out and met only the rough wood of the table. Where were their drawings, their plans?

It took her a moment to find and light a lamp, holding it up to survey the contents of the shop. There was the sideboard, behaving like a normal piece of furniture. Loveday's implements and tools lay scattered about. Everything was where Celeste remembered it, except their plans.

Loveday must have put them somewhere for safekeeping. That was it. She set the lamp on the achingly bare table and cast about. Behind the stack of metal? *Non.* In the drawer in the worktable, then? A number of turnscrews and some sticking plaster, but no plans.

She eyed the sideboard. Surely not. Maybe? She edged closer, waiting for any rumble, any shift. The thing remained frozen. Passive. She reached for the latch on the top right box.

As if she had affronted it, the sideboard shuddered. She could swear the drop front of the box snapped like a turtle. No, that couldn't be. It must just have been the flickering of the candle.

Celeste controlled her breathing and reached out again to give it a nudge. *"S'il vous plaît, Monsieur le buffet?"*

The monstrous thing stood silent a moment. Then it shimmied and gears hummed as it reconfigured itself.

"Merci beaucoup." Celeste set about searching it, watching for any other sign of trouble.

But every box was empty. Even the topmost right one.

She drew back, mind humming as loudly as the gears. Where could their plans be? The image of Arthur Trevelyan, walking away with her journal under his arm, rose up to taunt her. She could not have lost her work again!

She snatched up the lamp in one hand and her silk skirts in the other and fled back to the house. Morwen unlacing Loveday's corset as Celeste barreled into her friend's room.

"Tell me you have the plans," she begged.

Loveday waved the maid back and turned to face Celeste fully, brow puckered. "No. I left them on the worktable in the workshop."

Celeste's hand was shaking, and she set down the lamp before she set something ablaze. "They're gone."

"Gone?" Loveday took a step forward. "What do you mean? How can they be gone?"

"I don't know. I was too excited after the assembly to sleep, and I knew I would have to wait for Morwen, so I thought I'd fetch them up to my room to review. But when I went to the workshop, the table was empty. The coach was empty. Even your sideboard was empty."

Loveday shook her head as if she must have heard incorrectly. "This cannot be. Only the two of us ever go into the workshop, and the staff knows not to clean without my permission. I don't think anyone else in the neighborhood even realizes I *have* a workshop."

"Begging your pardon, Miss Penhale," Morwen put in. "But that Mr Thorndyke from Truro knows."

Loveday's gaze darted to Celeste, then back to the maid. "How can you be sure?"

"He asked if you and Miss Aventure were in the workshop the last time he called. I thought that odd, for I never knew anyone but you call that space a workshop."

Celeste's legs gave out, and she sank onto the bed. *"He stole our plans."*

Loveday turned to the maid. "We'll help each other change for bed, Morwen. Thank you."

Brow puckered in obvious confusion, Morwen nonetheless bobbed a curtsey and left them.

Loveday regarded Celeste. "It's possible Emory Thorndyke stole our plans," she said, with far more calm than Celeste could muster. "He's never appreciated my presence at the steam works, has tried to beat me to any advance. But I always thought it was a game to him. Perhaps he simply cannot bear to lose."

All the sweets she'd eaten at the ball threatened to march back up and spoil the symmetry of Loveday's Aubusson carpet. "I trusted him. I thought he liked me, that he enjoyed my company. A game, you say? He plays it very well."

Loveday came to take her hand and draw her to her feet.

"I said it was possible. But we must consider all possibilities."

Why did her traitor heart leap at the thought? "What other possibilities?"

Loveday released her to pace the width of the carpet. "Another of the engineers? Mr Clement might not have known I had my own workshop, but he might have reasoned as much. And after this week's disaster, he could use a boost in his standing at the steam works."

Celeste shook her head. "Tin on the boiler design."

Loveday winced.

"But Monsieur Clement adores you, Loveday," Celeste said with a sigh. "I cannot see him sneaking out here to cause you trouble."

"My sisters?" Loveday suggested. "Out of spite for ignoring them?"

"Rosalind and Gwendolyn would never be so horrid!"

Loveday grimaced. "Likely not. And they were at the ball. So was Emory, for that matter."

"*Non*," Celeste reminded her. "He left early. So did your Arthur."

"He is not my Arthur. Papa said Emory left to take him home." Loveday stared at her. "But what if he didn't? What if it was a ruse? I think our first call tomorrow morning should be to see what the good captain knows."

"And the engineer," Celeste said.

AT BREAKFAST, no sooner were the words, "I should like to call upon Captain Trevelyan, Papa, to inquire after his health," out of her mouth than both Gwen and Rosalind demanded to go along.

In the ensuing hubbub, Mama put her fingers to her forehead. "My dear, please do take them. If I hear one more word about Miss So-and-So's gown and how handsome Lieutenant Somebody Else was, I shall go quite mad."

"Loveday," Celeste said, looking woebegone, "surely you have not forgotten my engagement with Madame Racine? I cannot break it now—there is not time to send a message."

Oh, how clever she was. "Of course we must keep it. She so longed to hear how the ball went. Perhaps there will be time to call at Gwynn Place afterward."

In other words, they would mount a two-pronged attack. One would interrogate the captain, the other the engineer.

The day was very warm—at midsummer, Loveday supposed as they bowled up the lane to the Trevelyan home, it was only to be expected. But there was a kind of dampness in the air, and, far out to sea, a line of puffy white clouds was advancing that made her suspect they might see some weather before long.

Celeste left her at the door, where Loveday allowed her to drive out of sight under the trees before she lifted the knocker. She was shown into the sitting room where Mrs

Trevelyan was reading aloud to the captain. She put the book aside immediately and greeted Loveday with the warmth of long-standing friends, almost of family.

"Captain," Loveday said, perching up on the edge of her chair, "I wonder if you might lend me that treatise we spoke of last night?"

He gazed at her. "We spoke of a treatise?"

His leg was up on an ottoman, and while his injuries were concealed by his trousers, his position certainly did look awkward. His face was still pale, and his hair was a little more disarranged than usual, as though he had been running his hands through it in frustration.

"I realize you were in considerable pain, so I do not blame you for not recalling it. But it sounded so very interesting that I thought I might ask. However, I can see that to move would make you uncomfortable."

She should have thought of this. Of course he would be immobilized and quite unable to go hopping about the house to find a quiet spot in which she might speak with him—and not about an imaginary treatise, either.

But to her astonishment, Mrs Trevelyan rose. "May your father and I be deputized to find it for you, dear?" Mrs Trevelyan asked her son.

"No indeed, thank you, Mother." The captain's brows were still knit in confusion. "In fact, I don't—"

"Perhaps you and Miss Penhale might excuse us, then. I should very much like a stroll outside with your papa. It is such a beautiful day."

Mr Trevelyan looked startled, but stood nonetheless. "It is a lovely day. Perhaps Miss Penhale will not mind entertaining you for a very few minutes."

Within moments the captain and Loveday found themselves inexplicably alone, quite with the permission of both his parents. Mrs Trevelyan quietly closed the French window behind her.

Loveday turned to the captain, only to find him staring at her. "What just happened?"

"I cannot tell you," he said, his gaze turning to follow the retreating forms of his parents. "And I, like you, was a witness."

She took a deep breath and seized her opportunity. "I must confess that, in fact, it was my aim to speak with you privately, if not theirs. On a matter of urgency."

"You appear to be quite at liberty to do so," he said mildly and settled back in the chair.

"Captain, when you left the ball last evening, did Emory Thorndyke take you home? My father says he did."

"Mr Penhale is in the right."

Loveday concealed her disappointment at this abrupt end to their speculations of the previous evening. "Did you notice what time you left?"

"Ten o'clock, I believe. I simply could not stay any longer, and Emory, good friend that he is, loaded me into his phaeton like a delivery of lumber and brought me here. Why is this your concern, Miss Penhale?"

Ten o'clock. That would put Emory at Gwynn Place around a half past. He could have been at Hale House by eleven. And they had not returned until after midnight.

"Can anyone corroborate this?" she asked.

He waved to indicate all the inhabitants of the house. "Ask Father's valet—he helped me down. Though it disturbs me that you require corroboration."

With a sigh, she realized she must be honest or he would take offense. "I apologize for causing you concern. But a most disturbing event has occurred. I— We— Celeste and I are attempting to build something to compete for the prince's prize. The designs for our entry are missing."

Again she found him gazing at her, a pleat between his brows as he connected her disjointed inquiry. "And you suspect Emory of removing them?"

"Please do not take this the wrong way. He has always been interested in my work at the steam works and otherwise. My ideas have not only furthered his own inventions, but he often asks me for suggestions as to their improvement. He knew we were planning a project to be presented to the prince—what better time to remove the designs than when everyone was at the ball?"

"Except that he did not. He was removing *me* from the ball."

"Yes." She sighed. "He was."

"Does that solve your mystery?"

"No, indeed. It merely reduces the number of suspects. Sadly, we only had the one." And she wasn't entirely willing to eliminate that one.

"I am happy to have been able to clear my friend's name and trust that we will not need to return to such a painful conversation again." He gazed at her until she lowered her lashes and nodded. "Now, the only mystery left to solve is why my parents, dear sticklers that they are, have taken it into their heads to leave us alone."

〜

CELESTE SAILED into the Trevithick Steam Works, her anger fueling each step. Mr Trevithick raised his head, but his smile of welcome popped like a second-year student's trial balloon when he met her gaze, and he quickly found something he must do on the other side of the manufactory.

Emory was crouched beside the boiler, turnscrew in hand. Celeste came to a stop a few feet away.

"What have you done with our plans?" she demanded.

He frowned as he stood. "Plans?"

"Stop pretending. I know now why you befriended me, and I find it utterly repugnant."

He paled, but he set the turnscrew down carefully on a nearby workbench. "I'm afraid you have me at a loss, Miss Aventure."

Her stomach knotted. "How can you act so indifferent? I trusted you."

She hadn't realized all work had ceased around them until the silence pressed in on her. He glanced around as if noticing it as well, then took a step toward her.

Oh, no. If he touched her, she would crumble. Celeste moved back, out of reach.

He stiffened. "Perhaps we could discuss this outside."

And spare him the embarrassment? As if he felt any! Celeste held out her palm. "Give me the plans, and you will see no more of me."

"I don't know what you're talking about," he insisted. "Plans? For what? Everyone associated with the steam works has the current plans for building the steam engine."

So, he would play the game until the end. She wasn't sure why that disappointed her. She already knew him for a liar and a thief.

"Very well," she said, dropping her hand. "We will go outside, as you requested. But I am on to your ploys." She spun on her heel and stalked from the shop. If one of the other engineers glanced her way, she did not notice.

Emory joined her outside. A smudge of grease marred his cheek. Another time she would have been tempted to wipe it away. Now she straightened her spine and met his gaze straight on.

"Please, Celeste," he said. "Tell me what happened to upset you so."

That face was so earnest, those sea-green eyes so concerned. Did he practice in front of a mirror? At least she should feel no remorse that she had been taken in so easily. He was clearly a master.

"Loveday and I have been working on plans for an air ship," she told him. "Last night, while we were at the ball, they were stolen."

"That's terrible," he said. "I can see why that would worry you. What I don't see is why you think I might have them."

"You want me to prove I know the truth?" Celeste held up one gloved hand and ticked off the reasons on her fingers. "You resent Loveday's place here at the steam works. You were cool to me until you discovered I was the daughter of Madame Blanchard and might be of use to you. You discovered the location of Loveday's workshop, and you left the ball early, giving you adequate time to secure the plans before we returned to Hale House."

"You take remarkably large leaps of logic for someone with an engineering bent," he said, his voice returning to that terse tone he'd first used in her presence. "First, I do not resent Miss Penhale's place here. I question why the daughter of so ancient a landed family would want to dirty her hands, but at the same time, we have important work to do. Every pair of hands is valuable, and everyone must commit to the effort."

"So much commitment that you take every opportunity to advance," Celeste accused.

"Second," he continued as if she hadn't spoken, "I was cool to you because you showed every indication of being nothing but a disruption. When you proved you had a mind behind that dainty façade, I was willing to welcome you."

"You honor me," Celeste clipped out, dripping sarcasm.

"I did," he said solemnly. "As for the location of Miss Penhale's workshop, I took no pains to discover something I didn't know existed. Mr Penhale mentioned it when I requested the opportunity to pay my respects. And I left the ball early to escort a friend home."

"Arthur Trevelyan," she said. "Monsieur Penhale told us. But it would have taken little time for you to reach Hale House from Gwynn Place."

He shook his head. "Allow me to present additional facts. You claim to be the daughter of the commander of Napoleon's aeronauts. You reach our shores by mysterious means. You show an inordinate interest in our scientific advances. You speak French when it suits you to hide your words from others. And your plans to use balloons to invade England were discovered washed up on the beach."

"I explained about that," Celeste reminded him.

"You did," he acknowledged, eyes darkening. "And I accepted your word on the matter. It seems you cannot allow me the same courtesy."

Oh, but he was clever. How he twisted the situation to

meet his aims. She would not let him win. She raised her chin, and he stepped back once more.

"I don't have your plans, Miss Aventure. I like to think I have a sufficient number of ideas of my own that I don't need to steal them from others. Arrogant of me, I'm sure. And since you find my presence so offensive, I will endeavor not to single you out again. Good day."

With a curt nod, he turned and strode for the workshop.

Celeste stared after him. For a moment, watching him go, she almost called him back. But he had to be the culprit. A shame she had no proof. If he had stolen their plans, she had no way to discover where he'd hidden them—and she was hardly about to demand a search of his home.

Fists tightening at her sides, she walked back to the stables, where a young man held the whiskey ready. And then she had six lonely, despondent miles to consider how she might have spoken differently before the sight of Loveday standing at the crossroads cheered her just a trifle.

"No plans in your hands, I see," Loveday ventured as Celeste moved over to the passenger side and she climbed aboard.

"He denied all responsibility," Celeste said, tucking her skirts around her.

"Captain Trevelyan says it is impossible," Loveday said, "though I can't help thinking there was still time between when Emory dropped Captain Trevelyan off and when we arrived home from the ball."

Celeste turned her gaze forward over the horse's head. "Then we must accept that while his friends believe him innocent, we must still be on our guard against them all."

Loveday clucked to the horse, who obligingly set out at a trot. "All?"

Celeste nodded. "We can expect no help from the Trevithick Steam Works, Loveday. I have burned that bridge to its very foundations."

But to her surprise, her friend did not immediately agree. "We shall see."

CHAPTER 20

There was nothing for it—they must simply re-create the drawings from memory. Loveday spent the next day scouring the house for more paper and earned Rosalind's outrage by removing a length she had been going to use to make a pattern for a frock. To add insult to injury, she cut it into pieces easier to manage, and two days later, Rosalind still had not spoken to her.

The single advantage to having to do the drawings over was that her ideas had time to solidify. She and Celeste bent over the paper, pencils in hand.

"With the steam engine in the rear, we may dispense with manual levers. What if we installed narrow-gauge piping and used the steam pressure to perform those operations?" Swiftly, she sketched in what she had in mind. "If we run them along the sides, they give the advantage both of conveying steam pressure and of strengthening the gondola."

"You mean carriage," Celeste said with a smile, glancing over her shoulder.

"We ought to call it a gondola," Loveday said. "A gondola is a form of ship in the Duchy of Venice, is it not? When this is built, it will be closer to a ship than a carriage."

"Quite right." Celeste applauded.

"Piping will not present a difficulty," Loveday went on. "I shall simply pick through the rejection pile behind the steam works."

"The what?"

"That is what Emory calls it. The pile of failed experiments and discarded materials. I will lay odds that all those bent pieces of tin were tossed out there. Those, however, will have been picked over already. I hear that there are craftsmen who can pierce patterns in it to make spinning lanterns. A ship, for instance, can be created on the walls of a room and made to sail around and around."

"Never mind pictures of ships," Celeste said. "Can tin be used in our project? To strengthen the hull, perhaps?" Then she corrected herself. "Ah, *non*. The weight, of course. It is far less than iron or copper, but still."

Loveday nodded in agreement. "This carriage—gondola— has stood up to any amount of bad roads and bad weather. I think we may trust it."

She stood back to allow Celeste to examine the sketch. Then the latter took up her own pencil and began to draw call-outs to show greater detail. "The steam engine in the luggage rack, with a division to either side here and here," she murmured. "*Alors*, we must have a lever still, to control the pressure to the vanes." The pencil moved swiftly. "And the firebox, she must use a gravity feed, here, from the sword case."

"Oh, good idea. And a corresponding lever, then, here." She tapped the opposite seat. "Do you know, we might convert that seat into a control box. All within easy reach, yet contained."

"Agreed." Celeste sketched one in a call-out, then drew a circle around it as though it were being viewed through a spyglass. "We will be sitting forward, not looking back, in any case."

"And with what I learned from the construction of the articulated sideboard, I think we might use a system of pulleys and gears for the steering, too, all controlled from the box within the gondola."

Soon the plans would be completed, and carefully re-drawn in ink so that they might—if all went well and the prince were ever to request it—be shown in public.

But when would that glad day ever come?

CELESTE PACED about Loveday's workshop, the snap of her skirts in harmony with the *scritch* of her friend's pencil. The articulated sideboard stacked itself against the wall in a single layer as if concerned she might overrun it.

"We still have some important decisions to make," Loveday said, pausing to write calculations on another sheet of parch-ment. "We must find a source of lifting gas. I've never been keen on hydrogen, and I doubt hot air will be sufficient for the weight."

"It won't," Celeste confirmed. "We already confirmed that at *l'École*."

Loveday frowned at her. "So, what did you use?"

Celeste drew in a deep breath. She could almost hear the Emperor howling, *Traitor! To the guillotine with you!* How could she even consider revealing the secret to France's airpower?

Because this was her home, and Loveday was her family.

"In France," she said, stopping beside the worktable, "we bottle our lifting gas at the source—the mineral water spas."

Loveday stared at her. "A spa? Like Bath or—" She drew in a breath. "Could *that* be why the prince was visiting Lyme Regis?"

Celeste held her gaze and nodded slowly. "Anywhere the water bubbles hot from the earth. Do you have such places in Cornwall?"

"Not spas," Loveday said. "Mines. Why do you think Emory Thorndyke wants the boiler so badly? The copper and tin mines here flood too often, and often with hot water from deep in the earth. Then there's that terrible gas. Its invasion claimed fifty lives at his father's mine a few years ago."

So that was what drove him. He, too, wanted to see his father's work improved. She could admire him for that. But she would not allow this news to soften her heart. He could not be forgiven for what he'd done, no matter what his friends believed to the contrary.

"Perhaps if your father explained to the mine owners what we need, we will have our lifting gas," Celeste said. "I can explain the harvesting process."

Loveday nodded. "It will take some convincing for Father to agree, but it might work. That's one problem solved."

Celeste smiled at her. "Why do I sense there are more?"

Loveday tapped her pencil on their plans. "Even with the carriage for our gondola, and adding the lighter engine, we're more likely to be towing the balloon than the other way around unless we can better secure it to the craft."

Celeste resumed her pacing. "Agreed. The construction of the envelope is key. What we created at *l'École* was of silk, but it was too easily battered by the weather. Changes in temperature could cause it to shrivel prematurely."

Loveday made a face as she looked at her sums. "Perhaps some sort of covering, then? You protect a silk dress with a cloak or pelisse when it rains." She glanced up and grinned at Celeste. "Of course, how could we possibly coordinate our outfit?"

Celeste laughed. "You should have seen our balloon! I did my best to try to convince *Maman* I would wear nothing except blue, because the silk she bought for my gowns I gave to my friend Josie to sew into the envelope. But I don't think my mother believed me. We had every shade of color by the time we were done."

"Well, we'd have to convince my father we both need new gowns—"

"Many new gowns," Celeste corrected her.

"—many new gowns if we're to amass enough silk this time."

Celeste came back and eyed the recreated drawings. Loveday had placed the smaller high-pressure boiler on the shelf at the back of the carriage, which had originally been used to hold luggage. Ropes from the frame lashed the gondola to the balloon above.

The very large balloon.

"Your father would buy new gowns for you?" she asked, calculating square footage in her mind's eye.

Loveday sighed. "If he thought a new wardrobe would catch Arthur Trevelyan's eye, my father would likely buy out the local linen draper."

It hurt to see her friend so despondent. "He seems a fine man, Captain Trevelyan," Celeste ventured. "Handsome. Thoughtful. A shame he is so dictatorial, taking my journal as if we could not be trusted."

"A very great shame," Loveday said. "But enough of him. We must solve this issue with the envelope. We might not be able to cover it with an overcoat, but what about some sort of parasol? Didn't your father use one on his trip across the Channel?"

"He did," Celeste told her. "But it was intended to protect the passengers, not the balloon, and I think he positioned it too high to be of much use even for that."

"Like some ladies who misposition their corsets," Loveday said dryly. "Not the effect they were hoping for."

Celeste stared at her. *"Magnifique!* That is what we need. A corset for the envelope."

When Loveday frowned, Celeste took up one of the pencils and edged in beside her to begin a sketch on the back of their first draft. "An internal structure—a barrel-shaped frame over which to stretch the envelope. It would stabilize the silk, keep it from shriveling in poor weather. It would provide something stronger than rope on which to attach the gondola. It might even speed filling time."

"No friction from the material as it stretches because it will already be stretched," Loveday realized, eyes shining. "This could be just the thing, Celeste!"

Celeste beamed at her. "Who knew all that fashion nonsense would turn out to be so useful?"

They spent the rest of the afternoon hypothesizing material, size, and weight of the corset as well as the size of the envelope needed to lift it all. That final number made Loveday drop her pencil.

"I can't imagine Father ever buying so much silk, not even if Gwendolyn and Rosalind were set to marry dukes. We have to find an alternative."

"There is none," Celeste told her. "The early aeronauts tried canvas, but found silk to be the lightest and strongest."

Loveday frowned down at her work. "Perhaps I miscalculated."

"*Non,*" Celeste argued. "Your calculations are correct. They are very close to what Marcel devised when we looked into building a balloon to carry a similar weight. We did not have a structure such as this, but we had hoped to carry many more than two."

"For the invasion," Loveday surmised.

Celeste nodded. "Yes, to my sorrow. So, you see, the silk must be found."

Loveday pushed back from the worktable. "Let's think on it tonight. Something may come to us."

It did, just not in the way Celeste had expected.

They had been out in the workshop only a short time the next day before they received news of a caller.

"One of those engineering fellows," Morwen declared when she came to tell them they were wanted in the house.

Celeste's pulse gave a leap, as if ready to run. Silly thing. The visitor would not be Emory. The cinders of the bridge she had burned with him were still smoking.

As if she understood how Celeste felt, Loveday gave her arm a squeeze. "We'll be right there, Morwen."

They found Mr Clement waiting in the entry hall. He held out a rolled sheaf of paper. "Miss Penhale, Miss Aventure.

Thank you for seeing me. Mr Trevithick wondered if you would have a moment to look at these. Just to see if we missed anything," he hurried to add.

Loveday accepted the plans. "You may tell Mr Trevithick we will examine them at our earliest convenience."

"Oh, good." His smile faltered. "That is, I'd be delighted to relay that to him. I was afraid you'd ask me to wait, and I'd prefer to head straight out."

Celeste and Loveday exchanged glances, and Celeste knew her friend was thinking along the same lines. What had their rivals discovered in their absence?

"Oh, what a shame, Monsieur Clement," Celeste lamented with a moue of her lips. "I was hoping you could stay to converse. I so enjoy our discussions."

He stared at her. "You do?"

"But of course! Such a clever fellow. Have I not said so, Loveday?"

"Repeatedly," Loveday assured him.

He colored. "You are too kind, miss."

Celeste sidled closer. "But if you cannot stay, can you at least tell me how our *cher amis* at the steam works fare? Have you nothing new to report?"

"Not at the steam works," he said with such regret she could not doubt him. "I'm off to St Mawes at the moment, where my parents live. Some sort of skin washed ashore, they tell me, like a rainbow collapsed in the sea. I was asked to come help determine what it is, where it came from, and what to do with it."

Celeste did her best to keep smiling at him, though her pulse had begun to gallop. Could the balloon have washed ashore? Emory or Captain Trevelyan would know its source with one glance. Would others begin wondering whether an aeronaut had come to Cornwall with it? A *French* aeronaut?

"Mademoiselle Aventure and I will come with you," Loveday announced. "We have a particular interest in such skins."

He blinked. "Well, I—"

Of course! Celeste leaned closer to him. "*Oui*, Monsieur Clement. You must allow us to accompany you. I would very much like to see this marvelous skin. Loveday and I may know just the way to dispose of it."

Loveday and Celeste drove themselves in the whiskey behind Rudolph Clement's horse, since Loveday would in no way encourage him by allowing him to drive her anywhere. The short journey had never seemed so long. She and Celeste were positive that the "rainbow collapsed in the sea" was the latter's balloon, and by taking a little trouble, it could be theirs for the asking.

They tied up the horse outside the milliner's shop, which for a wonder was deserted. They soon found out why—half the town was standing along the stone breakwater, gaping down into the sea, quietly heaving with the high tide that had brought in the skin.

Mr Clement located his parents without difficulty. "Dad's a rope maker, you see, with my oldest brother. They outfit the vessels that sail from St Mawes harbor," he said proudly, "and my brother found it. Would you—" He hesitated. "May I introduce you to my family?"

"I should be very happy to make their acquaintance," Loveday said.

"As would I," Celeste agreed.

Introductions were swiftly carried out, Mrs Clement all of a dither at being introduced to Miss Penhale of Hale House. "Indeed, miss," she said, "I'm not sure I know what possessed our Rudolph to inform you of this strange event. It is so singular."

"Ma'am," Loveday confided, "I am of the opinion that it is a miracle. For you see, a skin like this is exactly what is required for a project we are working on for the prince's prize."

"The prince, miss?" Mrs Clement's cornflower blue eyes widened. "This mess in the water is to be shown to our prince?"

"Indeed it is, and believe me, your son will get the full credit of it."

Trembling fingers were pressed to her lips. "Oh, miss! To think of our Rudolph being recognized by royalty!"

At which point no one but Loveday Penhale and her foreign friend were to touch the skin, and certainly not carry off so much as a single inch of it as a souvenir. Mr Clement and both his sons waded into the harbor to pull the enormous thing in to shore.

"It's like a ruddy great sail," Mr Clement shouted. "We're going to need help reefing her in."

"This must be properly managed," Celeste said, hurrying along the breakwater to the harbor shore, where the small boats on their long mooring ropes now floated on the waves. "It is far too heavy to pull out. They must squeeze the water from it while you and I, Loveday, organize the women to drape it somewhere to dry."

"I can help with that, miss," Mrs Clement puffed along behind them. "We must arrange it on the roof of the sail loft, where they stretch the canvas."

"Excellent," Loveday said. "Mrs Clement, you are a treasure, just like your son."

And so it was that once they located the grommets where ropes had once been tied to connect basket to balloon, they fit well enough over the stretching hooks to draw the entire skin up the front of the loft to the roof. On the catwalks, the sail maker's apprentices shook it out as well as they could, rather like a woman would shake out a sheet upon a bed.

Celeste's hand fell away as the last bedraggled blue length slid through her fingers and was cranked up into place, water cascading from it to splash on the flagstones below, worn nearly smooth from generations of the same operation.

"My silk," she mourned in a whisper for Loveday's ears only. "What damage do you suppose it has sustained?"

"I expect we will find out once it dries," Loveday replied. "We will examine it closely, for who knows how many rocks and barnacles it has encountered."

"How are we to get it home? A wagon?"

"I will have Pascoe find us a hay wain," Loveday decided. "And a pair of horses to draw it. Not because of its weight, mind, but because there is simply so *much* of it."

Accordingly, the next day Rudolph Clement supervised the loading of the dried silk on a hay wain borrowed from the Trevelyan home farm. When it trundled down the lane and the horses came to a halt in the stable yard, Loveday and Celeste were there to meet it. As was Mr Penhale, standing with his arms akimbo as Cowan, the Trevelyan farm manager, lowered the rear gate.

"I heard you tell me of this at dinner, maidey, but I must say you left out a detail or two."

"It is a marvelous find, Papa," Loveday said, doing her best not to reach out and gather the fabric to herself in glee. "How clever Mr Rudolph Clement was to tell us immediately. It is the very thing for the vessel we are making for the prince's prize."

"Does it have something to do with my grandfather's sad excuse for a carriage?" he asked, watching the stable boys form a kind of snake under Celeste's instruction, to carry the silk out to the lawns where it could be laid flat and examined.

Loveday stared at him. "You know about that?"

Her father shook his head at her. "Pascoe would no more dream of taking apart a carriage without my permission than fly to the moon, my dear."

"Of course not." He had known from the beginning, then, what she harbored in her workshop. "You have shown great forbearance with us, Papa."

"I resigned myself long ago to having two ladies and a hobbledehoy for daughters," he said with a sigh. "Forbearance was part of the bargain."

"I am not a hobledehoy! And I am far more of a lady than Gwen, if one counts the fine inner qualities that distinguish such a person."

"I look forward to seeing them one day," her father said pleasantly.

"You may ask Captain Trevelyan, then, for his observations," she retorted with rather more spirit than wisdom.

Her heart sank as Papa turned, hope in his eyes. Oh, why had she said that? What a fool!

"What is this?" he asked. "Have you furthered a closer acquaintance with the captain after your dance together?"

"I— We—" Oh, dear. "We have spoken. Once."

"I am glad to hear it." He stepped forward. "That is the last of it. You'd best go with Miss Aventure to supervise laying it out. And then perhaps over dinner you can tell me what you plan to do with it all."

"You do not need to wait that long," Loveday said. She must tell her parents sometime. "You know the half of it. Let me show you the whole, Papa."

In her workshop, she removed the drawings from the top right box of the sideboard. Her father frowned at it.

"I thought your mother told you to have that thing removed."

"I did remove it. Out here. It is useful, Papa, and I know how you dislike throwing things out when they are still useful."

He turned away, the sideboard immobile behind him. "Like Grandfather's carriage?"

"Yes. Here is what it will become."

Her father was no engineer, but he had been to the boys' college in Truro and knew rather more than the average Cornish squire; for instance, about things like mechanics and weather and how to put drains in cottages. His gaze roamed over the drawings from left to right, taking in the call-outs while he rubbed his chin thoughtfully with one hand.

"I see," he said at last. "This is what you plan to build and demonstrate for the prince?"

"It is. With the skin, we have two of the three main difficulties surmounted."

"Where do you suppose that skin came from?"

Casually, she lifted a shoulder the way she had seen Celeste do. "It could have come from anywhere. The tides being what they are, it could have been aboard a ship bound for London that capsized or a cargo captured by a smuggler. It is impossible to know."

"Perhaps it was on that ship our young friend was on, from Portugal. The vessel could easily have come to grief after she was swept overboard."

"Possibly." Loveday needed to change the subject.

"What is the third difficulty you must surmount?" her father asked, turning from the drawings to gaze at the motionless sideboard.

"Lifting gas," she said. "Celeste says that it is found where there are hot water springs in the ground. She knows how to process it."

Papa turned, his gaze focused on Loveday with an intensity she rarely saw. "Does she indeed? How could that be, and she a gently reared young lady?"

She must tread very carefully now. "Who knows what gently reared young ladies learn in France, Papa? For all we know, such things are as common as our learning to drive a pony cart."

"I doubt that." He considered her, and she began to wonder if Papa knew more about Celeste than he was letting on. Had they been so indiscreet?

"This lifting gas," he said. "You may think me just a farmer who does not bother his head with your educated treatises—"

"I do not think that, Papa," she said with such conviction he nodded.

"But Trevelyan and I talk together of new developments,

especially the ones that aid the French army. I have heard of this lifting gas."

"And?" she ventured.

"If air vessels such as this project of yours turn into something the army needs rather than silly entertainments for people with nothing better to do…"

"I believe the possibility exists." If the Emperor believed an invasion could come by air, it was more than a possibility. It was a race between him and the Prince Regent to see who would get there first.

"Wheal Thorne," he said, his gaze steady. "Wheal Morvoren. Both struggling and all but unworkable because of the hot springs and the poison gas in the tunnels."

A bigger canvas than she had previously known existed opened to Loveday's mind's eye. "But eminently usable if the world changes, and lifting gas becomes necessary for flight."

Papa's face mirrored her own—a combination of awe and excitement.

"I must speak with Trevelyan," her father said, clearly controlling himself the way he controlled a spirited horse, "and see if we might go in together to buy Wheal Morvoren. Just in case you two girls prove to be right, and the world does change."

He hurried out. The sideboard seemed, somehow, to relax.

Loveday stood in the middle of her workshop, visions filling the skies of her imagination. It was not until Celeste called her some minutes later that she came to herself and left the workshop to walk at a fast clip down to the lawns.

Any great change must begin with a hundred small ones. The state of the silk skin was first on the list. And a barrel of lifting gas was the second.

CHAPTER 21

*T*he feast day of St James in July was still a week off
when Pascoe and all the stable boys carried the
gondola out through the stock doors. They staggered around
the walls of the kitchen garden to where Loveday and Celeste
stood on the most level section of the lawns that stretched
down to the cliffs. By some magic Loveday could not put her
finger on, since the Midsummer Ball, her father had begun to
take her rather more seriously and had given his permission
for the air ship to be assembled out here. It was all very
strange, but Loveday was not about to disregard his
generosity.

And that was not all. She and Celeste were no longer
forbidden to visit the steam works. Which was a good thing,
because where else could a person build a steam engine small
enough to fit on the luggage rack of a carriage? To say nothing
of fabricating lengths of piping strong enough to withstand
steam pressure yet light enough to allow the prototype air
ship to lift.

Papa and Mr Trevelyan had, to the amazement of their

neighbors, become the joint owners of Wheal Morvoren, changing its name from that of the legendary mermaid to that of a seagull—Wheal Golan. The mine had come at such a bargain price that Papa rather lost his head and bought another derelict mine a little distance down the coast with the same troubles with poison gas. He called it Wheal Garan, after the cranes that flew long distances and brought good luck when they built their nests. And he had met with old Mr Thorndyke and practically forbidden him to sell or even improve Wheal Thorne.

Mama had taken to her bed with a fit of the vapors, convinced he had gone mad and the girls' dowries had been thrown into the pit.

And now they were so close to the completion of the vessel that Loveday could practically taste it. She and Celeste had spent a week going over the silk skin and making meticulous repairs to each tiny tear or puncture it had suffered. Gwen had screeched and not allowed Loveday to have a single one of her castoff silk gowns for patches, even though many were too small for her. Loveday had simply turned away and used two of her own.

Not the new ones, though. She wasn't completely obsessed.

From the terrace, Gwen and Cecily Trevelyan watched the stable boys inflate the envelope with a hand pump, taking turns as their strength gave out. Loveday speculated the girls were less interested in the envelope than in mourning such a colossal waste of expensive fabric. The fact that it had spent two weeks in salt water and was no longer fit for wear did not assuage their feelings in the least.

Loveday and Celeste, meanwhile, had made so many

calculations that Mama had refused point blank to buy any more paper. Not after the mine debacle. Not after they could be thrust into the poorhouse at any moment, now that half the family had been touched by the piskies.

But it was a complex problem, rebuilding an envelope and stretching it over an internal corset made of wicker.

"It's working." Loveday clutched Celeste's wrist. "It's really working."

Celeste had shown Papa how to extract lifting gas from the underground springs, a process as simple as making whiskey, only instead of putting liquid into barrels, one put gas.

"The gas will expand," Celeste said. "We must tie down the gondola, quickly, before it floats away without us."

Loveday was ashamed to admit to herself that she had doubted the gas distillation process would work. That the very thing Napoleon held close as a state secret was actually the reason so many of the Cornish coastal mines had gone under. But here was the proof that Celeste had been right— and additional proof, had Loveday needed any, that she had a lot to learn from her friend.

To say nothing of the possibility that, if the prince were truly investigating Lyme Regis for the same reason, Papa and Mr Trevelyan and Mr Thorndyke were about to become very rich men indeed.

She instructed two of the stable boys where to pound the stakes into the ground, and even though the gondola lay on its side like a beached fishing boat and did not look like it would tilt upright, never mind float into the air, she and Celeste looped the lightweight mooring ropes around the stakes anyway. With only a hand pump, and even with the expansion of the gas, it took most of the afternoon to fill the envelope.

Every man who showed his face to see the proceedings was dragooned into a turn at the pump. Mr Clement came to see what in the name of heaven they were doing with his skin and was told in no uncertain terms that he was up next. Even Loveday and Celeste did their part. Loveday would never make such a poor showing in front of the staff as to ask that someone else do the job for her.

She was used to dirty work. But she had only dared hope for results. And as the envelope puffed and filled and rose, she and Celeste stared upward, as awestruck as any of their helpers at the fact that their sketches, drawings, scrubbed-out plans, and broken equations were actually coming to fruition.

"*C'est incroyable,*" Celeste whispered. "How lovely she is."

The silk envelope stretched over the internal corset, and she and Celeste sprang into action, adjusting the lie of it, taking up slack, smoothing it over the ribs within. It fit perfectly. And like a miracle, it began to lift.

The ropes became taut.

The gondola tilted upright.

And left the ground.

Spontaneously, all the stable boys cheered. Loveday grabbed Celeste and shrieked as the two of them jumped up and down. Mr Clement tossed his hat in the air.

And there she was, their beautiful vessel, balancing on the ends of her ropes like a bird tethered to the earth when she wanted to spread her wings and fly.

"What shall you call her, Miss Penhale?" Mr Clement called gaily.

"Call her?" Loveday looked at Celeste, who shrugged.

"Every vessel must have a name, miss," Pascoe offered,

unable to keep the grin off his face, his head tilted back to take in this marvel.

"Well…" she said at last, "in all our calculations, I do not believe we took that one into account."

"A bird, perhaps?" Celeste suggested. *"Alouette?"*

"What is that in English, miss?" one of the stable boys asked.

"It means *lark*," Loveday said. "I like that. *Lark* she shall be."

"Singing as she flies." Papa walked across the lawn just in time to hear. "The question in my mind is, who will fly her?"

"Why, we ourselves," Celeste blurted. "Who knows her better?"

"Loveday, Celeste, my dears, I owe you an apology," Papa said, gazing upward. "I must confess that I did not believe you would succeed."

"That is quite all right, Papa," Loveday said, taking his arm. "I had my doubts at times, as well, particularly when our designs disappeared so inexplicably."

"But now that we are at the sticking point, I have to say I do not want either of you putting yourselves in such danger. Is there not someone who could take her up in your stead?"

Loveday felt as though her chest had been clamped in a vise. Not take their vessel up? Oh, no, no… surely he would not forbid it now, at their moment of triumph?

"How will we demonstrate *Lark*'s ability to the prince if she is not taken up and put through her paces, Papa?" How very rational she sounded. Even though she wanted to scream the words. "If adjustments are necessary for complete success, we ought to be the ones to observe and make them."

"I am sure that some sailor could be found to do it. Think

of your mother's nerves should she catch sight of you a hundred feet in the air."

Loveday had never given her mother's nerves a single thought in all her life. Until the purchase of the mines, she had never known Mama to have any.

"We could send to Lyme Regis, I suppose, to ask advice of His Royal Highness, since he is to be our principal witness." She breathed deeply, reaching for calm. "But Celeste and I suspect he is there investigating the properties of hot water springs and lifting gas."

Papa's eyes widened.

"I very much believe that Mama's nerves will be miraculously cured if our suspicions prove true."

"From your lips to God's ears, maidey," he said fervently. "But returning to the point, what about the aeronauts proposed for St Michael's Mount? Surely there is someone trained for this kind of work."

"There is. Standing right here. Celeste was one of the foremost balloonists in France." This was the moment. Her secret had to be revealed. "One of two. The other is her mother, Madame Sophie Blanchard."

Papa gazed at her blankly. "Isn't Celeste's mother in Portugal?"

Celeste, who seemed to have turned to stone at Loveday's words, shook herself into life. "I have been in your home under an alias, Monsieur Penhale, for both my safety and yours. My real name is Celeste Blanchard, and Loveday is correct. My mother and I are the foremost balloonists in France. Further, in this country, no one is more fit and capable of flight than your own daughter. We have shared our knowledge, and other than practical experience, she knows everything she needs to know to take the air ship up with me."

"Your mother is Sophie Blanchard?" He seemed to be having difficulty apprehending the facts. Loveday could not blame him. She had been in his position.

"Yes. I fled France, not Portugal, to escape an unwanted marriage. I came in a balloon." She turned to look up at the envelope swelling against the sky. "That balloon. When that terrible squall blew up, I had to abandon ship and ended my flight on the beach below Hale Head."

"But Sophie Blanchard is Boney's Chief Air Minister." Papa grasped at a fact the way Mama caught a dove in the dovecote. As though she would never let go once she had it in hand.

"She is. But I am not. I am merely a flight instructor at *l'École des Aéronautes* in Paris."

"That's how you knew about the lifting gas."

"Yes."

"The existence of which, I have been reliably informed, is a state secret."

"Yes."

"Yet you have revealed it to me without a qualm."

"I had several qualms. But yes."

He gazed at her. "You have betrayed Napoleon Bonaparte in the way most likely to harm him and his infernal ambitions."

Celeste stood motionless, clearly uncertain if this was a condemnation or not.

Papa took a step forward… Celeste flinched… and he took her into his arms, patting her back as though he sensed she needed comfort.

"No one will ever know it from me," he said against her

hair. "But if I were our Prince Regent, I would award you the highest honor a ruler could bestow."

"Then may we take *Lark* up at the earliest opportunity?" Celeste asked.

He examined her face, holding her shoulders at arms' length. "Does it not give you pause, considering how your father died?"

"Papa fell after a seizure of the heart," Celeste said quietly. "Neither his balloon nor his skills were at fault."

"Then if you have no objection, I suppose I cannot." He released her, and Celeste began to breathe again. "For it is abundantly clear that in this case, both balloon and skills are in excellent working order."

Such good working order that he agreed to allow the two of them to take it out as soon as the weather was favorable. Celeste felt a little like Amélie, checking the conditions every few hours, until they were perfect.

"Now," she told Loveday that evening.

After dinner, they all assembled on the rear lawns. Mr Penhale had agreed to allow them the use of the stable hands for a ground crew. They scampered from one of the stakes to the other, checking lines and nearly tripping over each other. Celeste felt the same giddy feeling sweeping over her. Time to return to the skies.

A crescent moon had just risen, offering no more than a soft glow against the torches flaming along the Penhale terrace. The balloon swelled on the lawn, the gondola tied on short ropes so that it could be entered by means of a mounting block. All that lovely silk looked more silver than a rainbow in the starlight.

"I'll start the boiler," Loveday said, lifting her wool skirts to climb the steps to the door of the carriage. She paused at the top and glanced back at the terrace, where her sisters, mother, and father watched, along with a good number of the staff. After all, it wasn't every day an air ship made an ascent from your own lawn!

"I'll instruct *les garçons* in casting off the mooring lines," Celeste told her. "Once we're down to one she'll jump, and I'll only have a few moments to climb aboard. So tell me as soon as we're up to full steam."

"I will." Loveday's face was pale as she glanced out the open door. "I wish I had been able to convince Mama to have the modiste make me an outfit like yours."

Celeste smoothed her *pantalons*. After all this time in skirts, it felt odd to have the silk around her legs again, her redingote warm about her.

"If we succeed at this, the prince will buy you a dozen like it," she predicted.

"That would be highly improper. I'll buy my own with the prize money." She disappeared inside, where a lamp flared.

Celeste circled the craft, smiling at the stable hands, who were fairly hopping in place. The carriage was well secured to the frame, and she knew the silk had been stretched taut. They had tied the air ship off in no fewer than six directions, the braided rope looped over the stiff wood in the ground. What, did the stable boys think she would gallop away like a thoroughbred let out to pasture?

They weren't far off.

"That one first," Celeste said, and one of the boys removed the loop closest to the door to the rattle of coal dropping into the firebox. He dropped the rope as if fearing it would sting him.

Celeste moved to the opposite rope.

"We have enough fuel and water for a six-hour jaunt, by my estimation," Loveday called out. "Longer if we use the flaps and propellers judiciously."

"Perhaps we should include a manual propulsion option, like the pedals I had," Celeste suggested with a smile of encouragement to the jittery stable boy on that rope. "For emergencies."

"Next iteration," Loveday promised.

"Release her," she told the boy, and he tugged free the line.

Celeste came around to the cliff side in time to see something flash at sea. A blue light, there and gone so quickly she might have imagined it. Marcel's voice echoed in her mind. *Watch for the light. That will be my brother, checking to see if the coast is clear.*

Smugglers were coming in. Englishmen, bringing forbidden brandy and perfume. When would they return to France? How often did they sail?

For a moment, she hesitated. Somewhere between Hale House and St Mawes, free traders would land tonight. Could she find them? Would they take her with them on their next voyage? Was it possible she might return home after all?

Her gaze rose to the belly of the balloon, filled with English lifting gas. No. The door that led home was closed to her now. She had revealed the Emperor's secret, and he would know it the moment an English air ship was spotted in the sky over the French coast. And then her life would be worth less than a—

From the carriage came a clank. "Drat! A piece of coal stuck. I knew that drop to the firebox might be too curved. Another change for next time."

Next time. A bigger air ship, a finer air ship. An air ship her father had always dreamed of building, one she had dreamed of building. It had taken her and Loveday combined to bring it so close to reality. If she returned to France, she would lose her chance to see it truly finished.

And she would lose her best friend.

She turned her back on the tantalizing light and moved to the next rope.

All that remained were the stern and bow lines when Loveday called, "Full steam! Ready to lift."

"Hang on to something," Celeste advised. She dashed to the mounting block, then nodded to the young man who was on the stern line. "Loose!"

He pulled off the rope and scrambled back. The air ship reared like a stallion, and she heard gasps from the Penhale ladies. She pointed to Pascoe, who was holding the bow line. "As soon as I'm inside, let her free."

She dove for the door, and the air ship shot skyward. The momentum dropped her onto the floor.

She lay there a moment, trying to find her breath.

Loveday peered down at her, the lamp behind her making a halo about her hair. "We must find a better way of boarding."

She took Loveday's offered hand and pulled herself onto the seat. "Readings?"

"Holding at full steam," Loveday reported, glancing at one of the dials embedded in the control box where the opposite seat had been. "Though we may be able to go to half steam if we don't require propulsion just yet."

"Let's test the wind first." She scooted to the port window and lowered the glass. Cool, moist air rushed in.

Loveday already had the anemometer in hand. She edged to port and thrust it out the window, steadying it on the sill.

Celeste tensed. Would the two of them to port mean too much weight on one side? No, the structure was keeping the carriage level. Something to note in their journal.

"Wind from the southwest," Loveday reported, gaze on the rotating instrument, "approximately five knots."

She drew in another breath. Out the window, stars sparkled over the rugged silhouette of the Cornish coast. Brighter was the flash from the Porthkarrek Light. She lifted the sextant and calculated the angle and elevation. "One thousand feet and climbing."

"We should note that." Loveday turned to her journal and pencil, waiting on the seat beside her.

"If we are right about the weight," Celeste said, lowering the sextant, "we should start to slow our ascent at about fifteen hundred feet, then hover at two thousand. My father said the winds at that elevation blew predominantly from the west."

"Then we'll continue as planned," Loveday said. "We'll take her as close to France as we dare without alerting the coastal defenses, then bring her around and head back. That should prove our ability to cross both directions and maneuver at a basic level."

Celeste glanced at her. "Will they believe us, do you think?"

Loveday tossed her head. "They had better. And if they don't, we'll insist on a second trial, in full view of His Royal Highness."

Celeste smiled.

As the air ship continued to rise, they took turns monitoring the wind speed and direction as well as the altitude, dropping coal into the firebox as needed to keep the engine at half steam.

"Two thousand two hundred and fifty feet," Loveday called. "And still rising. And we're about out of sight of the Porthkarrek Light."

Celeste frowned. "Could we have included more coal in our calculations? More water?"

"If anything, we included a little less," Loveday informed her. "We should have been at or slightly above our ideal weight."

"Could our calculations with the sextant be in error?" Celeste reached out, and Loveday handed the instrument to her. It took only a moment to check. "Two thousand five hundred feet and rising!"

Loveday pushed the anemometer back into place. "The wind's shifted as well, from the south now. At least it won't send us into France this way."

"No, but it might make returning to England more difficult." Celeste lowered the instrument and met Loveday's gaze across the coach. "We may overshoot our goal and land in Bristol. Start the propeller. We turn and head back now."

"Agreed," Loveday said with a sigh. She swiveled toward the instrument panel and began opening the valves that pumped steam to the propeller and flaps. Celeste slid across the seat and pushed the lever to release the starboard flaps. They unfurled from the sides easily, like gossamer wings in the moonlight, and the air ship's bow began to veer toward the north.

"Propeller engaged," Loveday called.

Celeste felt it, like someone had shoved the air ship from behind.

Loveday went to check the anemometer. "Wind speed five knots."

Celeste glanced to the dials. "And our speed is eight knots." She grinned at Loveday. "We're going faster than the wind!"

Her friend's smile slipped. "But we're still turning."

Celeste slid over to the port flap and pressed on the lever, but it refused to budge. She grimaced. "I can't open it."

Loveday popped up and over to the other side, coming in behind her. Together, they shoved on the lever.

"It must have frozen," Loveday said. "Oh, for some lubricating oil!"

Celeste let go and threw herself across the cabin to the starboard flap. "Perhaps if we let it keep turning, we can reach the right degree, then stop."

Loveday put a hand on her belly. "Not before I cast up my accounts, I fear."

Celeste's own stomach was beginning to protest the imbalance, the spin. Worse, though, was her heart. She'd worked so hard, done so much.

Was she truly no better an inventor than her father?

CHAPTER 22

*F*rom his outpost on the cliffs, Arthur Trevelyan saw the blue blink of the light.

On/off.

On/off/on.

The smugglers out of St Mawes, led by the genial but dangerous Barnabas Pendragon, a man shaped like one of his own brandy barrels and with a fringe of black whiskers recognized from Falmouth to the Lizard.

The revenue officers had been after him for years with little success. As large as he was, Barnabas still possessed the ability to vanish like smoke in the night, taking refuge in fishing shacks and church crypts in exchange for a small share of coin for people who liked the revenue officers as little as Barnabas did. There was a reason that the Crown and Compass in St Mawes harbor served brandy as fine as anything served at the Prince Regent's court, but without the crippling taxes that made it impossible for ordinary people to enjoy it.

Ordinary people like Emory Thorndyke, who had called this evening and had departed not thirty minutes ago after refusing to accompany him next door to see what was going on upon the Penhale lawn. What would his friend think of him if he knew for certain that Arthur was in the smuggling business up to his neck? Not for barrels of brandy, but for information. Arthur might not work incognito behind enemy lines any longer, or serve as a soldier, either, until this blasted leg was in working order again, but he could still do his part by gathering information in the French ports. Barnabas Pendragon needed a translator to manage his French counterparts in the hidden coves and bays of the isle of Guernsey, which provided a kind of way station just outside the range of the French coastal emplacements. And in exchange, Arthur milked both sides for information about the movements of the French army and its *sous-marins* as skillfully as any maid ever milked a cow.

He picked up the lantern behind the flat rock. Using his coat sleeve to block the flame, he signaled back: On/off. On/off/on.

In the time it took Barnabas's landing crew to put a longboat in the water, row across, and pull it up on the sand, he had made his slow way down the cliff path to the beach where Celeste Aven—Blanchard's journal had been discovered.

Celeste Blanchard.

Had he not seen her face when he had removed the journal from her reach, he would never have believed it. But now there was the additional proof of the wildly colored balloon just visible over the treetops between their two estates. He had watched the strange vessel lift on its ropes and marveled at the determination and intelligence of its inventors. Those two young women had the grit and skill of any of the scientists employed by the Army.

He hoped Penhale would hire an aeronaut to test the ship with all possible speed, for the prince needed to know of it as soon as it proved workable. Thinking of how he might contrive to help with the location of such a man helped keep his mind occupied until he reached the bottom of the cliff. It was not an easy journey, and his leg ached like the devil by the time his boots landed in the sand where the crew was waiting.

Arthur lifted a hand in greeting, and the boatswain nodded. They saw him into the longboat and shoved off, rowing silently back out to where the two-masted brigantine waited. Voices carried over water. So no one spoke until they were within hailing distance of the ship.

After he was pulled over the gunwale in the boatswain's chair, having endured the harrowing lift up the side of the hull with his teeth gritted, Barnabas Pendragon showed him into his cabin and offered him a glass of brandy. There was no way Arthur could have climbed a rope ladder up the side in his condition, so he had swallowed the humiliation of being treated like a woman or an invalid and simply ignored any remarks the men made under their breath about the extra labor the toff cost them.

"Fair winds tonight," Barnabas said. "But me ankle says that we shall see some weather afore long."

"Not that I do not trust your ankle, but can you be certain?" A paring of moon rode high, and stars frosted the sky in countless numbers, with not a wisp of cloud to dull their brilliance.

"Aye, as certain as a man can be who has seen summer

storms all along this coast and been out in as many." Barnabas indicated the bench along the rear of his small cabin. His was the only cabin on the brigantine—the other men slept in hammocks below, or wherever they could make a dry bed on deck. Valuable space was reserved for the cargo. "'Ave a seat, me 'andsome."

When Arthur did so, Barnabas sprawled upon the bench with his own brandy while the low calls of the sailors readying the vessel to get under way sounded above them. Arthur's gaze fell upon something fixed to a shelf that had not been there on their last voyage. "I didn't take you for a clock watcher, Barnabas," he said with a sip of his brandy. "Is that a new timepiece?"

The other man's gaze swung to him with an intensity that might have made him step back had he been standing. "Ent a timepiece."

Arthur rose with difficulty and hobbled over to the wall. Now that he was closer, he saw that it certainly was not. It was a low box of similar size in which a number of tubes and metal coils were fixed, but to what end he could not imagine.

"We been sailing with 'ee some time," Barnabas said thoughtfully from behind him.

"Aye," Arthur said, sensing the other man was not simply exchanging pleasantries.

"Seem a trusty 'un."

"I hope so." His instincts and his senses sharpened.

"D'ye really not know what that is?"

Something in Barnabas's tone, some amusement, set Arthur's teeth on edge, but he would never show it. "A barometer of some kind?"

Barnabas chuckled. "Nay, tez what all the Frenchies have

been looking for these many long months. This un's Old Job's Pisky. Latest model. Heard of it?"

"I've heard of Old Job," Arthur said slowly. "Zephaniah Job, the smugglers' banker."

"Aye, well, 'e do more'n banking. He be a tinkerer, like our Prinny."

With a nod, Arthur examined the instrument again. "And what does this do?"

"What's a pisky do, me 'andsome?"

"He mazes people," Arthur said, resisting the urge to fall into the vernacular of his childhood. "Confuses them, causes them to feel they're insane."

With an outright belly laugh, Barnabas got up. "Aye, you've the right of it. If 'ee were a French *soo-marran*, and got within a hundred feet of yon Pisky, ee'd be right mazed and lose yer course. Might even run aground or broadside another of yer kind."

And suddenly, with a flash of understanding, all the pieces fell into place in Arthur's mind. "*That's* why the smugglers have been so successful and Boney's *sous-marins* have not. You've been mazing their navigation with Old Job's Pisky."

Barnabas clapped him on the back with such force that Arthur's bad leg nearly collapsed. It was only sheer will that kept him on his feet. "'Ee be a good 'un, Arthur Trevelyan. Smart, too. Mum's the word, now. Don't want them Frenchies gettin' wind of our tricks, do 'ee?"

"Certainly not. I must say, Barnabas, Job's done a proper job of spoiling Boney's ambitions for undersea vessels. Why has he not approached the War Office? Imagine if all His Majesty's ships were outfitted with one of these!"

They would own the Channel and the Atlantic, too. Every *sous-marin* harrying the shipping lanes would be chasing its rudders, whirling in helpless circles while the English vessels passed without harm. And then could be blown to bits with good English deck cannons.

But Barnabas shook his head, and Arthur's visions collapsed. "Can't 'appen, and if I hear a word has passed yer lips, me 'andsome, I'll be comin' to find out why. We'd lose our trade, sure as it's going to blow up a squall tonight." Again that intense glare from under those black brows that could surely sear a man's skin. "I'll 'ave your word on't."

Arthur had no choice; Barnabas would put him over the side as soon as look at him if he didn't agree.

"You have my word. I shall say nothing in my official capacity. I shall only wish you and your fellow captains good hunting."

Satisfied, the man turned for the door. "Best make yerself to 'ome. We've an hour's swift sailing ahead."

He went topside, leaving Arthur to contemplate the Pisky and all its possibilities, the singing of waves under the hull in his ears... and to notice when they left off singing and began to slap. Arthur straightened on the bench, listening to the sea, to an increasingly disorganized note that resembled nothing so much as the bass drum in an orchestra, beating against the side of the ship as the swell lifted and tilted the vessel with alarming strength. A *frisson* of alarm darted through his belly, and he limped out on deck. The sight that greeted him was not the orderly management of a brigantine under full sail, but the chaos of men leaping and scrambling to save their vessel.

On the horizon lay the lights of Guernsey. But in the two miles between them lay waves the size of Boney's behemoths. The size of the barrows on the Cornish hills that guarded the dead.

"What are you thinking, man?" the first mate shouted down at him as he staggered, trying to keep his footing. "Get below decks! We've no time to look after you!"

"Where is Barnabas?" Arthur shouted.

But the man merely flung an arm upward, where Barnabas and half his crew were reefing in the topgallants and foresails as fast as they could. And then with a crack of thunder, the skies opened up and a torrential rain drenched Arthur as thoroughly as if he had been tossed into the sea. The deck was suddenly awash, the water foaming over his boots, and then it tilted at such an acute angle that if Arthur had not leaped for the shrouds, he would surely have slid down the deck and into the waves.

There was no hope of getting back to the bulkhead or the door to the captain's cabin, where he might rescue the Pisky from certain damage. For he was not the sort of man who hid inside while work needed to be done that might save his life and that of his companions. The wind was howling in the rigging now, that haunting sound he had heard only once before. Their sloop had gone down, that time, and it was only by the grace of the sturdier frigate escorting them that any of the crew survived at all.

Barnabas shouted something, but in the scream of the wind Arthur could not hear him. And then the sea seemed to heave, as though something utterly dreadful were coming up from the depths to capture their frail craft and drag it down.

Two of the sailors shouted in alarm as the sea rose. The wave lifted them up on its crest and for one frozen moment Arthur hung in the air, clinging to the mainmast shroud with both hands, staring into the awful depths of the trough below.

The brigantine shrieked like a live animal as it heeled into the trough and turned turtle. Its timbers tore with a rending crash. The mainmast came down, and Arthur was flung off the shrouds and into the sea.

Get clear of the rigging.

The brigantine and the wonderful Pisky would go down. There was no hope for them. The men might yet make it to Guernsey. But not he. He, a spy well known on this coast, could not be captured. It was hopeless—it was ridiculous—the thought of swimming the long miles home with his leg in its condition—he may as well fill his lungs with water and sink to the bottom now.

But he did not. Some spark of hope or sheer stubbornness still remained in his heart, so instead, he seized a chunk of torn spar stripped of both sails and rigging and heaved himself over it.

He could not swim so far. But he could kick, and hope for an ebb tide that would carry him toward England before his strength gave out. And perhaps in his last moments before he sank, he might see that dark and beautiful shore, and think of a girl with hair like ripe wheat and a mind like a calculating engine, and a life that would never now be his.

"So, this is one of the famous Channel squalls," Loveday said, fingers braced on the padded bench. "I've only seen them from the land side. And usually from within doors."

If only Celeste could be so calm as the air ship bucked and swung. Even with the envelope sheltering them, rain pounded the windows. Between the cracks of thunder, she could hear the spit and hiss of the steam engine in protest.

"Yes," Celeste managed. "And it will only blow us closer to France."

Loveday nodded, face striped by light and shadow as the lamp swung with the ship. "Let's try the port flap again. Perhaps the water loosened it."

Celeste slid to the opposite side of the seat, and Loveday fell across the coach to join her. Together, they shoved and pushed, but the lever only shuddered.

"It's no good," Loveday said, collapsing beside her. "We have to think of something else."

Celeste stretched up to peer out the window, trying to catch a glimpse of where the flap was fixed to the side of the carriage. Why wouldn't it open? The lamplight shining through the glass showed the piping leading from the steam engine back to the flap, with no hint of steam escaping in the wind.

The flash of lightning was mirrored in another sort of bolt.

"Someone's screwed it to the carriage!"

Loveday pressed in beside her. "What? Where?"

Celeste pointed to the wood frame of the flap. "There. And we can't possibly reach it from here, even if we lowered the window."

Loveday sat back. "Perhaps the workers wanted it out of their way. Or decided to secure it for safekeeping."

"Or," Celeste said, "someone didn't want us to succeed. We are like a pigeon flying with only one wing."

As if giving up, the air ship canted. For a moment, Celeste was weightless, then she tumbled to the floor.

So did Loveday. "We must get out of this squall," she said, head in Celeste's lap, as the ship righted itself.

Celeste levered her friend up so she could perch on the bench. "*C'est vrai*. But it may not be possible to descend out of it. When I flew from France, the turbulence reached almost to the waves. And rising above this squall might compromise the integrity of the air ship."

"Then it's fight our way back or try to outrun it," Loveday said.

Celeste managed to regain the seat as well. Lightning flashed, and thunder rolled, deafening to the point that she could not hear herself speak.

"If we outrun it," she repeated in the brief quiet that followed, "we reach France. Even if we can slip through the coastal defenses, there is great danger."

Loveday raised her chin. "I trust you to keep me safe."

Celeste put a hand on her arm. "*Merci beaucoup*, my friend, but we must think of our work. The Emperor *cannot* be allowed to see this ship."

And Loveday could not know what it cost her to say that. If Celeste came home with this marvelous ship, there would be parades, speeches. She'd be awarded the Grand Golden Cross for Advances in Engineering, *l'École* renamed in her honor. Her mother need never hang her head or try her dangerous stunts again.

But Celeste would be giving Napoleon everything he needed to invade England. And that she could not do.

Loveday's face was ashen. Perhaps she did understand what was going through Celeste's mind.

"Agreed," she said. "We turn and fight our way home, and the storm be hanged. You work the good flap. I'll staff the propeller."

It took some effort just to position themselves correctly in the carriage. And they had to endure three sickeningly full rotations before Celeste managed to point them in the right direction. Now the air ship really bucked, nose pointing skyward at times, then plunging like a ship on the waves. The carriage shuddered and creaked as if determined to break free from its restraints.

"We have to descend," she called to Loveday.

"That means taking on weight," Loveday called back. "We can't. And every moment we burn more coal and water." She started. "Water! The rain! Open all the windows. Take in as much as we can."

"Brilliant!" Celeste lowered the windows on her side, sending rain coursing down the paneling, soaking the cushions. She slid over to the other side and did the same there. Water began to pool on the floor.

She could no longer see the light at Porthkarrek, but flashes of lightning showed the waves drawing closer. "We're losing altitude. It's working!"

Slowly, the air ship eased toward the sea. The movement of the water in the cabin proved that at least some was leaking through the seams of the doors, but still the cabin filled, until the chill liquid lapped Celeste's ankles and left damp spots on her *pantalons.*

She checked the anemometer. "The wind is shifting. From the south now and only three knots."

Loveday peered out the window. "It's too dark to spot the waves at the moment, much less land, but we appear to be heading in the right direction."

"Thank a merciful God," Celeste breathed, leaning back in her seat. "If the wind holds, we may make it."

Loveday maneuvered across the carriage to her side. "This is too much like your crossing, isn't it." It was not a question.

"*Oui*. But this is more bearable. I did not have a friend beside me then."

Loveday smiled. "Happy to face the elements with you."

"Happier not to face them at all." Celeste swung her feet and splashed in the water. "I will never take a hot bath for granted again."

Loveday glanced toward the coal bin, which would be so much emptier now. "I should feed the firebox. See what you can make of our surroundings."

It did seem less turbulent here, as though they were in the lee of an unseen land mass. She was able to shift on the bench without fear of falling into the water, which now reached her shins. The silk clung to her like a second skin. She craned her neck to peer out the window, and rain ran down her cheeks. They were low enough now that she could catch the swell and ebb of the waves, cold and grey and angry. A shiver went through her.

Lightning flashed, high above, anointing a shape in the water.

Celeste blinked as darkness swallowed the light. Surely the denizens of the deep had dived for safety. And the center of the storm would just now be meeting the French shore. Too early for driftwood to have been pulled this far out to sea. She focused on where she had seen the shape, counted off the seconds.

Lightning flashed again.

Celeste whirled to face Loveday. "There's someone down there! In the sea!"

CHAPTER 23

*W*hat on earth...?" Loveday leaned out of the window and was slapped in the face by a gust of rain. Lightning flashed again, and she saw the figure as if frozen in a monochrome painting. Clinging to a spar, the flotsam of some kind of wreck floating for some distance behind him, he rose and fell on waves that looked like mountains. He was certainly a man, beaten by the rain, but not yet dead.

He would be soon, if they did not do something.

"Celeste, take her down!"

"What? Are you mad? We shall capsize!"

"We cannot leave him. He'll die."

"Where is his ship?"

But there was no answer to that, and Celeste knew it. But Loveday saw the moment she made up her mind.

"We have all the water we dare hold. We'll use the propellers. A quick dive, and you haul him in. When you open the door, our water ballast will release and we will shoot up as we did on lift. You must be prepared. Tie yourself to something."

Loveday's hands were stiff with cold, but she saw the wisdom of it. The mooring ropes hung from the corners of the gondola, so she stuck her arm out of the rear window and fished one in. Knotting a length about her waist, she said, "Thank you."

"You may thank me when we find out he is not a pirate— or worse, a French sailor who will knife us on sight and steal our vessel for B-Boney." Celeste's teeth chattered, but whether from cold or fear of what they were about to attempt, Loveday could not tell.

She leaned out of the window. "Twenty feet, then come about. We shall be directly over him."

Celeste sent more coal to the firebox and set the pressure to full steam. They would need all the maneuverability they could muster, if they did not succeed on the first pass and were forced to come about for a second. Or a third.

They could not risk more. Loveday knew to an ounce the contents of the coal bin, and if they spent more time at full steam, they would not make the English shore.

Their chances of that were not good in any case. But she would never say that aloud. Celeste knew it, too.

Celeste brought them down in a tight circle about their target. By some miracle, he turned his head and looked up, his mouth forming a rictus of astonishment.

Or perhaps it was a scream.

And by a second miracle, Loveday recognized him.

"Celeste!" she screamed over her shoulder. "It's Arthur Trevelyan!"

Celeste shrieked a word in French Loveday did not know

—probably should never know—and then stopped herself, gasping. "Can he catch the tail of your rope?"

Loveday yanked it toward her and flung it out the carriage window, half her body hanging out after it. "Lower! Come back around!"

The rope dragged toward him and in vain he reached for it, likely blinded by water. It whipped out of reach, and he and his spar slid deep into a trough between the waves.

"Again!" Loveday shouted. "We must time it so he is at the crest when I open the other door."

"You ask for the very hand of God," Celeste gasped, pushing with both hands the lever that controlled the propeller.

"I do," Loveday said, a determination that was half rage— against the storm, against France, against their own feeble abilities—building in her chest. "We will not let Arthur die the way Jory did."

"No, we shall not. Coming about. Ready!"

She hauled in the rope, coiling it as fast as she could so its central weight would take it to its target. Arthur rode the spar, his face a white blur. Up... down... and here came the great wave, lifting him up—up—

Loveday threw the rope and Arthur flung himself off his spar to catch it. Treading water, his face a mask of pain, he knotted it under his arms.

She threw open the other door and their water ballast spilled out in a cataract that was instantly shredded to pieces in the wind.

Lark threw Loveday to her knees with the force of her sudden ascent. The carriage tilted and held, throwing what water remained out the door.

"Pull him up!" Celeste shouted. "We must capture more water!"

To the day she died, Loveday never knew how she had the strength to haul a waterlogged man half again her size up through a wild storm into a half-capsized air ship. But something—the rage—the hand of God—enabled her to do it, and when she hauled for the last time and Arthur's head and arm came through the window, with the last of her strength she grabbed him by the armpits and dragged him through.

She landed flat on her back. The force of the fall brought him down on top of her and crushed the air out of her lungs. Celeste hauled in the remaining rope, slammed the doors shut, and the water cascading down from the envelope began to fill the gondola again.

"Get him on the seat!"

"Can't," Loveday gasped. "Heavy."

Slowly, as though moving in nearly congealed ice, he got one elbow under him, then another.

"Beg... pardon," he croaked.

A knee. And more by chance than design, he heaved himself backward and fell onto the seat.

"Loveday, m'aidez!"

They were not out of the soup yet.

"Heading!" Celeste cried. She hauled the side flaps in.

Loveday scraped her soaked hair out of her eyes to peer at the compass. "North by west. Barometer is rising, thank the dear Lord."

"More coal. She has only one run left in her. We must get as far as we can before—"

"Before *what?*"

"We go down," Celeste rasped. "Poor Arthur will get another soaking."

Loveday thought he mumbled, "How will I know?"

At least they could use the water draining out of his clothes. He seemed to have brought half the ocean in with him.

She kept the engine pressure high while Celeste did her best with the rudder flaps. *Lark* heeled as though she were a sailboat in a high wind, but she did not fail. A rope snapped and struck the top of the carriage with a sound like an angry fist.

Oh, dear. Never mind. They had eight more.

They plunged into a nightmarish eternity in which Loveday lost track of time. Even of her own body. The rope about her waist sagged to the floor, no longer tethering her to the ship, and she barely noticed. All that existed were the rudder flaps and the compass and needle that showed they were heading for home like a wounded pelican, yawing and dipping and sloshing in the crests of the topmost waves.

And then Celeste cried, "The light!"

The Porthkarrek Light flashed out, once, twice. Loveday knew now how the sailors must feel, with their first sight of home and safety that blessed, faithful light.

"Two degrees west," she managed to choke out, her throat closing and hot tears warming her wet, cold face.

Lark heeled to the west, but not enough. "I cannot hold her," Celeste said, her whole body trying to control the rudder flaps.

"All the coal," Loveday said, opening the drop and hearing the last of their coal tumbling in. "This is it."

The light subsided to their right as Celeste struggled to keep her on their heading. Five minutes crawled by. Then ten.

Then the keel of the gondola crashed into the top of a wave and did not recover.

"Lighten ship!"

Again Loveday opened the doors, but it was already too late. The wave snatched them to itself and dragged them down with it into a trough. Flung them up to the heights, ripping off the flaps. Loveday hung out the window, coughing up water, and heard the boom and rush of waves striking rocks. At the same moment, the clouds parted and she saw the peculiar, crouching lion shape of Hale Head.

"Land!" she shrieked. "The Head! We will overshoot!"

The greedy waves reached up and grabbed their beautiful envelope out of the air. The gondola tilted into a whirling maelstrom.

"Abandon ship!" Celeste grabbed her hand—she grabbed Arthur's—the three of them fell out the door. "Swim!"

But of all the ways for the hand of God to reach down, Loveday would never have believed this one had she not felt it herself. For the riptide grabbed them and carried them past the Head, where an eddy took them from its inexorable grip and pushed them into the cove. Loveday's knees scraped on a rock, then her hands sank into the sand of the beach.

She crawled out of the waves like an exhausted crab. And realized a moment later that the rope was still knotted about her waist, and Arthur was dragging on it like a boat anchor as he pulled himself along on his elbows. She hauled on it to pull him farther up the beach and he collapsed across her legs.

He lifted his head, his chest heaving.

"Ties—that bind—" he gasped, and passed out cold in her lap.

~

DAWN WAS BREAKING. They were safe. Celeste wanted to throw herself down to kiss the speckled rocks on the beach, run up onto the cliff and dance. Oh, what a blessing to reach home.

She nearly stumbled as she helped Loveday and Arthur, who had come to himself a moment ago, up from the waves. Home? Yes, Hale House, this family, had become that. Some part of her would always miss Marcel and Josie and Amélie, all her former students at *l'École*, dear Dupont and *Maman*. But she had a place here. A chance to change the world. Her life had been snatched from the teeth of the storm and given back to her. Again. Easy enough to be content with that.

The storm had already passed over Cornwall, washing more debris onto the shore, tearing leaves and branches from the trees above. The remaining breeze pressed the wet silk of her *pantalons* to her body, raising gooseflesh all along her arms. She sucked in mouthfuls of the clear, crisp air.

Arthur, poor man, hung heavily between her and Loveday, his feet shambling over the rocks. The zigzag path up to the cliff top was a purgatory—worse, she knew, for him. But as they emerged from the path to the tussocks of grass on the top, he dug in his still booted heels as if to stop them.

Loveday looked at him askance, but he pulled himself upright and out of their arms. His whole body shook with the effort.

"Must... continue home without you," he got out, chin up. "Un—unseemly for us... to be seen... together... like this."

As Loveday raised her brows, Celeste started laughing. "You barely survive with your life, and *this* is your concern?"

His face took on the haughty look she now knew was no more than a mask to hide behind. "Propriety must be... preserved, mam'zelle." His cold lips could not pronounce the word.

"And your secrets, I think," Celeste mused. "Why we found you in the water."

"True," Loveday said, fists on her wet hips. "What were you doing so close to France?"

Balancing precariously, he bent and retrieved a slender length of wood from the ground, clearly torn from one of the trees nearer the house, then leaned on it. "Perhaps we can... come to an agreement. I'll say nothing about the marvelous craft that rescued me... or that it was flown by two young ladies. Without the approval of their family."

Loveday coughed into her hand. "We had approval, sir. Though we were never to go so far."

"I am glad... you did. You say nothing... about where you found me." He looked from one to the other.

"Agreed," Loveday said.

"Agreed, with an amendment," Celeste put in. "Did Monsieur Thorndyke have anything to do with your appearance in the water?"

He frowned. "Why... do you ask?"

"I am ashamed that we suspected him of stealing the plans for our... marvelous craft, as you called it. But we discovered that craft had been tampered with. Very likely shortly before we lifted. That is one of the reasons we struggled to reach home safely."

Loveday gazed out at the waves. The so very hungry waves that had been deprived of their prey.

"So," Celeste concluded, "I would very much like to know if Monsieur Thorndyke was in the area at the time."

"He was," Arthur confirmed, and her heart shriveled. "But he cannot be your villain. We were together most of the evening. Until… nine-thirty. He would not have had time… to reach Hale House. And he was driving his phaeton. Not easily hidden."

Celeste sagged even as her heart soared. "Thank you."

He nodded. "I must go… before we attract notice. My everlasting thanks, Loveday, Celeste." He took Loveday's hand and bowed over it, as much as he could on his ungainly crutch. Then he turned and began picking his way along the cliff path—slowly, agonizingly—toward Gwynn Place.

Loveday rubbed her hand absently. "Why do you think he was in the water?"

"You have seen him on the headland often enough," Celeste said, turning for lawns behind Hale House. "Could he be spying on France?"

"From Cornwall?" Loveday had not the strength even for a laugh as she gathered her sodden skirts. "Unless he has found a way to augment his spyglass, no. Hmm. Now, that would be a useful invention. Far vision. We might even have spotted the squall before it did us in." She cast one more despairing look out to sea.

Celeste laid a hand on her shoulder. "We can build another air ship. A better one. With all the improvements you noted."

Loveday nodded, and together they started for home. Mr

and Mrs Penhale would likely raise a fuss, but Celeste did not doubt that Loveday would find a way to calm them.

Eventually.

In the meantime, she had to find a way to visit Truro. The very air tasted sweeter now that she knew Emory was not the one who had stolen their plans. Surely the thief and the vandal were the same person. She and Loveday must discover their hidden enemy and stop the villain before someone was hurt.

But first, she must bathe. Give thanks. Sleep. Recover.

And then humble herself and apologize to Emory.

CHAPTER 24

*I*t was simply beyond Arthur's ability to rise from his bed a few hours after he fell into it and behave as though the previous night had never happened. His mother was the easiest to fool. If she had things her way, he would be wrapped in cotton wool and put away safely in the closet until Gabriel blew his trumpet or Arthur married, whichever came first. The servants were well trained to look the other way at the vagaries of their employers. But his father was not the kind of man to accept things so easily.

Luckily, he *was* the kind of man who made his observations, came to his own conclusions, and then kept his lips firmly closed. If the ruined boots and the rime of salt in his son's hair had not been enough evidence, then Arthur's grey face and exhaustion was enough for him to conclude that some skulduggery had occurred the night before. While Arthur had long known that his father suspected he consorted with smugglers, there was no proof of it and he would never ask.

SHELLEY ADINA & R.E. SCOTT

He merely ordered hot water for Arthur and removed his ruined boots on his way out.

It was some two days later that Arthur was able to leave his bed and make his slow way down to the cliffs as usual. He had very jumbled memories of everything that had happened after he had looked up and seen that impossible contraption floating above his head like some kind of dilapidated angel. But curiously, he could still feel Loveday's drenched body under his on the floor when she had hauled him in. Could remember the look in her eyes as she had pulled him up the beach on the end of her rope, only to collapse upon her in a highly embarrassing fashion.

She and Celeste had saved his life, that much was obvious. But what was he to do with that life, was the question he now must answer. Far better men than he had met their end in the service of king and country. He had been given his life back not once, but twice, and must somehow see his way to making more of it than merely being his father's heir and the squire of a beloved property. Or even a spy who now carried a secret that would be of utmost interest to the government.

His halting steps took him down the lawns to his favorite flat rock on the cliff edge. The sun was shining as though the killing storm of two nights ago had been only a figment of his imagination. The rock felt warm beneath him, and the usual haze that lay over the Channel had cleared away, giving him a long view halfway to France.

Two girls had brought him across that vast expanse and dropped him practically upon his own beach.

How was that even possible?

How much had everyone around them underestimated

their intelligence, their ingenuity, and—deuce take it—their astonishing skills?

And further, added the Army man that lay all too close to the surface within him, how might they contribute all of the above to the final defeat of Napoleon and the safety of their beloved country?

A feminine voice hailed him from some distance away, and he lifted his head to see Loveday approaching along the cliff path. "Good afternoon, Captain," she called. "I was coming to see how you were."

She wore a white dress embroidered all over with small yellow flowers, and her green spencer matched the ribbons tied in a jaunty bow under her chin. Her eyes took him in, blue as the sea stretching into the distance to meet the skies over France. How was it possible that both the sea and the girl could have recovered so completely, and look so utterly lovely?

"I am as well as can be expected," he said, doing his best to regain his equilibrium. It was as though he had never seen her before, yet he had known her since she was born. "And I believe you should be able to call me by my first name. After all, you saved my life."

"Very well, Arthur." She seemed to be trying the word on for size. "Then you must call me Loveday."

He could not help his smile. "You will forgive me if I do not rise. My leg has objected strenuously to all that has been required of it lately and is being very miserly about what it allows me."

"I do not blame you at all. I hope you will not think me forward, then, for sitting without an invitation." She seated herself on the rock beside him, a modest foot or so away.

He had to smile. "Certainly not. But I do wish to beg your pardon for making rather free with your person during my rescue."

Her cheeks, which were blooming with the exercise and the fresh breeze, reddened still further.

"I can't remember much of what happened," he confessed. "If you like, I will pretend that I was mostly unconscious the whole time. Though that is not far off the mark."

"I am just glad that by some miracle, our courses happened to cross," she said quietly.

When she looked up to meet his gaze, something inside him resonated, as though he had been a bell struck by a mallet.

"I do remember very clearly that I refused to let the storm win," she went on. "We lost Jory, and I do not think I could bear it if we lost you, too."

It took him a moment to get his mouth working. "I shall do my very best not to cause you such distress of that kind again. I find that I value my life more than ever I did before, now that I have had it returned to me twice in one year."

When she smiled, he saw that she had a dimple as small as a seed, right there at the corner of her lips. He dragged his gaze away, slightly out of breath.

"I was on Barnabas Pendragon's brigantine," he blurted. "When they go to Guernsey to collect their illicit cargo, I go as translator… and to gather what information I can."

"I see," she said slowly, taking in this abrupt change of subject with a long breath of sea air. "How did you come to be in the Channel?"

"A devil-spawned king wave." He owed her the truth, and a

little speculation for garnish. After all, he had only sworn that he would not pass the information along to *official* channels. He was under no such restriction in conversation with the young lady next door. "But before we were swamped, I winkled a secret out of our Barnabas. The *sous-marins* have brought their own doom upon them."

"You will not see me drop a tear at that," she said. "Their harassment of English shipping has made them as hated as the behemoths, I'm sure."

"But it has enabled the smugglers' trade. And the smugglers have made certain they hold on to it. You've heard of a man called Zephaniah Job?"

She nodded. "Though my mother would be appalled at such knowledge."

"It seems that besides acting as the smugglers' banker in Polperro, he is also something of a tinkerer. Each smuggler who does business with him carries aboard a small device the size of a mantel clock. It interferes with the navigation systems of the *sous-marins*. Hence the unprecedented level of the smugglers' success."

"Good heavens," she whispered. "Should not the War Office be informed?"

He shook his head. "I have no proof, and Pendragon's device is at the bottom of the sea. I must get my hands on another if I am to propose that naval ships carry one, too. But that is by the bye. Your air ship is more important. I have written this morning to the Admiralty about your achievements. We may find the Prince Regent becoming more serious about his visit here."

"I won't hold my breath," she said, then flashed that smile

at him again. "But it is a wonderful prospect. As is your recovery. I will leave you to your solitude. Sunlight, I hear, is good for the soul."

"Good morning, then, Loveday."

As she walked away with only a little stiffness in her stride from her night above and in the sea, half of him wanted to call her back. To speak further. To become better acquainted with the workings of that extraordinary mind. To find out what she wanted from life.

But he did not. For what woman would consider such a badly used hulk of a man the way he was now, as scarred as any driftwood tossed up on the beach? Loveday Penhale was a woman with the heart of a lion. A woman even the worthiest of men would be grateful to have beside him in the grand adventure of life.

He would just have to make good and sure that he became that man.

One week later

The staff of the Trevithick Steam Works seemed delighted to see Celeste and Loveday, when Mr and Mrs Penhale had calmed sufficiently to allow them out by themselves again. Well, not entirely by themselves. They'd come in the family carriage rather than the whiskey this time, and both the coachman and a groom had been waiting their return to escort them home after their visit to Madame Racine. Loveday had convinced her staff that a brief stop at the steam works was entirely warranted.

Now Mr Clement offered them a toothy grin, and Mr

Trevithick went so far as to incline his red head in a bow, dripping lubricating oil from the can in his hand on the battered floor.

Only Emory regarded her cautiously as Celeste made her way in his direction. Oh, but she wasn't ready. She paused beside Mr Clement's workbench.

"The piston is coming along nicely, I see," she said, gazing down at the dented brass in front of him.

"Yes, thank you, Miss Aventure," he said, hands shaking as he picked it up.

She knew that tremulous feeling.

She allowed him to gush about the swift pumping action, the pounds per square inch of pressure it could withstand, all the while trying not to gaze overly long in Emory's direction. Did that slender frame look just the least bit thinner? Had he been pining for what might have been as well?

"So, you see, it will be just the thing," Mr Clement finished, like a watch winding down.

"I am certain under your inspired efforts, it will be *magnifique*," Celeste assured him. She picked up her muslin skirts and swept toward Emory's workbench. Her heart was pounding faster than Mr Clement's high-pressure piston, and her hands inside her gloves were damp, as if she'd held them over a lifting gas vent in the mine.

"And what are you working on, Monsieur Thorndyke?" she trilled as Loveday went to talk to Mr Trevithick about a new small-scale boiler.

He regarded her. "I continue to persevere on the weight-to-thrust-ratio problem, Miss Aventure."

So formal. Her mouth was dry; she could scarcely force

out the words. "Could you spare a moment to discuss a matter with me?"

He leaned closer and lowered his voice. "Only if it does not involve you impugning my honor further."

Celeste swallowed. "I promise you it does not."

"Very well, then." He straightened and wiped off his hands, then led her out of the shop to the testing field at the rear. Every gaze followed them.

Out in the sunlight, Celeste wound the reticule strings around her fingers and dove into her reason for coming. "I must apologize to you, Monsieur Thorndyke. You rightly pointed out that my logic was not sufficiently strong to support a conclusion regarding who had stolen our plans, particularly when I know you to be a man of character."

He crossed his arms over his chest. "And what makes you question your logic now?"

"Other... evidence showed me you could not be the thief," Celeste admitted.

"Ah." He dropped his arms. "But in the absence of proof, my honor is still not sufficient."

"No, I..." Celeste drew in a breath. "I was wrong, Emory. Your honor should never have been in question. Where I was raised, seldom is anyone all that they seem, so it was too easy to assume the same of you. But the truth is that you are one of the most genuine people I have ever met. I should have accepted you as such, and I did not. Please forgive me."

He nodded. "Very well."

That was it? He believed her? Once more relief gushed up through her chest, leaving her giddy. She stuck out her hand. "Friends?"

He regarded her hand a moment, and she froze. Was there

some English custom she was missing? Did a lady not offer friendship to a gentleman?

He took her hand and shook it. "Friends. And I do hope that means you'll feel comfortable allowing me to see what you and Miss Penhale have been working on."

Loveday came out the door just then and gave Celeste a nod. Celeste sent her a smile.

"We've had a little... how do you say... setback," she told Emory. "But I'll let you know when we have something worth viewing. I promise."

She and Loveday regrouped at the door of the steam works.

"I take it Mr Thorndyke was willing to accept your apology," Loveday said as they headed for the coach.

"He was," Celeste marveled. "And was Mr Trevithick agreeable to help with the new boiler?"

"Indeed, yes. We may have it ready by the end of next week. But we'll have to find another form for our gondola. A larger form. I could not like the cramped space for maneuvering."

"Mais oui," Celeste said as the groom came around to lower the steps and assist them into the coach. "And we have a number of improvements to factor in."

"Squalls like that will always play havoc with the flaps and the silk," Loveday acknowledged.

"All that lovely silk!" Celeste moaned.

"It might yet wash ashore, perhaps even with the corset still inside." Loveday tapped her chin as they settled into their seats. "Unless we can encase it with something, with the gas held in an interior bladder. We have a lot to do to be ready to present the ship to the prince when he visits. If he visits."

"If he doesn't," Celeste said. "We can always fly the ship to London to see him. *Voila, Monsieur le Prince*—your air ship!"

Loveday laughed as the carriage jerked into motion and took the road home. "I can hardly wait."

THE END

AFTERWORD

Thanks for reading the first book in The Regent's Devices series. To make sure you know when the next book is out, sign up for Shelley Adina's mailing list at https://www.subscribepage.com/shelley-adina and begin the adventure with "The Abduction of Lord Will."

Sign up for Regina Scott's mailing list at https://subscribe.reginascott.com/ and learn what happened in France while Celeste was in England.

Now we invite you to turn the page for a sneak peek of the next book in the series: *The Prince's Pilot*.

Fair winds!

—*Shelley and Regina*

EXCERPT

THE PRINCE'S PILOT © 2022 SHELLEY ADINA
AND R.E. SCOTT

Chapter 1

Truro, Cornwall
Late August 1819

"Is there anything else I might do to assist you, Loveday?"

Such a civil inquiry to be made in such a roar, but this was red-bearded, irascible Thomas Trevithick, who had probably proposed to his wife at the same volume.

"Thank you, Thomas, but no," Loveday Penhale said over the ringing of Rudolph Clement's hammer as he battled a sheet of copper. "This small boiler is even better than our last one, thanks to you and your men here. Now that we have installed it in the gondola, I believe we may call it complete."

What a change three months had wrought—free rein at the steam works for herself and her friend Celeste Blanchard, actual civilities falling from Thomas's lips instead of criticisms, and tolerance of their presence that was now almost cordial.

It was as great a miracle as finding lifting gas in the depths of the Cornish bedrock.

"Aye, it's a fine bit of work," he agreed. "Better this be done in the full light of day, and not cobbled together with bits and bobs and hope."

"We still have hope," she reminded him with a grin. "*That* did not wind up in the sea in the spring, at any rate."

He hesitated, his ham-sized hands pushed into the pockets of his leather apron. "Tez glad I am, Loveday, that you made landfall on your own doorstep. It would have been a sad loss to us all if you'd gone down with your air ship." His face turned even more scarlet than usual. It looked almost painful.

She resisted the urge to pat his shoulder, for that would have embarrassed them both to no end. "We will not distress ourselves with the might-have-beens," she said bracingly. "Come, tell me what you think of my work on this narrow-gauge copper piping."

Relieved, he bent to inspect it, and they returned to a congenial discussion of hydraulics and pressure. Celeste sent her a commiserating smile from where she was inspecting the installation of the steam engine.

Yes, how far they had come in every part of their lives since May! For once the original *Lark* had been launched and her remains subsequently washed ashore near the St Mawes harbor—truly, there must be some reason why the tides so consistently brought in large floating objects that she and Celeste had misplaced—there was no keeping secret any longer what the two of them meant to do.

Compete for the Prince's prize. And win.

She and Celeste were young and unmarried. Neither of

them were permitted to attend a university to take a degree in engineering, like Emory Thorndyke over there at the metal forge. Neither possessed the means to build an air ship, only the imagination and the will.

And yet they had done it.

They'd built it, and flown it nearly to France and back, and lived to tell the tale.

Now, as though the district had been shaken awake by the novelty and sheer nerve of such an endeavor, Loveday and Celeste were suddenly—well, perhaps not the belles of the ball, but certainly the apple of their neighbors' eyes. Why, even Sir Robert Jermyn, the terribly severe magistrate for Truro who used to frighten Loveday half to death as a child with his beetling eyebrows and abrupt manner, had stopped his landau in the street two days ago to greet her and Celeste as they walked back from visiting their friend, the elderly émigré Madame Racine.

"Good day, Miss Penhale, Miss Aventure," he had said, lifting his hat.

Loveday curtsied and hoped the two seconds with her head bowed would be enough to wipe the astonishment from her face. And for Celeste to remember she still went by an alias.

"How is that flying vessel of yours coming along?" he boomed.

A pair of women with baskets over their arms had slowed to hear the reply.

"Very well, sir," Celeste had answered when Loveday could not find her tongue. "We obtained the silk for the new envelope for a very good price, since we could not use the old after its second sea bathe. Thank you for recommending that mill in Bristol."

He looked pleased, though the silk was such a revolting shade of brown it was no wonder no lady had wanted to purchase it. They'd had all the bolts for next to nothing, for they could not be particular at this late date.

"And we have had a new gondola built to specifications and have not had to importune our neighbors for their old carriages to be cut up for the purpose," Celeste went on.

"Capital," he had said, his face creaking into a smile. "We'll have that prize, won't we?"

"I certainly hope so, Sir Robert," Loveday finally managed. "Though it seems the high-pressure pump built for the mines by the Trevithick Steam Works may give us a run for our money."

He had nodded sagely. "You have the right of it, Miss Penhale. Either way, we'll put Cornwall on the map."

"We will indeed, sir."

And he had tapped the floor of his landau with his cane to signal his coachman and rolled away, leaving that little word ringing in Loveday's ears.

We.

Oh, dear. If something went wrong, it would no longer simply reflect badly on her and Celeste. Or even Emory, who had perfected his pump at last.

Their failure would reflect badly on all the county.

But she must not think of that. She had spent far too many hours of her life feeling like a failure. A failure to be graceful and accomplished. A failure to be a good marital prospect. She and Celeste were something else now. Something England had all too rarely seen.

They were aeronauts.

A glow of happiness suffused her that had nothing to do with the sun pouring in the isinglass windows of the workshop. She and Celeste were *aeronauts*. What other young lady in the country could say the same?

"Miss Penhale, Miss Aventure," Colin Treloar called from the big double doors of the workshop that faced the street. "The wain's come for your flying boat."

"It's come early! Celeste, we shall have to finish installing the pipes at home." Thomas and Rudolph were already rolling the overhead pulleys into place to hoist the gondola into the wagon behind the Puffing Jenny.

While Celeste rolled up the pipes in canvas, Loveday hurried over to Colin. "Have them back the wain up to the turntable and we shall have our Jenny deliver it directly."

"Tisn't any old *them*, miss. It's Captain Trevelyan from Gwynn Place and your Mr Pascoe."

She tilted her head back as Pascoe, the Hale stable master, backed the big Percheron borrowed from one of the Jermyn farms so that the wain could receive the gondola. "Captain Trevelyan, I did not expect you today."

Arthur Trevelyan dismounted a little awkwardly from the vehicle's bench and bowed once he had reached the ground. "It has been some years since I rode in a wain, I must admit. But the excitement of collecting the gondola was too much to resist."

"What, no racing curricle?"

"And be thought of as an obstruction in the road compared to the triumphant progress of the new and improved *Lark Deux*? I think not." His hazel eyes twinkled, and not for the first time, she marveled at his utter lack of pretension or self-importance. Instead, he entered into the spirit of the thing with the gravity of a man and the enthusiasm of a boy.

The sound of rapid footsteps made them turn. *"Vite*, Loveday!" Celeste cried, her arms full of canvas-wrapped piping. "Stand aside or you will be run over."

To put punctuation to her words, the Puffing Jenny let off a gout of steam with a whistling sound that pierced the ears. And here she came, the tiny locomotive engine with the tall stack that was stronger than a brace of oxen. She ran back and forth on her track in the workshop to take heavy equipment to the street. Coupled to her was a flat-bed wagon, on which the gondola had been roped. Their Puffing Jenny was very similar to Richard Trevithick's original engine, the *Catch Me Who Can*, built right here in this shop by the great man.

"Oh, but this is exciting," Celeste whispered. "I can scarcely breathe."

After all their work, all their revised plans, their dreams were now coming to fruition. No more cut-up carriages for them—the new gondola had been financed by Mr Trevelyan and Loveday's father, in a humbling show of confidence in their abilities.

Loveday took her arm. "Isn't it marvelous? Careful, now, the turntable is about to move."

The Puffing Jenny rolled onto the turntable, and with a jerk and a puff of steam from the engine below the floor, it began to move. When it locked into place, the Jenny now faced back the way it had come, the wagon neatly lined up with the rear of the wain. The pulleys and winch rolled down their track to the door, and their new gondola was lifted on to the wain, to be cradled in a generous bed of straw. How lovely it was—as smooth and sleek as a seashell, its wooden curves gleaming in the sunlight.

Celeste gave a sigh of happiness.

"It is a lovely sight," Emory said as he walked up, his gaze resting warmly upon her friend.

"It is," Arthur agreed. "Pascoe, are you sure you trust me with this great beast?"

"His name is Hugo, Sir Robert's man tells me. It is more a matter of his trusting you, sir, and I believe our journey here made it clear he does. Now, Miss Celeste, if you will step up, I will go back and tie down your vessel."

With a smile of thanks, Celeste laid the bundle of pipes in the straw and held out her hand to Emory so he might help her up. "We must not keep the captain waiting any longer."

Pascoe made short work of the ropes, making sure the gondola would not fall over or suffer any damage on the way, though goodness knew the apparatus was sturdy enough that it would take more than a pothole in the road to move it. Sturdy, but light, its form would sail through air more easily than a ship through water. As easily as the lark for which it was named.

Not for nothing had they taken two weeks of unrelenting work to create a scale model of the *Lark Deux*, right to the silk envelope with its internal corset made of wicker and a second, more durable bladder of treated canvas inside the corset to hold the lifting gas. Each pipe, each tiny control, was created from clock parts and scraps of copper and tin. Even the vanes operated, to control direction and altitude. Loveday had built an engine no bigger than her clenched fist, and when the whole was assembled, Loveday's family had joined her and Celeste on the lawn to test it.

And it had flown, on the end of an entire spool of Mama's silk thread, which Loveday subsequently had to spend the evening rewinding. The landing was not quite as successful as they had hoped, and had broken both the bow vanes, but she and Celeste had soon made an adjustment to their placement. When she came in at full size, nothing on the hull would interfere with *Lark*'s ability to moor or launch, including their mount and dismount.

"Miss Penhale, may I assist you up?" Arthur held out a hand.

Oh, that rascal Pascoe! He had engineered it on purpose so that Celeste would sit on the outside and she in the middle, next to Arthur. But she kept her head high. "Thank you, Captain." She waved to Thomas and Emory, and they were off.

Somehow, though they had told no one that the gondola would be going home today, word had got out. People stopped in the streets to cheer, and children came to their garden gates to wave as they went by. Even Hugo, Loveday was quite certain, had a livelier step as he pulled a wain as full of hope as it was of their invention through town and out on to the road that led to their village and home.

"I wonder if the Tinkering Prince himself will have such a reception when he rides through town." Arthur's voice held laughter.

"I should hope he would have quite a lot more." Loveday turned to face the front after checking that all was well with Pascoe in the bed of the wain. "I feel equal parts proud and dismayed."

"What do you mean?" Celeste asked. "For me, it felt quite

like old times, when my mother would be cheered in the streets for her latest ascension."

"But did Madame Blanchard have quite so much riding on her shoulders as we do?"

"Before my flight, she did," Celeste said soberly. "Every bit as much, and perhaps more. For the villagers and townsfolk here do not have the power to have us imprisoned or even executed for our failure to perform."

That certainly put her worries in perspective and shrank them to the size of their scale model in comparison.

"Surely you are not losing your nerve now," Arthur said, glancing at her.

"No indeed. But what if something goes wrong?" Loveday said. "It was bad enough when our hopes went to the bottom of the bay. It seems infinitely worse to think of the hopes of the entire district doing so as well."

Celeste regarded her, concern in her dark eyes. "This is not like you. What has happened?"

Loveday straightened her shoulders and sat up straight. "Nothing. Perhaps I am simply weary of always hearing that the Prince Regent will come and never actually seeing him arrive."

"Have you heard nothing, Captain?" Celeste asked, squeezing Loveday's hand in a gesture of comfort.

"Not a word," Arthur said. "Not since he was sighted in Lyme Regis earlier in the summer, and we thought he might come to the Midsummer Ball. After that, not a whisper or even a rumor. I suspect he has been called back to London."

"Perhaps the King has taken a turn for the worse," Loveday suggested. "Or he must deal with some fresh scandal of the Princess of Wales."

"It is a shame, whatever the cause," Arthur went on. "Here is Emory's steam engine and pump working as well as they are designed to do, emptying the mines of water. Even if powered flight were to come to nothing, at least the mines will be fully operational again by Michaelmas. To the miners, that is worth more than any royal recognition."

"But the gas must still be removed," Celeste said. "I hear in a number of drawing rooms much speculation about the mysterious warehouse built by your fathers in St Mawes and the barrels being filled with the gas and stored."

"The fishermen and miners must think us mad," he said with a laugh.

"Mama still thinks so," Loveday said. "She will not even let us say the words *lifting gas*. Which is difficult, since we must fill our lovely envelope with it, and there it will be, staring her out of countenance upon the lawn."

"She will change her mind soon enough," Celeste said. "When we win the Prince's prize and Mr Penhale and Mr Trevelyan become the richest men on the Cornish coast."

Hale Head came into view, the promontory that resembled a crouching lion thrusting out into the Channel that had given her family its name, and soon they were turning off on the road that led home.

It was no easy feat lifting the gondola from her comfortable bed and into the place cleared for it in the carriage house. The hay hook was dragooned into bearing pulleys and winch, and with the help of Pascoe and the stable boys, the gondola was guided to its place, where it was held upright with triangle-shaped blocks.

After Arthur had called at the house to give his regards to her parents and then departed, Papa had come out to watch the operation as Loveday and Celeste directed their crew. At length it was completed, and the wain taken back to the Jermyn farm with a promise that Hugo would get an extra ration of oats for his unusual duties that afternoon.

"Thank you for allowing us to complete the final steps in the carriage house, Papa," Loveday said. "I know it is an inconvenience."

"I am committed to the project now," he said with gruff affection. "Besides, with your grandfather's old coach out of the way, there is plenty of room for it. When do you propose to take her up?"

"Well," Celeste said, "we must fit the pipes and be sure the engine performs as well as it did in the steam works, and the vanes react as they did in our model. Then we must rig it, fill the gas bags, and finally fit the envelope over all."

"So, by Christmas, then?" Papa said with a smile.

"No indeed," Loveday told him, tilting her chin. "Two weeks at most."

"So soon?" Had he been the sort to wear a pince-nez, it would have fallen off his nose.

"No need to look so amazed," she said. "The most difficult parts are complete. Oh, Papa," she said, clasping her hands in delight, "the boatwright has done a masterful job, has he not? Have you ever seen anything so lovely?"

Her father contemplated the gleaming gondola. "Not in the realm of mechanical devices," he said at last. "But see here, Loveday. This is more important than I think you realize. I believe that if your project is to be taken seriously, it must be witnessed and documented."

"Our journals have documented each step, sir, down to the

screws and nails," Celeste assured him. "And your entire family witnessed our last ascension."

"That is not what I mean," he said. He motioned toward the double doors, and they followed him outside into the sunshine. "I believe that in order for this air ship to be taken as seriously as it deserves, you ought to have someone with you as witness. Like Captain Trevelyan, or Mr. Thorndyke. Or both, for that matter, unless this marvelous craft won't hold more than two."

"Of course it will," Loveday blurted, stunned. "But that is not the point! Papa, surely you do not mean we must have an audience."

"Is our word not enough?" Celeste added. "Why must a gentleman's observations carry so much more weight than our own?"

"You mistake me, my dears," Papa said. "No one contests your observations and achievements. In fact, it is all I hear of when I go into the village. But this is your home, where you are known and respected. If these same achievements are recounted in London, it is a simple fact that they will be discounted on hearing, simply because you are young and female."

Celeste said something in French that Loveday was quite certain should never be expressed in polite company. Whatever it was, it could not do justice to her own feelings at this moment. It was a very lucky thing that the crowbar was inside the carriage house, for she wanted to hit something—or at the very least, throw it.

"I can see you boiling over, maidey, like your own steam engine," her father said mildly. "But apply that brain of yours to what I have said, and you will see the truth of it, right or wrong. I shall call on the captain and Mr. Thorndyke with all dispatch. I would trust none other but those two with such a challenge—and such a privilege. For the ship will carry precious cargo indeed." With a smile, he left them simmering.

For more, find The Prince's Pilot at your favorite online retailer!

OTHER BOOKS BY SHELLEY ADINA

The Magnificent Devices series

Lady of Devices

Her Own Devices

Magnificent Devices

Brilliant Devices

A Lady of Resources

A Lady of Spirit

A Lady of Integrity

A Gentleman of Means

Devices Brightly Shining (Christmas novella)

Fields of Air

Fields of Iron

Fields of Gold

Carrick House (novella)

Selwyn Place (novella)

Holly Cottage (novella)

Gwynn Place (novella)

The Mysterious Devices series

The Bride Wore Constant White

The Dancer Wore Opera Rose

The Matchmaker Wore Mars Yellow

The Engineer Wore Venetian Red

The Judge Wore Lamp Black

The Professor Wore Prussian Blue

REGENCY ROMANCE as Charlotte Henry

The Rogue to Ruin

The Rogue Not Taken

One for the Rogue

A Rogue by Any Other Name

OTHER REGENCY-SET BOOKS BY REGINA SCOTT

Grace-by-the-Sea Series

The Matchmaker's Rogue

The Heiress's Convenient Husband

The Artist's Healer

The Governess's Earl

The Lady's Second-Chance Suitor

The Siren's Captain

Fortune's Brides Series

Never Doubt a Duke

Never Borrow a Baronet

Never Envy an Earl

Never Vie for a Viscount

Never Kneel to a Knight

Never Marry a Marquess

Always Kiss at Christmas

Uncommon Courtships Series

The Unflappable Miss Fairchild

The Incomparable Miss Compton

The Irredeemable Miss Renfield

The Unwilling Miss Watkin

An Uncommon Christmas

Lady Emily Capers

Secrets and Sensibilities

Art and Artifice

Ballrooms and Blackmail

Eloquence and Espionage

Love and Larceny

Marvelous Munroes Series

My True Love Gave to Me

The Rogue Next Door

The Marquis' Kiss

A Match for Mother

Spy Matchmaker Series

The Husband Mission

The June Bride Conspiracy

The Heiress Objective

ABOUT THE AUTHORS

SHELLEY ADINA

Shelley Adina is the author of more than 40 novels published by Harlequin, Warner, Hachette, and Moonshell Books, Inc., her own independent press. She writes steampunk as Shelley Adina; as Charlotte Henry, writes classic Regency romance; and as Adina Senft, is the *USA Today* bestselling author of Amish women's fiction.

She holds a PhD in Creative Writing from Lancaster University in the UK, won RWA's RITA Award® in 2005, and was a finalist in 2006. She appeared in the 2016 documentary film *Love Between the Covers*, is a popular speaker and convention panelist, and has been a guest on many podcasts, including Worldshapers and Realm of Books.

When she's not writing, Shelley is usually quilting, sewing historical costumes, or enjoying the garden with her flock of rescued chickens.

www.shelleyadina.com

R.E. SCOTT

R.E. (Regina) Scott started writing novels in the third grade. Thankfully for literature as we know it, she didn't sell her first novel until she learned a bit more about writing. Since her first book was published, her stories have traveled the globe, with translations in many languages, including Dutch, German, Italian, and Portuguese. She now has had published more than fifty works of warm, witty historical romance.

Regina and her husband of more than 30 years reside in the Puget Sound area of Washington State on the way to Mt Rainier. She has dressed as a Regency dandy, learned to fence, driven four-in-hand, and sailed on a tall ship, all in the name of research, of course.

www.reginascott.com